For Maggie.
I love you more than chicken.

THE NIGHTSHADE CABAL

CHRIS PATRICK CAROLAN

THE PARLIAMENT HOUSE

Edited by Kelly Beyus and Katelynn Watkins

Parliament House Press

www.parliamenthousepress.com

"I don't think he ever told her he loved her.
He probably knew the words would sound too small."
- Hugh MacLennan, *Barometer Rising*

1

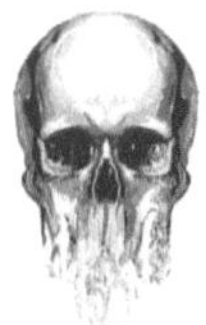

HALIFAX, NOVA SCOTIA, 1881.

"I'm telling you, Jonathon, these so-called stage magicians are nothing more than charlatans and hucksters of the highest order," Isaac Barrow said, raising his voice to be heard over the din of the crowded Theatre Royale. "The act is nothing but mirrors and wires and other trickery making you think you've seen something you haven't."

Inspector Jonathon Eddings chuckled heartily, shaking his head. "And I keep telling you, Barrow, being fooled is the whole point of the bloody show!" Fifteen years in Halifax had done little to blunt the edge of his thick Mancunian brogue.

His friend's retort failed to quell Barrow's annoyance. The inspector's invitation had had all the cordiality of a press gang. Eddings had bought the tickets to thank Barrow for his help with a recent investigation. He hadn't skimped, either; they sat just three rows back of the orchestra pit. The notion of putting down hard-earned coin with the express intention of being hoodwinked by some sham of a magician struck

Barrow as inordinately foolish. He knew of the occult and the dangers of flirting with its deadly secrets. Real magic being his stock-in-trade, he considered the pretend variety, popular on stage, mildly offensive at best. It was only on his friend's repeated insistence that he had finally, against his own better judgment, agreed to attend the performance.

"Besides all that," Eddings continued, smacking his rolled-up playbill against Barrow's knee, "they say this Oriental mystic Lai Jūn can conjure up illusions unlike anything you've ever seen before!"

Barrow snatched the pamphlet from his friend's hand. He knew Eddings was given to overstatement, even exaggeration. "I highly doubt that, Jonathon." He looked down his long nose at the inspector, then unrolled the playbill and read.

He had to admit that the show's promoter had a flair for the dramatic, making fantastical claims about Lai Jūn's mysterious origins and otherworldly talents. "*Thrill to the Spectacle of the Spectral Chinese Dragon and Other Wonders,*" read the headline. "*Straight from the darkest corners of the mysterious Orient, Lai Jūn shocks and amazes audiences by conjuring fantastic beasts from the very air. Not for the very young or faint of heart!*"

Barrow couldn't hold back a mirthless chuckle as he scanned the playbill. Real magic remained taboo, its practitioners the target of scorn and hatred, yet here he sat in a room with five hundred people who had paid to watch these pointless illusions. *The lure of the forbidden is a powerful thing, I suppose,* he mused.

The playbill also promised *An Opening Act of Unspeakable Evil,* but the first entertainer to take the stage—a young magician performing as The Amazing Antony—failed to impress the audience, trotting out tired tricks and illusions it had seen a hundred times over. He clashed a set of three large brass rings together, then held them up so the audience could see he had linked them like a chain, drawing little more than polite applause. A pretty young woman was placed in a wooden box, then apparently cut in half with a comically oversized blade. The trick was performed flawlessly, but it was nothing new. The illusion had been an old saw when Barrow was just a lad. No doubt sensing the audience's growing impatience, The Amazing Antony rushed his way through his final two feats. The illusionist seemed as glad to leave the stage as the audience was to see him go. Heckles and jeers followed him as he departed.

"I hope this mystic of yours has something more interesting to offer than that poor display, Jonathon," Barrow said over weak applause, again looking down his nose at the inspector.

Eddings remained impassive. "Wait and see, Barrow. Wait and see."

The lights dimmed as reedy flutes played a mysterious tune and the hubbub in the crowded theatre died away. With a deafening crack, a swirling column of flame erupted from the center of the stage, sending thick red smoke billowing up. More than a few people in the audience shrieked in surprise. The flame soon subsided, revealing the mystic.

Standing in the center of a single spotlight wearing long robes of red silk, Lai Jūn appeared younger than the wizened figure Barrow had envisioned while reading the playbill. The man on the stage was no graybeard, but a well-built figure of maybe twenty-five. From his place above the audience, he regarded the auditorium coolly, wordlessly, his expression distant.

Pounding drums struck up a frenetic rhythm as Lai Jūn stripped off his scarlet robes, leaving him bare-chested under the glaring stage lights. His skin was tracked with several tattoos depicting exotic animals, though from this distance

Barrow could make out only a scant handful. There was a large tiger on one shoulder, and a cobra on his chest. Most impressive was a massive, colourful Chinese dragon, snaking the length of the mystic's torso. Even from this distance, the level of detail was astounding.

As impressive as the tattoos were, Lai Jūn allowed little time to admire them as he launched into an acrobatic display unlike anything Barrow had ever witnessed. As if borne upward by some preternatural wind, he leapt high into the air, catching a hanging ring in each hand, twirling and spinning at dizzying speeds before coming to an abrupt pause. He hung there for a full half-minute, his arms straight out in a crucifixion pose as the audience held its breath. Sweat beaded on his brow as he held the agonizing pose, the taut muscles of his arms twitching beneath the skin. Finally, without seeming to move at all, he slowly inverted the position, hanging upside-down in midair for just as long. With a cry, he flipped himself over once more, released his grip on the rings, and landed on the stage to thunderous applause.

As the drums went silent, Barrow could hear Lai Jūn softly chanting. He watched as the mystic touched two fingers to the tattoo of the tiger on his shoulder. The image seemed to peel away from his skin, glowing faintly as it took form. It grew slowly, morphing from a flat illustration into a fully formed projection that appeared to have substance. It stood on the stage, easily the size of an actual tiger.

The audience cheered as the music swelled once more, the spectral tiger padding its way from one end of the stage to the other under Lai Jūn's determined gaze. Aside from the soft glow surrounding the beast, everything about it—the way it moved, the way it regarded the audience with those fierce hunter's eyes—seemed real and alive. The illusion was phenomenal.

Sweat, visible in the spotlight's glare, beaded on Lai Jūn's brow. Maintaining the image clearly took a great deal of concentration and effort on the mystic's part. He continued his chant as the beast prowled, all the while holding two fingers to the spot on his shoulder where the tattoo had been just moments before. As he raised his free hand in a fist, the tiger came to stand obediently at his side, bringing another chorus of cheers from the captivated theatre audience.

The drums pounded, their deafening beat working towards a frenzied tempo. With a barked command, Lai Jūn threw his free hand out towards the audience. The drumming ceased as the phantom tiger sprang forth from the lip of the stage, leaping outward over the front rows of the breathless spectators with a mighty roar.

The airborne beast vanished, swallowed up into nothingness. In the same instant, Lai Jūn removed the two fingers he had pressed to his skin to conjure the tiger into being. The tattoo reappeared on his shoulder.

Rapt silence filled the cavernous theatre, replaced a moment later by a deafening rumble of applause. As one, the audience leapt to its feet. Barrow was surprised to find himself out of his seat, part of the ovation.

"Well, Barrow? What do you think of that?" Eddings shouted over the noise of the crowd as he clapped his big hands together.

"Very impressive," Barrow replied, also shouting. "Very impressive indeed, though I've no idea how he was able to create such an illusion."

"Bah! Scoffer!" Both men laughed.

The lights dimmed once more, the sound of the flutes urging the audience back to their seats in attentive silence. Still in the spotlight at the center of the stage, Lai Jūn began to chant once more as he raised his right hand above his head, displaying the tattoo of the Chinese dragon for all to see. He pressed two fingers to the image.

As the tiger had done before, the image of the dragon glowed softly as it peeled away from Lai Jūn's skin. As the audience was stunned once more into awed stillness, the ethereal beast grew larger and larger until finally, it stretched the full length of the stage.

The serpentine dragon took to the air, flying up toward the theatre's ornate ceiling. It swooped and coiled its long body through the space above the rows of seats, astonishing and delighting the audience. As the dragon passed overhead, Barrow could feel the draft it left in its wake. *It has physical mass*, he realized. *This is no mere projection.* The hairs on the back of his neck bristled.

As the dragon danced in the air above the audience, Barrow regarded Lai Jūn with growing suspicion. The mystic was locked in intense concentration as he worked to keep the ethereal beast under his control.

Gently, carefully, Barrow extended a small part of his own mind out toward the stage. He had come to the theatre expecting naught but cheap illusions and trickery, but was beginning to believe he had discovered something much more. If there was real magic at play, he should be able to sense it.

The tricky part would be doing so without Lai Jūn noticing his probing.

Near the very edge of the stage, Barrow found what he was seeking. The aura of magic emanating from where Lai Jūn stood was intense, swirling around his feet like a ragged, churning maelstrom. It wasn't a thing that could be seen by human eyes; only those trained in the transmundane arts would sense the radiating circles of raw power that focused wherever occult energies were being channeled.

With an audible gasp, the mystic's head whipped around. He locked eyes with Barrow across the rows of oblivious spectators. Disbelief and anger mingled on his face.

In that moment of distraction, Lai Jūn faltered and dropped to one knee, losing control of the spectral dragon. It turned in midair, fixing its stare on its human master with a wicked grin. With a startled cry, Lai Jūn flung a hand toward the airborne beast.

The spell broken, the dragon vanished instantly. As the tiger before it had done, the tattoo reappeared on the mystic's body. The column of otherworldly flame erupted around Lai Jūn's feet once more as the audience burst into applause, thinking what they had seen was but part of the show.

Lai Jūn stared through the flames directly at Barrow, pure malice evident on his face. When the flames died away a few moments later, Lai Jūn was gone.

Fog had started to roll in from the harbour by the time Barrow and Eddings left the Theatre Royale, taking on an oily and unwholesome aspect as it swirled in the yellow glow of the gas lamps lining Spring Garden Road. Hansoms lined the street waiting for fares, and a bare handful of steamcarriages ranged among their number. Nervous horses shied away from the low rumbling of the steamcarriage engines and their acrid exhaust fumes. The hansom drivers eyed the newfangled vehicles with mingled curiosity and disdain. The lure of the unfamiliar was enough to draw some passengers to try the steamcars at least once, but there weren't yet enough of the vehicles on the streets to be any real threat to the hansom drivers' livelihoods.

Eddings was still gawping as they emerged from the theatre lobby. "Bloody brilliant, weren't he?" he proclaimed, wrapping a red scarf around his neck. It was early June, but the coming of spring in Halifax simply meant rain instead of snow. Days were milder, but evenings remained chilly and damp.

A small group of vociferous protestors huddled across the street from the theatre, their enthusiasm undampened by the soggy weather. The placards they carried quoted scripture and denounced the evils being performed within the Theatre Royale. They didn't care that stage magic was an act; the demonstrators drew no distinction between the real and the pretend, and thought any public act of magic was performed in concert with the devil himself. To their way of thinking, mere discussion of the occult was as bad as the practice. One good thing about the brutal Halifax winter was that it kept most of these sorts of debates indoors.

Narrow-minded bigots, driven by nothing more than base fear and a lack of understanding, Barrow thought as he glanced across the cobbled road. *Have they no better way to spend their time?* He wondered what the demonstrators would think if they had seen Lai Jūn's conjurations for themselves. He scarcely knew what to think of what he had seen, and he knew a great deal more about such things than these busybodies.

"Come now, Barrow," the inspector chided, swatting the technomancer on the shoulder and calling his attention away from the display. "You can't tell me you've ever seen anything to compare to those illusions before."

"What we saw tonight was no mere illusion, Jonathon," Barrow said. "Those creatures were as solid as you and I, and conjured into being by some very real magic."

"Wait a minute," the inspector said, stopping in his tracks. "Are you saying those great glowing beasties in there could've come down off that stage and, what? Taken a bite out of us?"

Barrow nodded. "I believe so, but I can't be sure. I have no idea what magic could be used to create and control those...those monsters. Not only have I never seen the like before, I've never even heard of anything like what we saw on that stage tonight." He frowned, annoyed at having to admit his ignorance in the matter.

"Then how do you know it was real magic?"

"There's an energy connecting all things," Barrow explained, frowning as he tried to conceptualize the truth for his friend; the inspector was worldlier than most, but still had little experience with the transmundane. "No one knows what it is, really, but you can think of it like the surface of a pond. Most of the time the water is placid, the surface flat as a pane of glass. When a spellcaster taps into that energy, it's almost like a stone has been thrown into the pond. Another spellcaster can often feel the ripples from that spell breaking the surface. The more powerful the spell, the further those ripples radiate."

"And you felt those ripples tonight?"

"It was more like a maelstrom," Barrow said. "Most magic is primarily a means of manipulating elemental forces and playing off their interactions. There's nothing I know of— nothing I've ever heard theorized—that would allow such creatures to be conjured out of pure nothingness. I don't think he called the beasts forth from the Otherwhere, either. Whatever it was, though, was some quite potent casting indeed."

Eddings exhaled deeply. "Bloody hell."

That brought a small smile to Barrow's face. "Indeed, Jonathon."

"Well, you're a right clever fellow. You'll suss it out soon enough," Eddings said. As ever, he showed great confidence in Barrow's talents. He turned the collar of his heavy wool coat up against the chilly night air, then jammed his hands into a pair of black leather gloves. "In the meantime, how do you fancy joining me at Carleton House for a late meal?"

Barrow shook his head. "I would, but I'm afraid I have an early appointment in the morning," he said, drawing a curious look from the inspector. "I've got to be at Henry Feele's home in Point Pleasant for eight o'clock, and I'd rather not keep him waiting."

"Henry Feele, of Feele Trans-Atlantic? I should say not, Barrow!" Eddings whistled, impressed. "That's one wealthy client. What does he want with you?"

"Mechanical services of some sort, I would assume." Barrow shrugged. Henry Feele's message had arrived earlier that day and, other than the time and address, the note had been maddeningly vague. Absent of any details, only the shipping magnate's solid reputation—to say nothing of his deep pockets—had held Barrow's interest. "Maybe he has one of those new steamcarriages in need of repair. The engines that power those things will be keeping mechanics busy for years to come, I'd wager."

He reached out and clasped his friend's gloved hand. "Have a good night, Jonathon," he said with a smile. Almost as an afterthought, he added, "And thank you for this evening's entertainment. It was certainly...intriguing."

"By which you mean you've found yourself faced with a question you don't know how to answer," Eddings said with a grin, clapping one big hand on Barrow's shoulder.

Barrow tipped the brim of his bowler hat to his friend, conceding the last word. He turned to stroll into the roiling fog, another shadow in the chiaroscuro night.

2

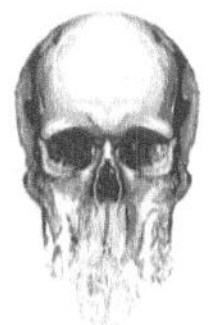

STEPPING OFF THE POINT PLEASANT STREETCAR INTO A gray Tuesday morning, Barrow popped open his umbrella to fend off the light rain that peppered the cobbles. He thanked the conductor as he hopped down from the car's bottom step, instantly feeling foolish. The automaton that sat behind the controls clicked and whirred as it sketched a jerky salute before putting the streetcar into gear to continue along its route, but the emotionless machine had no sense of professional pride.

Barrow's courtesy came from habit. He was used to interacting with the human operators that still ran the Gottingen line; few streetcars in Halifax had the expensive new autonomous conductor units installed. Any time he happened upon one, he wondered why the transit commission insisted on dressing the automata in the same uniform their human counterparts wore. Clothing a machine struck him as inordinately wasteful. He supposed it was in part to set their passengers' minds at ease. Not everyone was enamoured with the idea of the streetcars driven by mechanical operators. But with the spinning mirrored discs of their round eyes set into featureless, polished brass faces, the mechanical men didn't look remotely human. No clothing would change that.

There was talk that a British airship company was planning to use the new automata to pilot their transatlantic routes, but Barrow had trouble believing the story was anything more than a clever marketing ploy. The technology was too new, too untested to make the idea palatable to any but the most enthusiastic of technophiles. Conducting a streetcar along a set cable track and piloting an airship with more than five hundred passengers across an ocean were very different propositions.

Despite his own misgivings, Barrow had to admit the idea had merit. Nonstop flights across the vast ocean took several days, requiring three shifts of crew members to make the journey. Airship pilots worked in pairs, so each flight meant training—and paying—no fewer than six men on the flight deck. Add to that the mechanics in the engine rooms and the crew tending to the passenger cabins, and it quickly became a very expensive operation. Powered by their compact internal voltaic batteries, automata worked around the clock, requiring no rest.

His thoughts came crashing back to earth as a steamcarriage rattled past, its chassis squeaking as it sped over the uneven surface of the cobblestone roadway. The driver capably handled the steering from his seat behind the long barrel of the steamcar's tapered boiler, keeping the vehicle on a more or less straight course as it pitched and jounced over the cobbles. Dark velvet curtains were drawn over the windows of the passenger compartment, concealing the identity of the steamcar's wealthy owner inside. Even with the noise the vehicle made, Barrow took a moment to admire the machine as it passed. The artistry that went into designing the miniaturized boiler engines the new steamcars used was no small thing, and advances in materials engineering over the last few years had reduced the number of explosions to almost nil. The astronomic cost of the vehicles was the only factor keeping them from overcoming their novelty status as playthings of the wealthy.

Pausing at the gate, Barrow checked the address on the note Henry Feele had sent the day before. Visiting the home of a client wasn't normally a notion he willingly entertained. He offered mechanical services mainly to local industry and the shipping trade at the wharves, leaving the broken-down home appliances to regular repairmen. Every hour he spent working on someone else's machinery was one he didn't have to devote to his own technomantic research. As much as he wished he could hole up in his own laboratory with his personal projects, though, the reality of his fiscal situation demanded he take on at least some outside work from time to time.

As much as Barrow hated the idea of playing to another man's tune, the backing of a wealthy patron could mean the difference between a technomancer eking out his days repairing worn-out valves while scribbling away in a basement somewhere, and becoming the next Edison. The American, backed by some serious capital, had been on a tear over the last few years, filing patent after patent.

Barrow's successes were nothing compared to Edison's, but neither did he have a fortune of resources to draw on. If he managed to suitably impress Henry Feele, the shipping magnate might very well be convinced to finance his future researches. Such politics galled him, but he knew it was a game he had to play.

Heading straight up to the house, he didn't take much time to admire the pristine landscaping. He was met at the door by Mr. Feele's butler. Gray-haired and a bit paunchy, he was English-trained if his accent was anything to go by, though Barrow supposed that could be an affectation. He handed the man his calling card.

"Isaac Barrow, *Technomancer*," the disinterested servant read aloud, an edge of disdain apparent in his voice. "The tradesman's entrance is located at the rear of the house, Mr. Barrow," he said shortly, handing the card back.

Barrow couldn't decide if the butler looked down his nose at working men in general, or if this condescension was held specifically for spellcasters. He didn't much care either way. "If I should happen upon any tradesmen, I shall let them know," he replied as he took a step across the threshold. He handed his coat, hat, and dripping umbrella to the butler. The stuffy servant bristled, but took the damp articles without protest. "There's a good man! Now, where might I find Mr. Feele?"

He followed the butler down a long corridor to Henry Feele's library. Even on a gray morning such as this, two tall windows at the south end of the room flooded the library with light. Barrow noted a number of taxidermied animals throughout the room. Several stuffed game birds were perched atop bookshelves, including pheasant, grouse, an eagle with its wings spread wide, and some others Barrow couldn't name. A small red fox stood between the two windows while a large wildcat, posed as if prowling through long grass, kept vigil on the transom above the door to an adjoining room.

A broad oak desk sat in front of the windows, its surface scrupulously tidy. Sheets of paper were piled neatly in labeled trays atop the desk, and an oversized ledger was laid open in the center of the blotter. Not a single item was out of place. Barrow almost wondered if the tableau had been set out for his benefit, but based on the fellow's reputation, he quickly decided Henry Feele was likely not the sort of man to resort to such empty theatrics.

A sturdy man in his early forties, Henry Feele had dark brown hair that was graying slightly at the temples. The sleeves of his crisp white shirt were rolled up past his elbows, and he wore a fine silk waistcoat. His suit jacket was slung over a nearby chair. Barrow didn't even try to hide a wry smile when he noticed the butler eyeing the rumpled jacket with something approaching resignation writ plain on his face.

Mr. Feele stood studying a large coastal map mounted on one wall. Several colored pins were scattered across the map, which Barrow assumed noted the current locations of Feele Trans-Atlantic's fleet vessels. His attention locked on the map, he didn't seem to take any notice of Barrow and the butler. Barrow admired a man who could become so engrossed in his work; indeed, it was a trait he shared.

The butler cleared his throat once, loudly. "A Mr. Isaac Barrow to see you, sir," he announced in a booming tenor, drawing Feele from his reverie.

"Ah, thank you, Coleman," Feele said as he crossed the room to clasp Barrow's hand. "And thank you for coming on such short notice, Mr. Barrow. May I offer you anything in the way of refreshment?"

"Coffee, if you have it. Bergamot tea if you don't, thank you," Barrow said as he shook Henry Feele's hand. The fellow's grip was firm and confident, his smile sincere. His ruddy face told of some years spent working outdoors; Barrow knew one of the conditions of his inheriting ownership of the company had been five years at sea as a young man. The condition of inheritance had been written into the company charter by his great-grandfather before his retirement, remaining in place through generations of family ownership, with the notion being that a man cannot properly run a company without some hands-on experience in its daily trade. Barrow thought the reasoning sound.

Feele nodded to the butler, once. "The Sumatran, please, Coleman. I trust you didn't have any trouble finding us, Mr. Barrow?"

"I'm not in the habit of visiting private residences, Mr. Feele," Barrow said, joining his client in looking over the large map on the wall. "Most of my clients require mechanical services in factories, offices, or other places of business." He flashed a crooked smile. "I hope you didn't call me here for the sake of a burned-out bread toaster."

Feele chuckled heartily, taking the comment for the joke Barrow had intended. "Of course, Mr. Barrow. The library here at home often does duty as my place of business." He shrugged. "Some days I find it easier to work here, away from the din and constant interruptions of the office. I'm sure you understand the virtue of solitude."

"Yes," Barrow said, and left it that. It was a generally held assumption that spellcasters tended to be withdrawn by nature. In his case, it happened to be true more often than not, but he didn't feel the need to play to the stereotype. "Why did you ask me here, Mr. Feele?"

Just then, Coleman returned, carrying a silver tray laden with a pewter carafe, matching vessels for cream and cubed sugar, and two porcelain cups. Barrow accepted a cup with murmured thanks, stirring in a small dribble of cream. The rich smell of the steaming coffee filled his nostrils.

Feele also took a cup, dismissing the butler. "I've been having rather a lot of trouble with my autotype machine lately," he said, gesturing towards the unit, which sat off to one side behind the desk. "It started acting up some months ago, peppering random letters in places throughout the documents I composed on it. At first I thought these were simply errors on my part, but it was happening when I dictated to my secretary as well."

Barrow nodded, taking a sip of the coffee. He tried his

best not to let on when the steaming hot liquid stung his lip, but he thought he saw Feele suppress a grin. "Was there any pattern to the extra letters?" he asked around his embarrassment. "Ks slipping in next to your Ls, things like that?"

Feele shook his head with a rueful smile. "No, I did check to make sure it wasn't a case of my fat fingers hitting two keys at once," he said, waggling the digits in question. "And as I said, the same happened when my secretary used the machine, and her digits are notably slenderer than my own."

"I'm sure they are," Barrow said. "My thought, though, was that frayed wiring underneath the keys might be causing the errors."

Feele shook his head. "I don't think so, and I'll tell you why not, before you start pulling the machine apart. The problem became more pronounced as the weeks passed. It wasn't long before entire extra words started to appear on the page."

Barrow felt an eyebrow quirk upward. "Whole words?"

Walking over to the desk and opening a drawer, Feele pulled out a sheaf of printed pages. "I was drafting a speech to deliver to my company's shareholders some weeks back. Have a look for yourself."

"*Third quarter moon earnings were up year over stinking year,*" Barrow read aloud. "*Modest cheese gains were made along the traditional transatlantic porridge routes, though investment in the French cabinet project in Panama has yet to bear out.*" He leafed through a few more pages, noting numerous other similar errors. "This was printed here? You didn't type it on this machine, then transmit it to have it printed it at the company office?"

"That's right," Feele said. "I've had to leave the paper carriage empty. Towards the end, the damned thing was spooling out reams of nonsense."

Barrow set the pages and his cup down on the desk and

crossed the room to inspect the autotype, a black behemoth of a device almost half the size of the broad oak desk and likely almost twice as heavy. "Do you know how an autotype works, Mr. Feele?" he asked, running his hand down the side of the machine.

"I never thought to consider the specific mechanics of the device," Feele said with a shrug. "I know there's an element of the arcane in it."

"You're not quite wrong," Barrow said, "though the word *arcane* doesn't necessarily imply anything of the occult. It only refers to something which is secret and unknown to most people." He smiled. "As long as a machine works as it's supposed to, most people will never stop to think about *how* it does what it does. It's enough for them that it works.

"When you hit a key on a standard typewriter," he explained, poking at the air with his fingers, miming the act of typing, "a hammer engraved with the corresponding letter swings upwards, striking an ink-soaked ribbon to transfer that letter onto a sheet of paper. It's instantly on the page, and difficult to correct if you've made an error. An autotype machine is similar in concept, though it puts a few intermediate steps into the process. Instead of mechanically swinging a hammer, each letter keystroke sends a unique electrical impulse into a storage medium, which remembers the order of their input while sending a working copy to a rasterized display screen as you type, rather than impressing it on the page. The great advantage is you can review what you've typed and make changes before printing the document, and unlike a single document drafted on a typewriter, someone using an autotype can create multiple identical copies when his document is finished."

"I've already purchased the machine, Mr. Barrow," Feele said with a patient smile. "You don't need to sell me on its merits."

"The storage medium is where the arcane factors in," Barrow continued, grasping the cold metal edges of the auto-type machine's outer casing. With an audible click, the top panel of the casing came free, and he gently lifted it off and set it aside.

Examining the machine's inner workings, Barrow whistled slightly. "Oh, but you are a beauty, aren't you?" he whispered, almost inaudibly. Hundreds of tiny brass gears and polished steel wheels and pistons sat idle, springs and pins ready to spin into life at a moment's notice.

Towards the back of the machine lay a glass tube, nearly a foot in length and as thick as a man's wrist, filled with a viscous gray fluid. There were electrodes attached at either end. The stuff inside looked almost gelatinous and glowed softly with a pale, pulsing iridescence as Barrow pointed to it. "That fluid is the machine's storage medium: brain tissue, suspended in a preservative solution of nutritive and conductive compounds."

"Brain tissue?"

"That's right," Barrow explained, "a cluster of cells from the brain's memory center, to be specific. No bigger than child's front tooth when it was extracted."

Feele swallowed once, hard. Barrow was sure he wasn't meant to have noticed the reaction. "What...what kind of brain?" he asked after a moment.

"Oh, an animal, always," Barrow said reassuringly. "Rodents are too small to yield much viable brain matter, so they use the tissue from livestock that would have been discarded or sold along with the offal. Sheep and cows are too slow-witted to be any use, but swine are actually quite clever beasts." He gently twisted the memory cylinder until it came free from its mounting, and held it up to the light of the gas lamp on the wall behind Feele's broad desk. "Enough viable tissue can be extracted from a single pig's brain to build nearly a hundred autotype machines."

"I had no idea."

"Arcane, as you yourself said, Mr. Feele." He tilted the memory cell back and forth in his hand in a seesaw motion, watching the viscous fluid within slowly swirl. "Do you mind if I take this with me? I've never seen a memory cylinder even half the size of what you've got here. I'd like to conduct a few simple tests on this."

"You may as well," Feele said, seeming to have regained his composure. "It's not any use to me, working the way it is now. I trust you'll return it to the machine when you have some answers?" His eyes narrowed slightly as he watched Barrow examine the cylinder. "You know something already, though, don't you, Mr. Barrow? I can see it in your eyes."

"I don't know anything yet, Mr. Feele, though I have a suspicion that what we have here is something rather more evolved than the brain of a hog," Barrow said solemnly, tucking the cylinder inside his valise. "I suspect that the brain tissue used to create your autotype machine's memory cell came from that of a human."

3

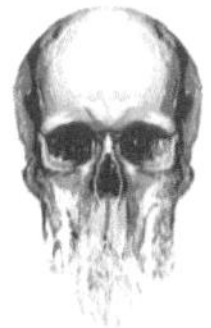

D ECLINING H ENRY F EELE'S OFFER OF A RIDE HOME IN A carriage, Barrow rode the Point Pleasant streetcar back into town and then transferred to the threadbare car that trundled and gasped its way up the Gottingen line. Choosing to stand in the aisle rather than sit in whatever murky fluid had puddled in the only empty seat, something sticky and unwholesome nonetheless smeared itself onto the bottom of his shoe by the time he stepped down off the streetcar. With a resigned sigh, he did his best to wipe the stuff off on the twisted rope matt at Higgins's door, with little success.

Higgins Mechanical Supply was a cavernous place, part chandlery, and part general store, taking up much of a city block. Upon entry, one's nose was assaulted by the mingled odours of machine grease and copper wire, oiled wood, and metal polish, wet paint, and Stockholm pine tar, old dust and damp dog. The latter was courtesy of Charlie, the dozy old basset that acted as the *de facto* mascot of the place. The musty warehouse potpourri was off-putting to most folk. To Barrow, the odour was one of comfort.

Higgins himself didn't seem to have a first name, or at

least not one Barrow had heard in the decade and more he had been coming here. The squat, red-faced Irishman's forehead was always beaded with perspiration, as though he had just climbed several flights of stairs. He was a jovial fellow with a thick orange beard and thinning hair in a matching hue, both that had started to frost over with white. No matter what gear or piston or gauge of lead pipe you were looking for, Higgins prided himself on being able to put it in your hand at a moment's notice. He also ran a full machine workshop, and could produce high-quality, custom parts with a remarkably short turnaround.

Customers were not permitted to browse beyond the service counter; everything in Higgins's hoard was meticulously organized according to a system that only the shopkeeper understood. The odd time a customer did manage to stump him, Higgins always made the same promise. *"T'ree days, shore as gun's iron!"* Somehow, he never broke it.

Barrow visited Higgins whenever he needed supplies for his experiments, which was often. The bulk of Higgins's trade came from the factories and workshops up the road, and among seamen and longshoremen, he also had a reputation for better prices and selection than the chandleries closer to the wharves.

Aside from the selection of materials, the warehouse was a short walk from Barrow's own workshop. More importantly, whatever he thought of Barrow's experiments and the odd items he purchased, Higgins had always regarded the technomancer with mild bemusement, never scorn.

Today, though, Barrow wasn't stopping in to make a purchase. He had brought the memory cylinder from Feele's autotype machine, hoping Higgins might be able to offer some insight to the piece's origins. "Well, t'ain't got no maker's markings anywhere on the casing, not that I can see," he said, carefully turning the piece over and over in one calloused hand as he examined it through a jeweler's loupe, finally handing it back to Barrow with a shrug. "I'm afraid I don't deal much in this sort of t'ing, y'understand."

"Thanks for taking a look all that same, Higgins," Barrow said.

Just then the bell above the door chimed, calling Barrow's attention to a tall, stern-faced man who marched into the shop. Finely dressed, wearing a black riding cape and matching silk top hat, his stride was full of purpose as he crossed the floorboards to the counter. He didn't even pause to shake the rain from his dripping cape.

The tall man's hair was bone white but his eyebrows were very dark, as were his eyes. A cold fire burned behind them. He regarded Barrow for a moment, a faint, tight smile crossing his lips. He nodded, almost imperceptibly. Barrow returned the stranger's unspoken acknowledgement, but he had the feeling the man was not in the habit of smiling often.

"Good day, Master Higgins," he said dispassionately. "I trust the item I commissioned has been completed?"

"Aye, sir," Higgins replied with a smirk. "It were done an' ready for pickup two days ago, like I told you it'd be. Hold on a minute, and I'll fetch it from the back." He hurried off, leaving Barrow and the stranger at the counter.

Silence lingered as the two men regarded each other. "Doctor Johan Morgentaler," the stranger finally introduced himself, extending a hand. He spoke with a slight accent. *Austrian, perhaps?* Barrow couldn't quite put his finger on it, but to his ear, it sounded as if years of speaking in English had rounded off the edges. Morgentaler seemed somewhat irked to have spoken first. Barrow didn't know why, but he felt he had won some small victory.

Charlie, the dozy basset hound sprawled on the floor nearby, chose that moment to yawn loudly. Barrow had to choke down a laugh as the sleeping dog rolled over with a groan.

Barrow took Johan Morgentaler's gloved hand. His grip was firm, as Henry Feele's had been earlier that morning, but there was something almost magnetic to Morgentaler's grasp. "Isaac Barrow," the technomancer introduced himself, hoping his voice sounded steadier than he felt.

"A pleasure, Master Barrow," Morgentaler said, though the frigid tone of his voice gave away the lie in the words as he spoke them. If anything, his eyes held mild curiosity as he minutely studied the technomancer. "I've heard of your work," he added.

"Then it would seem you have me at a disadvantage, Doctor," Barrow replied.

"Indeed?"

Barrow didn't answer. He had met many other spell-casters throughout his career; while Morgentaler had not revealed himself as such, Barrow recognized the man for what he was. The man's eyes were the colour of tempered steel, his gaze keen as a knife. Those eyes took in the world, it seemed, and gave little back.

Barrow felt he was being weighed and measured. He had never met this degree of scrutiny—not even when faced with Magisters of the Triune Congress, who felt the openness with which he practiced his craft invited public backlash against all spellcasters.

The handshake lasted several seconds longer than Barrow found comfortable before Morgentaler finally released his grip. Higgins returned then, carrying a large, oblong object wrapped in brown paper and bound with rough twine. If he noticed what had passed between the two men, he didn't let on. "There y'be," he said, placing the parcel on the counter in front of Morgentaler. "I trust you'll find it meets the specifications you provided."

"Of that, I've no doubt, Master Higgins," Morgentaler replied. "Your work never fails to exceed expectations. I trust you'll provide Master Barrow here with the same level of service."

"He always does, Doctor," Barrow said.

"Excellent," Morgentaler said. "Just excellent. What is it that brings you to Master Higgins's counter on a rainy Tuesday morning, if I may ask?"

Before Barrow could answer, Higgins did. "Barrow here's trying to find the maker of that memory cylinder," he said, pointing to the piece in question. "I've got to admit I wasnae any help at all."

"I know something of this technology, Master Barrow. May I?" Morgentaler said, holding out his open hand. With some reluctance, Barrow handed him Feele's memory cylinder.

"That's very fine work," Morgentaler said, examining the cylinder closely. "An odd size, though, wouldn't you say? The brass casing of the electrodes at each end must've been machined by hand, and look at how seamlessly they fit." He handed the cylinder back to Barrow. "I wish you luck with your enquiries, Master Barrow, but I'm afraid I can't be any more help than our Master Higgins was." The hint of a smile pulled at the corner of his mouth.

"My thanks, Master Higgins." Gathering up his parcel, Morgentaler touched the brim of his hat. "Master Barrow." He turned and left without another word.

"Cold fish, that one," Higgins said when the door had closed behind him.

"Not a man who makes friends easily, I'd wager," Barrow agreed.

"Nor a man who cares much either way, though some may very well say the same about yourself, Isaac," Higgins said with his tongue planted firmly in cheek to show the barb wasn't altogether serious. "Now, anything else I can be doing for you, *Master* Barrow?"

Barrow chuckled, relishing the moment of levity. "A roll of three-quarter-inch paper ticker tape, if you have it? I'll also need a few feet of telegraph wire and a few fresh ink ribbons."

Higgins disappeared into the bowels of his hoard. Returning to the counter a few minutes later, he wrapped the roll of ticker tape in waxed paper to keep it dry and tied it with some strong twine. "I'll add it to your account," Higgins said when Barrow reached for his billfold. "You're in often enough that it's just easier to settle up the once at month-end."

Taking the wrapped parcel under one arm, Barrow stowed the other items in his valise and headed back out into the dreary morning.

"Hey, Isaac Barrow," a small but enthusiastic voice called out as he walked down the block. "Got a job then, have you?"

"I'd say he has," called a second voice. "Look at that great lumpy parcel he's got!"

"He only buys up that much junk when he's got a job," said a third. "Unless he's inventin' another new rat trap, that is!"

The three lads came running up to meet Barrow. They had been playing a game of pitch-penny against the outside wall of Higgins's shop, but Barrow knew the game couldn't have lasted very long; he would've been surprised if the three boys had much more than three pennies between them. Either way, considering the trouble three boys of their age with too much free time on their hands could get into, the harmless bit of gambling was hardly worth fretting over.

Each of the three could've been poured from the same mold. Their clothes were shabby, but not in tatters, and the oldest of the trio barely had the hint of his first fuzzy whiskers on his chin. All three ran with the Gottingen Street boys' gang, the Collywobble Boys.

"Hello Mack, Will," Barrow tipped his hat to the threesome. "Liam, how's your mother this week? Feeling better, I hope."

"Yeah, she's alright," answered the shortest of the three lads. "Her fever finally broke on Sunday morning, but she's still been sleepin' an awful lot."

"Bed rest and plenty of water is the best thing for influenza," Barrow said. "You've been stirring the iodine tablets I gave you into her water, just like I showed you?"

Liam nodded vigorously. "I done it just like you told me, Mr. Barrow! But she says it tastes worse than the chamber pot." The other boys laughed.

Barrow smiled too. "I know it tastes bad, Liam," he said, "but the chemical cleans the water and makes sure there's nothing in it that can make her sick again. She's already weak from the flu, so anything nasty that might be in the water could make her worse."

"That doesn't make any sense." Mack, the oldest boy, made a face. "How could *water* make you sick?"

"Our well water here is rather clean to start with, but in many places, there are tiny little bugs swimming in the water, smaller than anything you or I can see with our own eyes," Barrow explained. Mack still looked dubious, but the younger boys' eyes were wide. As far as they were concerned, Isaac Barrow seemed to know everything about everything, and none of them had ever yet caught him in a lie.

"Most of these tiny bugs are harmless, and some are even

good; they help you turn the food you eat into the energy your body needs to keep growing. But there are some that can make you sick as a dog if they get inside your stomach." He jabbed a finger toward Mack's belly and dropped his voice to a conspiratorial whisper. "Some of them will even lay their eggs in you."

"Yuck!" all three boys chorused.

Barrow laughed, knowing that had caught their full attention. The Collywobble Boys were mostly harmless, though a disreputable lot of kids. Poor lads from poor homes, their mischief rarely went beyond petty theft and vandalism, though some of the older boys in the gang sometimes found their way into deeper trouble. Polite folk tended to turn their noses up at these unkempt urchins, and were quick to level blame at them whenever anything untoward happened in the rough corner of the city they prowled.

Barrow, however, kept on their good side. Most doctors wouldn't come to the neighborhood the Collywobble Boys called home, so he was often called upon to put his great scientific knowledge to use in a medical capacity. He used his understanding of herbs and chemistry to prepare remedies and preventatives, and—in rare cases—would resort to what he knew of healing magic. It was a service he provided without charge. In return, the boys often ran errands for him.

"Have any of you boys ever heard of something called a tapeworm?" he asked them.

Pausing a moment to put his parcel and valise down while the three boys shook their heads, he looked around on the sidewalk. Finally, he snatched up a fat earthworm from a puddle and held it, dangling, for each of the boys to see. "Sometimes what happens, you see, is someone will swallow a tapeworm egg when they take a drink of dirty water, and that tiny egg gets stuck inside their belly. It's warm and wet and dark in there, which is just what tapeworms like, so before too long it'll hatch out and grow right inside you." Holding each end of the writhing earthworm, he pulled it taut. Instead of snapping the thing in half, though, Barrow whispered a simple transformation spell focused on the worm, stretching it out as he spread his hands apart until it was as long as his arms were wide. It flattened out as well, looking much like a length of the paper ticker tape he had just now bought from Higgins. "This nasty fellow curls up in your belly, and he takes a tiny nibble out of every bite of food you eat, getting longer and fatter while you waste away to nothing."

The boys had seen Barrow's magic on display before, but relished every chance they got to see him do something out of the ordinary. Even a minor thing such as this was a splash of color in their otherwise gray day. He allowed himself a smile at the thought; he knew his transformation spell was nothing compared to the conjurations he had watched Lai Jūn perform the previous evening, but the boys had enjoyed it all the same.

The boys cheered as he let go of one end and the thing in his hand shimmered back to being a regular, wriggling earthworm. "You see now why clean water is so important?" he asked as he tossed the worm back into the puddle.

All three boys nodded vigorously.

"Now, boys," he said, gathering up his parcels, "if you'll excuse me, I have an experiment to get started!"

4

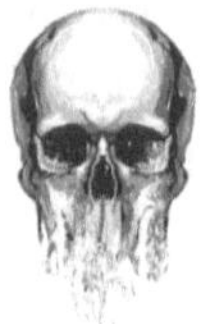

THE WOMAN WAS ALREADY WAITING FOR BARROW WHEN he arrived at his office a short time later. The morning rain was starting to let up and dissolve into a filmy gray drizzle that seemed to hang thick in the air rather than fall straight to the cobbles. She stood close to the side of the building clutching an umbrella, which kept her mostly dry but for the hem of her dress. Though he hadn't been expecting any callers, Barrow apologized for keeping her waiting in the rain as he unlocked the door and ushered her into his streetside office.

The narrow room within was small and sparsely furnished, but scrupulously clean. As he maintained the office primarily as a place to meet prospective clients, Barrow made sure to keep it spotless. Minimal furnishings and just enough in the way of decoration to make it feel homey allowed him to spend as little time as possible on keeping the office tidy. At the far end of the room, behind Barrow's broad oak desk, there was a plain wooden door marked PRIVATE. This was the entrance to his workshop, where his *real* work was done.

For décor, a handful of engraved portraits of some of the greatest minds mankind had ever known—Galileo Galilee, Leonardo da Vinci, Johannes Kepler, and others—adorned one wall. To history, these men were venerated as great thinkers, but behind closed doors, the Technomancer's Collegeum claimed them as their own. Had they practiced their gifts more openly in their own time, the Church surely would have tried them all as witches. Things had improved somewhat for spellcasters over the centuries, but even Barrow and his relatively benign colleagues still worked on the fringe of society.

"I am terribly sorry to show up at your door so unexpectedly, Mr. Barrow," the woman said, shaking the water from her umbrella in the doorway. Her voice held a soft, rather musical Scottish lilt, more pronounced than the Haligonian accent. She folded away her umbrella and reached into her reticule, handing him her card.

"Miss Meredith Skye," Barrow read aloud. "Please, let me take your overcoat, and have a seat near the stove." The drizzly morning couldn't be called cold, but dampness brought on its own chills, and the hem of her long blue skirt had soaked up a considerable amount of moisture. Barrow hung her coat along with his own and his hat, then set to reviving the smoldering coals in the small potbellied woodstove as Miss Skye settled herself into one of the big green chairs. The fire in the stove had burned itself quite low while he had been at Henry Feele's home, but he soon coaxed the remaining coals to life with a cheery orange glow before tossing a fresh log on top of them. The cast iron stove would soon be giving off proper heat. "Can I offer you anything? Tea, perhaps?"

"Tea would be lovely," she said, rubbing her hands together. She wore white lace gloves. While certainly fetching, they couldn't possibly have provided much in the way of warmth.

Give me gloves of leather and thick wool any day, Barrow thought to himself as he filled the kettle and set it atop the stove, then measured some dried leaves into a plain ceramic teapot. The teapot was nothing fancy to look at, but the spout never dribbled when he poured, and as far as he was concerned that more than made up for what it lacked in aesthetics. Whether teapots or gloves, or anything else for that matter, effectiveness mattered far more to him than appearance. "What can I do for you, Miss Skye?"

"It's my sister, Emily," she said simply, handing him a tintype photograph of a young woman. "I'm afraid she's gone missing."

The younger Miss Skye had rather narrower, more angular features than Meredith. In the picture, her hair looked darker and straighter than Meredith's brilliant, spiraling copper locks, but anyone could clearly see the two were sisters. Even in the grainy photograph, the young woman's eyes smoldered with keen intensity. Barrow examined the photograph carefully, committing the face to memory. "Surely a missing persons case is more of a matter for the police," he said gently. "I have a friend with the constabulary who could—"

"I'd rather not involve the constabulary, Mr. Barrow," Meredith interrupted. "The circumstances of Emily's disappearance are rather...unique, shall we say."

"When is such a disappearance ever mundane," Barrow said rhetorically, furrowing his brow. "Very well, but why come to me? There must be any number of private detectives in Halifax. This sort of case is hardly within the realm of my particular expertise, and I..." he trailed off. One eyebrow arched slowly upward as understanding dawned on him.

"You think there's something of the occult involved in her disappearance?"

Meredith nodded slowly. "You've a reputation for cleverness, and I see now that it's not unearned," she said appreciatively. "I'm ashamed to say it of family, Mr. Barrow, but Emily fell in with the Nightshade Cabal once before. I fear they may be involved in all this."

"I'm no necromancer, Miss Skye," Barrow said, his voice thick with distaste. "My expertise is intertwining the transmundane with science and technology, not the profane rites the Nightshade Cabal practice. Believe me, I've found trouble enough on my own without dabbling in blood magic, resurrectionism, and demon worship."

"I know," she said. "That's why I came to you."

"I'm not sure I see the connection."

"The Cabal would surely notice a fellow necromancer sneaking around their business, would they not?" she asked. When Barrow nodded, she continued, "So my thinking was that another type of magician, say, a technomancer such as yourself, might be able to get close without being noticed."

"I'm afraid it doesn't really work that way, Miss Skye," he explained gently. "Those with a knack for magic can sometimes sense when other talented folk are nearby, it's true, but the differences in how we use the talent are more a matter of individual choice and training than anything else. A specialization, as it were."

"I'm afraid it's my turn to admit I don't follow, Mr. Barrow."

Barrow frowned, pausing a moment to consider how best to explain what he meant. Trying to explain certain aspects of the occult to regular folk was often the most trying part of his career. "Think of a coroner and a surgeon," he said finally. "They perform very different roles, but both are doctors, as are the dentist and the veterinarian, yes? Yet each of these doctors has chosen an area in which to specialize, and in all likelihood wouldn't attempt the duties of the other."

Meredith nodded slowly. "But there are enough commonalities between them that each man would recognize a fellow as his equal. Is that what you mean?"

"Just so," Barrow replied as the kettle began to whistle. He rose from his seat to tend to it. "It's similar among occultists, especially when it comes to the sense we feel when another practitioner is nearby. As much as it galls me to admit it, when all is said and done there's little more than a matter of differing practice that separates what I do from the work of a necromancer."

"How so?"

"What you call *magic* is a manipulation of energies— both natural and transmundane—to effect a tangible outcome in the physical world. Spellcasters can do this in many ways," he explained. "It's something of an oversimplification, but basic spellcraft or so-called potions just combine ingredients to channel energy for magical effect, for example. A fortuneteller might use runestones or marked bones to predict future events. Come to think of it, casting the bones is a very rudimentary form of necromancy. Most necromancers go far further, though, using blood sacrifice to call upon powers from beyond the veil of death to achieve their ends." Barrow paused, watching Meredith to be sure she followed. Seeing she understood, he continued, "There are some spellcasters who don't need a physical conduit to work magic at all. It's exceedingly rare, but sometimes one can harness occult energies by mere thought alone."

"Is that what you do?

"I'm not that talented, nor so ambitious," he said. "As a technomancer, my work involves marrying transmundane elements with mechanical objects to improve their function, or using the principles of physics and the other sciences to strengthen my spellcraft."

"I see. I'm sorry to have wasted your time, Mr. Barrow," she said, rising to leave.

"I never said I wouldn't help you find your sister, Miss Skye," Barrow declared, pouring the hot water into the teapot. "I have little use for necromancers as a rule in general, and even less for those who serve the Cabal. Their very existence stokes the argument that all spellcasters should be put to the stake. Please," he said, urging her to retake her seat by the stove, "do stay."

Meredith inclined her head in thanks, her red curls bouncing lightly. She managed to force a tight smile as she settled herself once more.

Barrow crossed the room to his desk and pulled a small journal bound in red leather from one of the drawers, along with an inkpot and pen. He opened the book to a fresh page as he retook his seat opposite Meredith near the stove. "Tell me what you know of your sister's prior experience with the Cabal and anything before that which might be relevant."

"Emily always thought she had the knack for magic, Mr. Barrow," Meredith began, fretting at the cuff of one sleeve. "From when she was just a wee lass, strange things just seemed to...*happen* around her." She spread her hands wide.

"How do you mean?"

"Nothing drastic at first, you see. She couldn't revive her dead kitten when she was run over by the ragman's cart, or anything of that sort," she explained. "But she'd ask our mum what time our uncle Jimmy was coming to visit when she wasn't expecting him to show up at all, and then he'd turn up at the door in time for dinner with a bottle of wine in hand. That sort of thing."

Barrow nodded as he scribbled something in the notebook. "That kind of foresight is a common enough thing in young children. Most folk never bother to develop it past adolescence, and by adulthood it's all but forgotten. Like any talent, the capacity for magic withers where it goes unpracticed." He smiled faintly. "I would guess that's not what happened in Emily's case, though."

"You'd guess correctly," Meredith confirmed. "She never had any proper training in it the way you might've, mind, but by the time she was fifteen or so, it was known around the neighborhood that Emily could find lost items. She even made a few bob at that for a while, but things got truly ugly one day when she just out and told the butcher's wife that her husband was sneaking around with Miss Moseley, the fishmonger's daughter, right there in front of everybody in the market square."

"That must've been a rather dramatic scene."

"Aye, it was, but it was just the start of the strife. Mum thought Emily was talking to devils, and tried to thrash it out of her that very night." She cast her eyes to the glowing grate of the stove, unable to meet Barrow's gaze as she continued. "When the lash didn't work, she sent Emily off to the nuns at Saint Patrick's, hoping that would be the end of it. It were either the nunnery or the asylum, you see."

Barrow was silent for a moment. He had known his share of troubles when his knack for the mechanical had started to manifest in his youth. When he was eight years old, one of the nuns at his primary school drew blood with the strap when he took apart and reassembled a stopped clock without any tools. The pain of the lashing he had received was secondary to the confusion and betrayal he felt; he had thought he was helping, only to be punished for his efforts. As a child, he hadn't understood the raw, naked fear his preternatural abilities could trigger in others. The scar that remained on his left palm reminded him of it daily.

"Fear can be a very ugly thing, Mr. Barrow," Meredith

said. The sympathetic look she leveled at him said she had followed his thoughts.

He cleared his throat. "Fear of the unfamiliar is part of the human condition," he said, hoping his reply sounded off-handed. He checked the teapot, poured two steaming cups, and handed one to Meredith. "May I ask, Miss Skye, if you've you ever felt any twinge of the knack yourself?"

"Not a whit of it. Why do you ask?"

"The capacity for spellcasting tends to run in family lines," Barrow explained. "It's fairly common for the ability to be shared among siblings, but just as common not. The how and why of it remains a mystery, though." He waved the point aside. "Please, continue."

"Well, Emily ran away from the convent before too long, of course. My sister was never the sort to fit into life at the nunnery, and she knew she couldn't very well come back home after that."

"I would think not."

"She took a job in one of those taverns down by the harbour, one of the ones where seamen wash up to spend every penny of their earnings, if you take my meaning," she said pointedly.

Barrow understood her exactly, but let the sordid details remain unspoken.

"Lawrence MacGowan's place, it was. She was just clearing the tables and helping out in the kitchen, mind!"

"I know the place," he said vaguely, jotting down some notes. "Did you keep in touch with Emily through this time?" he asked.

Meredith nodded. "She wrote me in secret when she fled the convent, and we'd meet at the Commons near Citadel Hill every Sunday after Mass. I felt terribly guilty keeping it from our mum, but what else was I to do?"

"How did Emily become involved with the Cabal?"

"It was just about this time last year, soon after her seventeenth birthday. She was working at MacGowan's place, like I told you, when a man approached her. Said he could see the magic shining around her 'like an angel's halo,' he did." Meredith drew her fingers through the air around her head in mockery of the platitude. "She told me later that she didn't know what he was when she met him, else she never would've gone off with him. But you have to understand, Mr. Barrow, he was the first person she ever met who didn't treat her knack like the plague or some kind of curse."

"It's a common ploy devotees of the dark paths use to lure new initiates," Barrow said, contempt evident in his tone. "They prey on young people with the knack who have been ostracized by family and friends. How much do you know about the Nightshade Cabal, Miss Skye?"

She shrugged. "Only what Emily told me," she answered. "That they're a guild of necromancers who spend their time talking to the dead and trying to conjure up spirits to do their bidding."

"They are that, but they're also a dangerous band of fringe lunatics, chaos worshipers, and profane occultists with real power," Barrow said. "Some extremists among them engage in blood sacrifice, trying to win the favour of dark gods and demons."

"Gods and demons, Mr. Barrow?" Meredith asked skeptically, seeming cynical for the first time in the interview. "Surely you don't expect me to believe in such things?"

"Gods and demons are very real, Miss Skye," he said, a grim expression on his face. "I've had more dealings with both than I care to recall. I don't want to worry you unnecessarily, but if the Nightshade Cabal are behind Emily's disappearance, she could be in very real trouble."

"I thought as much myself," she said, rising from her seat.

"That's why I came to you for aid. I see now my trust is well-placed."

For once caught at a loss for words, he paused a beat before he answered. "I will do my best, but I can't promise your sister's safe return."

The slightest of cracks appeared in Meredith's brave façade at that moment as a single tear welled in her eye. By sheer force of will, she did not permit it to roll down her cheek. Instead, she raised her chin. "I trust you'll do your best for us, Mr. Barrow." Taking up her overcoat and umbrella, she turned and walked out into the afternoon sun without another word.

The rain had stopped.

SHORTLY AFTER MEREDITH SKYE'S DEPARTURE, BARROW locked the door to the street. Before anything else, he still had the matter of Henry Feele's errant autotype machine to investigate. He wasn't in the habit of taking on multiple clients at once, preferring to devote his entire attention to one matter whenever possible, but he had been without a paying job for several weeks. The time between clients hadn't been wasted, though. Barrow had his own research to attend to, and he had welcomed the time to devote to his own pursuits. With a sigh, he resigned himself to the fact that his personal studies would once again have to be set aside for the time being.

Taking up his valise containing Feele's memory cylinder, he headed for the door marked PRIVATE at the back of the office. The windowless room within was smaller by half than Barrow's tiny streetside office, its floorspace dominated by a large workbench in the middle of the floor. A few dusty hand tools were scattered on the surface along with some mechanical bits and pieces: a few steam fittings of various sizes, a coil of wire, the face of an old clock. These, like the tools, were covered in a fine layer of dust.

Reaching underneath the workbench's wooden top, he felt around. His blind fingers soon found the trigger catch they were searching for. As the heavy switch flipped over with a loud *clack*, the workbench raised itself a fraction of an inch as hidden castors pushed out from the base. The entire assembly slid quietly aside, revealing a winding stairway that led down to Isaac Barrow's true workshop.

Descending the iron spiral stair to his workshop always brought a feeling of calm. He kept a small apartment a few blocks away, but the subterranean workshop was where Barrow truly felt at home.

Gas lamps hissed quietly; Barrow had dynamos and alternators to generate electricity and several large voltaic storage batteries, but he preferred the softer light the older lamps cast. Though driven by discovery, he was in many ways fiercely nostalgic. Sparsely furnished but for a threadbare green chaise longue to one side, the cavernous space was scrupulously neat. Shelves of supplies ran the length of one wall, while others filled with leather-bound volumes on all subjects, from the mechanical to the arcane, ranged along another. He had lined the shelves with cedar to keep insects from nibbling at his books. But, being underground, he had also placed some simple magical wards in place as an extra precaution.

Barrow's underground workshop occupied the entire basement beneath the large building that housed his street-side office. He knew that the impressive space was nothing when compared to Thomas Edison's new facility at Menlo Park, but neither did he have a growing staff of brilliant young assistants working under him. He worked alone, with no one but himself to share in the credit for his triumphs or, as he felt was more often the case of late, the blame for his shortfalls.

The ceiling and walls, built of reinforced hydrostone, were lined with flame-retardant paneling behind the plaster. The engineered concrete slabs were designed to keep ground moisture out. If one of his experiments were to go terribly wrong, the sturdy hydrostone slabs would also contain any explosion. At least, that was the hope. He had not yet had the opportunity put the construction to the test as, thus far, he hadn't managed to set anything much more than his worktable alight. Thankfully, his catastrophes remained small ones.

"Maybe this time," he muttered sarcastically as he set himself to the task at hand.

Henry Feele had told him the autotype machine had been spooling out entire pages of gibberish text unbidden. Barrow's intention with the memory cylinder was to let it do just that. The paper rolls the autotype machines used for output were frightfully expensive, but ticker tape was cheap. All he had to do, he theorized, was improvise a way for the memory cylinder to connect to a stockticker printer and leave the thing to its own devices for a few days. With the stock-ticker doing the printing, he hoped, he didn't need the bulky autotype unit to test his theory. The ticker would only hammer out about one letter every two seconds – much slower than the autotype machine's output – but as he so often did, he would have to make do with what was available.

Had the memory cylinder been a standard size, he could simply have wired any powered cradle and matched the component to the ticker's input line. With the cylinder being an oversized custom piece, he'd have to craft a suitable makeshift. It didn't take Barrow long to cobble together a workable cradle to house the memory cylinder and connect it to the stockticker.

"After all," he chided himself as he caught himself admiring his own ingenuity, "this isn't a case of inventing something wholly new, I'm just adapting existing components to fit a new need." Wiring his makeshift unit to the stock ticker only took a few minutes. He fit the memory cylinder between the upright brackets he had set up, and connected the device to a fully charged voltaic battery.

For a moment, he wondered if anything was going to happen. Surely enough, after nearly a minute, the ticker began to hammer out letters in a slow, methodical beat.

Tick, tick, tick...

5

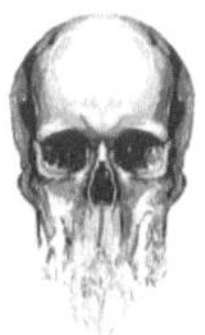

Hammering out one letter every few seconds, it would be several hours—if not days—before the ticker would print anything of use. With the rest of the afternoon and evening free, Barrow decided to use the time to start looking into the disappearance of Emily Skye. Before he could do anything else, though, a growl from deep in his stomach reminded him that he hadn't eaten anything solid since the few biscuits he had had with tea at Henry Feele's home earlier in the day.

He headed for a small café less than a block away. The place had a few seats, but mostly served carryout meals for workers from the brewery across the street and the nearby factories. It was exceptionally basic fare at best, but he was only looking for something to fill the growling emptiness in the pit of his stomach. He reviewed the sparse notes he had jotted down during his meeting with Meredith as he made his way through a wholly flavorless stew of ham and potato swimming in a sort of thin, yellowish broth.

The frown that creased his brow had less to do with the food and more to do with the exceedingly scant information

Meredith Skye had been able to provide. Aside from the address of the boardinghouse where Emily had rented a room, and her most recent place of employment, he didn't have much at all to go on.

When he had finished his meager meal, he set off for the Halifax Constabulary Headquarters, hoping it wasn't too late in the afternoon to catch Inspector Eddings at his desk. Meredith had her reasons for not wanting to involve the police in the matter, but Barrow thought he could count on his friend's discretion.

Located in the basement of City Hall, itself a converted and aging courthouse, the cramped and grimy offices the Halifax Constabulary called their headquarters were widely considered an embarrassment by police and civic officials alike. Proposals and plans to move the constabulary to a dedicated facility came and went, but funding the construction never seemed to make its way onto the city's list of priorities when budgets were tabled. Practical matters had a bad habit of dying on the desks of important men.

A portrait of Queen Victoria hung above the desk. Barrow always regarded it as a rather drab and lifeless effort, the artist leaving the queen looking dour and jaundiced. The Dominion of Canada had been granted its independence fourteen years earlier, but Victoria was still widely revered across the young nation.

A second portrait hung beside that of the queen, this one bearing the likeness of Prime Minister John A. Macdonald. Barrow had no love for the Tory, whose first tenure in office had ended in scandal. How the disgraced politician hadn't been ousted from his party entirely, Barrow never understood. Watching the story unfold had left him apathetic toward politics, where showmanship seemed to count for more than a man's deeds. He wondered if the constabulary had kept the painting in some storeroom somewhere for the five years Alexander Mackenzie had led the nation.

The duty clerk attending the reception desk was an older constable named O'Hara. He had the stooped bearing of a man who had done his years on the beat and then some, but the gleam in his eye said he wasn't yet ready to be put out to pasture. Constable O'Hara knew Barrow by sight, and welcomed him warmly before ushering him down the hall to the inspector's office. Barrow felt a momentary pang of guilt as he realized he had forgotten the older constable's first name.

An automaton carrying an armload of files clanked past as they walked the long corridor. It was very much a baseline unit, one of the cheapest available and not good for much of anything at all beyond filing and fetching, but with its gleaming skin of brass and steel, it still looked absurdly out of place as it ambled down the shabby hallway.

Unlike the transit authority, the Halifax Constabulary did not feel the need to clothe the mechanical man. Barrow took a moment to admire the automaton's exposed gears and pistons as it moved. "I'd pay good money for a chance to take that machine apart one day, just for a look at what's inside," he said wistfully to Constable O'Hara.

The constable chuckled as they watched the unit awkwardly negotiate a corner to head off to the file room. Walking in a straight line was easy for the mechanical man, but its limited hip mobility made corners more difficult. Stairs were likely an impossibility.

"You're not here to help the inspector with one of our cases, are you, Mr. Barrow?" O'Hara asked in a hushed voice as they resumed walking. "I hadn't heard of anything too out of the ordinary coming across the docket in the last few weeks – not since the Osgood case."

Barrow felt a moment of regret at the death of Edward

Osgood. Osgood had died while dining at the Carleton House, the apparent victim of a sorcerous attack. Barrow and Eddings had been there as well, witnessing the scene first-hand. The investigation revealed Osgood had been a spell-caster, a fact a colleague at his bank was planning to reveal to their manager. Fearing termination, Osgood cursed the fellow with a spell of bane, only to have the spell slowly backfire and burn up his lungs from the inside out. The case had been ruled a suicide, but prejudice and fear had killed Edward Osgood as surely as if the man had put a knife in his belly.

"Not this time, Constable O'Hara," he said. "I'm actually hoping Inspector Eddings can help me with an investigation of my own for a change."

"The good Lord above knows he owes you a favour or two, sure enough," O'Hara chuckled. It was no great secret around the precinct that Eddings called upon Barrow when the constabulary found themselves faced with anything involving the supernatural. Crimes involving the occult prop-erly fell under the jurisdiction of the Triune Congress, but as often as not lately, the metaphysical and the mundane over-lapped, with the constabulary knee-deep in troubles well beyond its ken.

Consulting with a known spellcaster on police matters ran against official policy. However, the constabulary resolved more of the paranormal cases with Barrow's aid than would be possible to crack without him. He invoiced the constabulary for his services under the ambiguous title of *Technical Consultant*. The ruse fooled no one, but as long as his participation yielded results, administrators were usually content to look the other way.

"The inspector will be with you in a moment I'm sure, Mr. Barrow," Constable O'Hara said as they neared the closed office door. "He's, ah...he's just dealing with a small disciplinary matter."

Barrow thanked the constable as he took a seat by the door. Whatever the matter was, Inspector Eddings's booming voice could be heard through the solid wooden door. He couldn't make out much of what was being said, but even through a few inches of oak, his friend's ferocity was easy enough to hear. Barrow made an effort not to eavesdrop, but he could hardly help but overhear some of the inspector's more colourful profanity; Jonathon Eddings had a tendency to punctuate his more scatological exclamations with increased volume.

Several uncomfortable minutes crept by. Barrow felt a deal of sympathy for the target of the inspector's rage. The conversation from within soon turned quiet, which from this side of the door felt worse by far for whomever was on the receiving end of the tirade. A few moments later, the door swung open and a shamefaced young constable shuffled out, hat in hand. Even hanging his head, the constable was easily a full foot taller than Barrow with a massive build to match his towering height, but he carried himself like a boy who had just been scolded by his mother for forgetting his jacket on the streetcar. Declining to make eye contact with anything but the scuffed floorboards, he hurried off down the narrow hallway. Eddings stood in the doorway, red-faced and glaring after the cowed young man.

"Right, then," he barked without looking in Barrow's direction. He jerked a thumb towards his office. "Get yourself on in here."

The inspector's office was small and rather sparsely furnished, especially given his rank. His maple desk took up nearly a third of the room, and a row of sturdy file cabinets filled one wall. A large painting of the White Cliffs of Dover hung on the opposite wall, and a few chairs filled the rest of the space. There was a small window at the very back of the room, high up near the ceiling, letting in a little light in the form of a thin and watery sunbeam, constantly shifting and broken by feet as people on the street above passed by.

Eddings dropped himself heavily into his big leather chair, one of the few luxuries he allowed himself on the job. It groaned under his weight. He pulled a half-empty bottle of scotch from one of the drawers of his desk, worked the stopper free, and poured himself a generous drink. He wasted no time offering Barrow a belt; he knew his friend better than that. Without a word, he drained the glass and refilled it.

Barrow hung his bowler and coat on a hook near the door and settled into one of the seats on the other side of the desk, one eyebrow raised in question.

The inspector rumbled a deep sigh. "There was a carriage collision on Buckingham Street this morning," he explained, jamming the stopper back into the bottle of scotch. "One of those blasted steamcarriages you're so in love with crashed into an offal cart. One of the horses was killed, and young Constable McCallister, who you saw just now, attended the scene. It fell to him to fill out the incident report."

"Was there some error in the report he filed?"

"The report was fine, but the bloody idiot dragged the horse's carcass three blocks to Duke Street before writing it up because he didn't know how to spell *Buckingham*."

Barrow did his best to hide a grin. His best, unfortunately, was not good enough.

"Aye, go on and laugh."

"I'm sorry, Jonathon. Didn't Constable McCallister think to look at the street sign above him and copy the spelling?"

"It didn't occur to him." Eddings sounded tired. He took another swig of scotch. "I suppose he was too busy playing at being the knacker's errand boy."

"In a way, you have to admire the young constable's inventive problem-solving."

"Don't start with me, Barrow. I haven't the patience for it today." He rubbed at his temples then drained the remainder of his glass once more. "It's not enough I've got McCallister dragging a dead horse all over town, now you go on and show up here uninvited."

"You wound me, Jonathon. I didn't realize I had to schedule an appointment."

Eddings sighed and apologized. "You know you're always welcome to stop in, but in my experience, it's rarely a social call when you do. What is it that brings you by this time?"

Barrow felt a moment of guilt and annoyance at having his motives so readily inferred. "I've taken a case," he said, pulling the photograph from his jacket pocket. "A missing girl. I thought I'd begin by asking if you had heard anything that might be pertinent."

"Pretty enough young thing," Eddings said as he studied the photograph. "She'd be, what, about sixteen years old? Who is she?"

"Seventeen, actually. Her name is Emily Skye. Her sister, one Miss Meredith Skye, visited my office this afternoon to seek my help in locating her."

"Why would she come to you? This isn't normally your sort of business. Why wouldn't she bring this to the constabulary?"

Barrow hesitated before he answered. "Emily Skye is...well, she's like me, Jonathon."

"An insufferable annoyance, you mean?"

Most men would've had the courtesy to wither under the glare Barrow shot at his friend for that remark, but Eddings only chuckled.

"I mean, *Inspector Eddings*, that the girl has magical talent. Her sister believes she may have been abducted."

"Nasty business. How long has the girl been missing?"

"A little over a week."

Eddings exhaled smoke. "Well, for what it's worth, I can tell you that she hasn't turned up in the city morgue," he said, looking at the photograph once more. "There's been no shortage of fresh bodies coming through lately, but I'm quite certain she's not been one of them."

"I'm glad to hear it. The thought that she might've met with some dreadful fate had crossed my mind."

"Hard not to think that when a young thing like her goes missing," Eddings agreed. "You hope to find them all safe and warm, but all too often it goes the other way." He shook his head sadly. "Do you have anything to go on at all?"

"Not much, I'm afraid," Barrow said austerely. "I have the address of the boardinghouse she was staying at, and I know she had taken work at MacGowan's Wheelhouse."

Eddings whistled. "She'd come up against no lack of unsavoury types in that place. Of course, I don't need to tell you that. I take it you'll be poking your nose in around there at some point?"

"I don't see that I have much choice in the matter."

"For God's sake, be careful, Barrow."

"In all the years you've known me, Jonathon, have you ever known me to take an unnecessary risk?"

"Do you want that list ordered chronologically or alphabetically?" Eddings grinned. "Need I remind you which of us leapt from the Devil's Island Lighthouse wearing a set of wings made out of canvas and brass, just to see if they worked?"

"That should've worked, Jonathon," Barrow said. "The elemental bonding—"

Eddings put up a hand to cut him off. "Some other time, Barrow. As much as I enjoy trading barbs with you, none of this helps the missing Skye girl." He scratched his chin. "There is another possibility, you know. She very well might've gone off on her own for some reason. It very well might be that Emily Skye doesn't want to be found."

Barrow considered that for a moment before deciding he didn't know enough about the girl to speculate. "I'll work on the assumption that's not the case," he decided.

"Suit yourself." Eddings shrugged. "If I hear anything on my end I'll let you know straight away, of course. The Skye girl aside, what happened with Henry Feele this morning?"

"A mechanical mystery is all. It's rather a puzzler, to tell you the truth, but I believe it's one that I can handle quite capably." Until he knew more about the memory cylinder, he decided to keep his suspicions regarding the device's potentially grisly origins to himself.

Inspector Eddings seemed quite satisfied with this short answer. The man had an uncanny ability to tell when he was being lied to, a skill which made him exceptionally effective in the interrogation room. If he suspected Barrow was holding anything back now, though, he didn't let on. "You should come by the house sometime," he said. "Jayne and the boys would like to see you. An evening's company and a home-cooked meal would do you a world of good."

Barrow nodded, feeling another pang of guilt. He knew he had a tendency to neglect his friendships when he was working, which seemed to be always. "I'll try," he promised with a thin smile. "Thank you, Jonathon." He shook the inspector's hand and headed for the street.

✿

THERE WAS NOTHING OUTWARDLY REMARKABLE ABOUT Mrs. Winslow's boardinghouse on Clarke Street. With its rolling green lawn and wraparound veranda, the blue three-storey house in the middle of the block looked much the same as the houses on either side of it, if a bit on the large side for the neighbourhood.

Mrs. Winslow herself was also on the large side, huffing and puffing a bit as she pushed herself up the stairs to the third floor. "I haven't seen Miss Skye in near a fortnight, Mr. Barrow. She's paid up through the end of the month, though, so I've not set foot in her room, and I don't make it my business to keep watch on the comings and goings of the girls."

Barrow didn't quite believe that last part; it seemed to be a rule that landladies loved gossip nearly as much as they hated scandal under their own roofs. He kept his misgivings to himself as he followed her up the stairs.

She stopped at the second door in a long hallway and fished a ring of keys from an apron pocket. A large window at the far end of the corridor stood open, linen curtains billowing lazily inward in the soft afternoon breeze.

"She seemed a bright sort of girl, of course. Never too busy for a friendly chinwag when you saw her, which is more than I can say for half the girls we get around here these days." She clicked her tongue in disapproval as she worked the key in the lock. "It does seem queer, her disappearing without a word the way she did."

"Thank you, Mrs. Winslow."

"Have you any idea what might've happened to her? I only ask for the sake of the other girls, you see."

Barrow idly wondered once more if that was wholly true. Either way, though, he had nothing to tell her. "I don't know much of anything. I'm afraid I only began my investigation this very morning."

"I'll leave you to it then, Mr. Barrow." She hustled off toward the stairs.

Emily Skye's room was more or less what he had expected it to be. The furnishings were simple, consisting of only a bed, a half-sized wardrobe, a mirrored vanity, and a small roll top writing desk. An empty coat stand stood by the door. There was also little in the way of decoration; a hinged diptych frame atop the dresser held tintype photographs of Emily's sister, Meredith, and an older woman Barrow assumed to be their mother.

A quick glance around the tidy room offered little in the way of evidence, but there were no apparent signs of foul play. Indeed, true to Mrs. Winslow's word, there were no signs the room had been disturbed at all since the girl's disappearance. Everything seemed to be in perfect order, and the bed had clearly not been slept in.

He checked the wardrobe. A small collection of simple linen blouses and skirts were folded away neatly in the drawers, apparently untouched. If Emily Skye had been snatched away, her captor had not rifled through her meager belongings. The vanity drawers were also unmolested, but aside from a pair of heavy sewing shears, he found nothing that struck him as out of the ordinary.

He turned his attention to the roll-top desk. There was a stack of letters from Meredith in one of the drawers, tidily folded back into the envelopes in which they had arrived. He briefly scanned a few of these, but found nothing in them that seemed relevant. Pay receipts from MacGowan's tavern, filed by date, filled another small drawer. Barrow examined these thoroughly. With a sigh, he replaced them in the drawer.

Expecting to find nothing more than another assortment of mundane items, Barrow pulled open a third drawer. There was only one item inside. With a low whistle, he tentatively picked up a small glass phial, half-full of a thick, indigo liquid. He didn't need to unstop the phial to know what it contained.

Eldersight!

But where would the young girl have come across even half a dose of the powerful psychoactive compound? The

Triune Congress had long since proscribed the import and use of the drug, while mortal authorities continued to deny its very existence. Even among the rogue fringe, eldersight hadn't been seen in the Halifax occult underground in over five years. If Emily Skye had even this tiny amount of the potent drug in her possession, it was a definite sign that whatever she had become entangled in was dire indeed.

Standing there examining the phial in his hand, Barrow was abruptly wrenched from his reverie by a clatter from the open doorway behind him. Turning sharply, he locked eyes with a shocked-looking boy. Dressed in patched dungarees, scuffed heavy boots, and an oversized wool cap, the lad could've easily been taken for one of the Collywobble Boys, had he not been a good five years older than the rest of the gang of street urchins. The youth had knocked over the coat stand as he entered the room.

Without a word, the boy turned and bolted.

"You there! Wait!"

Barrow started after him, but got caught up on the fallen coat stand that lay across the threshold. Muttering a curse, he picked the thing up and flung it into the hallway, then barreled out after it. In that time, the boy had made it more than halfway to the far end of the long corridor.

"Wait!" Barrow called out again.

The lad cast a quick look back over his shoulder but did not stop running. Redoubling his steps as he neared the end of the hallway, he leapt up and planted a foot on the sill, flinging himself forward through the open window.

Barrow sprinted after him, a twisting, sick feeling rising in the pit of his belly. They were on the third floor of the house. The fall might not be enough to kill the boy, but he'd surely break several bones in the landing.

Skidding to a stop at the window, Barrow threw aside the linen curtains and leaned out into open air, expecting to see the boy's crumpled form laid out on the ground below. Instead, all he could see on the flagstones was the lad's fallen wool cap.

Barrow looked up and across just in time to see the boy haul his legs up and onto the rooftop of the house next door, a building about a half-storey shorter than Mrs. Winslow's boardinghouse. Safe on the other side, the boy looked back across at Barrow, his eyes wide with panic. Without his lost cap, Barrow could see now the lad had short-cropped red hair, tousled and wild. Before Barrow could call out again, the youngster turned on his heels and ran off across the neighbouring rooftop.

Barrow swore under his breath. He knew he couldn't hope to leap the gap himself. The boy had barely made it across, and he had been running full bore when he heaved himself through the window, to say nothing of the fact that he likely weighed a good two stone less than Barrow. He turned from the window and raced for the staircase, taking the steps two at a time and careening past the bewildered Mrs. Winslow as he darted through the front door onto the veranda.

He looked up at the house next door, but there was no sign of the red-haired boy on the roof. He ran the length of the block, scanning the rooftops of each house as he went, but with no luck. A thorough search of the laneway and gardens behind each and every house on that side of the street came up empty.

The boy had disappeared.

6

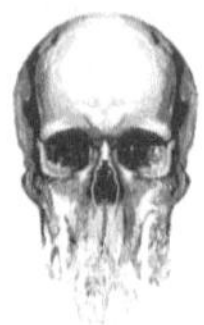

THE HARBOUR'S STINK FILLED BARROW'S NOSTRILS AS HE
neared the waterfront. The harsh tang of the salty sea air
mingled with the carrion reek of dead fish and the acrid
fumes belched out by the coal-fired steamships idling in port.
Here at the docks, the veneer of polite society sloughed away
like the skin of some ancient reptile, revealing the true heart
that drove Halifax.

Like all port cities, Halifax had been built on the
seafaring trades: whaling and fisheries, transatlantic shipping,
and the military. As much as the young city's rising elite may
have wished to keep such crass concerns at arm's length, the
true nature of things was never far from the surface.

In the earliest years of the settlement, raucous taverns
and brothels had ranged from the docks all the way up to
Knock 'Em Down Street in the shadow of the looming
Citadel. French and British soldiers alike, as well as sailors
in port, shared in driving the booming local economy of sin.
The harbour that drew them had only grown busier over
the last two hundred years, but the city's maturation over
the centuries and the establishment of a more genteel

society had pushed most dens of iniquity to the very outskirts.

MacGowan's Wheelhouse carried on the hedonistic traditions of those early days. It was the sort of place a man could find both drink and debauchery. Sailors on leave could spend their entire earnings in a week on dry land without going any further inland than MacGowan's. A great many regularly did just that, returning to sea as penniless as when they had first set sail. A man had to look no further than the Wheelhouse to find drink, a game of dice or cards, a bed for a night or a week, and someone to warm it. More exotic entertainments, and indulgences stronger than drink were also available if you knew who and how to ask; seamen traveled widely, after all, and they tended to bring unconventional and oft-times unsavoury tastes to bear.

The world had a lot to offer. Lawrence MacGowan tried his level best to match it.

The building itself was massive, having been built as a shipping warehouse before falling into MacGowan's hands. The two golem-like guards he had working the door were equally impressive. Both of the big men had the broad shoulders, thick muscles, and swarthy features of a Cossack from a storybook, while the tattoos and scars they bore told of the hardships they had lived through. The Wheelhouse attracted some rough customers, but even the most seasoned of brawlers thought twice about starting any trouble after seeing these two.

"Weapons in a locker," one of them grunted as Barrow drew near, jerking a big thumb towards several rows of small metal compartments. The other guard said nothing, focused as he was on digging something out from under a yellowed and cracked fingernail with the tip of a vicious stiletto.

"Do I look the sort to be carrying a sidearm?" Barrow asked with a show of indignity.

The second guard snorted as he tucked his dagger into a leather sheath on his hip and gestured for Barrow to raise his arms. He wordlessly, and rather roughly, patted Barrow down, front and back. Barrow thought the fellow was particularly thorough in searching his inseam, but decided it would be rather imprudent in the moment to mention it.

As he finished his search, the guard snorted once more and nodded to his partner as he pulled his wicked dagger from its sheath. He flashed Barrow a savage grin, then leaned back against the wall and got back to work on his manicure.

"Enjoy your evening," the first guard said with a sneer. Barrow nodded his thanks and headed inside before breathing a heavy sigh of relief. His concealment glamour had worked—the guards hadn't found the elementally powered Webley revolver hidden at the small of his back.

It was Tuesday night, but if the revelers here had anywhere important to be on Wednesday morning, they didn't seem to care. The sun had gone down little more than an hour earlier, but a riotous bacchanalia was already in full swing. A trio of musicians on the small stage at the far end of the cavernous room belted out a bawdy sailor's tune. Fueled by ale, a rowdy huddle had gathered near the stage and was singing along in various keys, few of which actually matched the notes being played. The resulting calamity would've made the nine muses weep and wail in horror, but no one present seemed offended by how bad the drunken chorus sounded.

The gaming tables were also doing brisk business. The Wheelhouse had separate, quieter rooms for poker, but here in the main room there were tables for blackjack and roulette, two-up and throwing dice, and a number of other games Barrow did not recognize.

He briefly observed a game where the players placed and shifted numbered tiles resembling dominoes around the table, but he couldn't make much sense of the winning patterns. Tiles bearing matching prime numbers and pairings adding up to nine seemed to be among the most desirable combinations, but he didn't linger long enough to watch the full game. The use of numbers in the game intrigued him, though. He resolved to find out how to play.

He was distracted from the game by that familiar extrasensory twinge cutting through the crowd and signaling the presence of a fellow magician nearby. Scanning the unruly room, he soon picked out a familiar figure. The man was tall, pale, clad entirely in black, and heading in Barrow's direction.

"Hello, Malleus," Barrow greeted the black-clad man with little warmth in his voice. "What brings you to the Wheelhouse?"

Malleus did not offer his hand in greeting, not that Barrow would have clasped it if he had. "Triune business," he said, his voice flat. Supposedly centuries old, Malleus was one of the few people Barrow had met who spoke with an authentic Acadian accent. In his hand, he carried a simple straight walking stick with a large green gemstone set in the pommel. The cane didn't look like much, but Barrow knew that in Malleus' hand, it was a weapon far deadlier than the one he had managed to sneak into the tavern.

He had no quarrel with Malleus and was not looking to start one. A Magister for the Triune Congress, Malleus was vested with authority over all occult matters. Once, that had simply meant ensuring practitioners adhered to a strict code of conduct when working magic, as much for their own protection as for that of the world at large. These days, however, the mundane and the paranormal had a way of overlapping more and more frequently. The Magister's role was becoming increasingly complicated.

"Triune business," Barrow repeated with a nod. "Which is to say, none of mine."

Malleus leaned in uncomfortably close and peered over the red lenses of his peculiar round spectacles. "I could ask what you're doing here as well, Barrow, and what madness compelled you to smuggle an elementally-charged weapon past security."

"As if I'm the only one," Barrow hissed, his eyes darting to the cane Malleus carried.

Malleus looked to the cane as though he had forgotten he had it, which very well could've been the case; Barrow had never seen him without it in his hand.

Barrow made a decided effort not to let Malleus get his hackles up. He reminded himself silently that he was here to ask after Emily Skye, nothing more. He hadn't come to get into a verbal spat with a Triune Magister, no matter how much Malleus personally irked him. "At any rate, I'm here on business of my own, which is not any concern of the Triune Congress." *Or their lapdog*, he thought, keeping that much to himself.

Malleus's craggy face twisted as though he had bitten into something sour. "Your business tends to have a way of becoming the Triune Congress's concern, Isaac. You flaunt your abilities far too openly for our liking."

That was too much to let slide. "What would you have me do, Malleus? Skulk about in the shadows and alleys? The world is changing! Science and industry are already accomplishing things mankind could never have dreamed of just a century ago, with or without magic. We have a very real chance to help shape things for the better." Caught up by his own speech, he reached out and gripped Malleus by the shoulder. "Not just a chance, Malleus. We have a responsibility!"

Malleus raised an eyebrow as he looked down at Barrow's

hand on his shoulder. He gently, but deliberately, used his cane to brush it aside. "Shadows and alleys are the only place men like you and I are safe, Barrow. You would do well to read your histories. Have you forgotten Trier, Basque, and North Berwick? Have you forgotten Salem, and even Ipswich?"

"I've read the histories, and it always comes down to the same thing: fear. Raw, naked fear. They fear us because they don't understand us and the things we can do. Maybe the world wouldn't be in the sorry state it is today if people didn't have to live in fear simply for being who they are."

Malleus was silent for a moment. "In a way, I have to admire your youthful idealism, but the world is not ready to accept us. It may never be."

Barrow sighed in resignation. He knew they could argue the point for hours and never come close to agreement. "Until it is, Malleus, it would appear you and I don't have much to discuss." He tipped the brim of his hat as he turned away, but he could feel Malleus's cold, dissecting gaze boring into his back as he crossed the raucous room.

LAWRENCE MACGOWAN'S PERSONAL SUITE WAS ON THE second floor, far away from the rooms where his girls plied their trade. Softly lit by gaslight, his orderly office drew a stark contrast to the general mayhem that reigned downstairs. One wall was lined entirely with sturdy oak shelves, heavy with books. Barrow stole a glance at a few titles as he entered the room. British writers dominated the shelves. Lawrence MacGowan owned several volumes of Carlyle, Dickens, and Swift. Among the few American works Barrow spotted, were a handful of Mark Twain's recent novels and *The Complete Works of Edgar Allan Poe.*

One book, in particular, caught Barrow's eye, an older edition of Marlowe's *The Tragical History of the Life and Death of Doctor Faustus*, bound in red leather. He had seen and coveted a similar copy two weeks earlier at a bookseller's called the Owl's Nest. The price of the book had been nearly a week's rent, though. He could've afforded it, but such an indulgence struck him as irresponsible. With no small degree of resignation, he had returned it to the shelf.

"You would've expected a merchant of degeneracy to seek out the same entertainments as his clientele, Mr. Barrow?" MacGowan asked as he shook Barrow's hand, slyly letting Barrow know that he had noticed him assessing his personal library. The practiced smile he unleashed would've been the envy of any traveling medicine peddler.

Barrow took a moment to examine the man. Lawrence MacGowan's bespoke suit was of the finest material, with an embroidered green silk waistcoat and matching pocket square. Everything fit him perfectly; his tailor had done remarkable work. A delicate gold chain disappeared into his pocket, no doubt connected to an impressively expensive fob watch. The scars that marred his knuckles were the only visible indicators of his checkered past.

"It's an impressive collection, Mr. MacGowan," Barrow said appreciatively, nodding to the bookcases. MacGowan inclined his head and smiled at the compliment, another clearly choreographed gesture. "If I'm not mistaken, there are quite a few British first editions on your shelves."

"One of the advantages of dealing with sailors. I have a handful of seamen who bring back the latest titles when they visit from afar. When they bring me books, they drink for free that night. I simply don't have the time to put up with shoddy American printings full of mangled text." He smiled again as he pulled a crystal decanter filled with golden brandy and two matching snifters out of a desk drawer. "Can I offer you a drink, Mr. Barrow?" he asked, working the stopper free. "Turkish, aged in oak for thirty years. It's very fine."

"No, thank you."

Barrow suppressed a smile. No matter how much coin he pressed into the hands of the city's best tailors, no matter how many first editions he had imported from England, a rogue like Lawrence MacGowan would never be accepted in the higher echelons of society he tried to mimic. All of his fancy clothing amounted to little more than an elaborate costume, his books and fine liquors little more than window dressing.

MacGowan eyed Barrow with seeming apprehension. "You're not one of those Temperance Leaguers, are you?"

"Not in the least, Mr. MacGowan. I believe everyone has his own choices to make in life, and if swilling himself into insensibility on the nightly is what a man desires, he ought to have the right to do so."

MacGowan laughed heartily and raised his glass in salute. "I'll drink to that. But you're not here to discuss temperance or my taste in literature, are you? Tell me, Mr. Barrow, what can I do for you?"

Barrow fished the photograph Meredith Skye had given him out of the pocket inside his jacket. "I'm trying to locate a young woman who was recently in your employ," he said, handing the photograph across the desk.

MacGowan studied the photograph for a brief moment. "Emily Skye," he said, handing it back. "She worked for me through most of last winter. I haven't seen her around here in a few months. Good lass, if a bit on the quiet side. She's gone missing, you say?"

"A little over a week ago, yes," Barrow said as he tucked the photograph back in his pocket. "Do you know if Miss Skye was in any sort of trouble? Can you think of anyone who might have wanted to harm her for any reason?"

MacGowan paused to think that over. "Nothing that I'm

aware of. I don't make a point of getting involved in my staff's personal affairs, of course, but as far as I know, Emily kept her nose out of trouble, which is more than I can say for a lot of other folks in my employ."

"I understand there's a lot that's troubling about this place," Barrow said, thinking back to his encounter with Malleus, but left it at that. "What about her time here? Did she get on well with the rest of the staff?"

"She kept to herself for the most part. She was rather quiet, as I said before."

"And when she quit, did you try to keep her on?"

"I didn't care much whether she stayed or left." MacGowan shrugged aloofly. "It's always easy enough to find another scullery girl. No shortage of girls out there looking for work these days. But if you're asking whether or not there was anything untoward in her departure, I can tell you Miss Skye didn't leave on bad terms. She owed me no debts, so I had no reason to coerce her into staying."

Frowning, Barrow jotted some notes down in his book. "What did Emily do around here?"

MacGowan shrugged again. "Kitchen help, mostly. Peeling potatoes, cooking a bit, running back and forth with the empty glassware." He smiled his practiced smile once more. "She didn't provide any entertainments if that's what you're asking. Even if she had wanted to, which she didn't, I assure you I wouldn't've put her to it."

"That wasn't what I was inferring, but since you've brought it up, may I ask why not?"

"I've never forced an unwilling girl into the skin trade, Mr. Barrow. I want that much to be abundantly clear," MacGowan explained, his expression gravely serious. "For one thing, there's enough who are willing that forcing one who's not, strikes me as more trouble than it's worth. For another, you get better work out of the ones who don't have to be forced into it, if you take my meaning."

Barrow coughed, embarrassed.

Amused at his apparent discomfort, MacGowan chuckled. "In Miss Skye's case, though...well, without putting too fine a point on things, she's a pretty enough girl but she was built like a twelve-year-old lad. A man who has just washed up at my door with money in his hand after sixteen months at sea is looking to spend his time—and his coin—making the acquaintance of someone who's going to remind him what a woman feels like.

"I'm afraid there's not much more I can tell you, Mr. Barrow. Emily is a sweet girl and I sincerely hope she turns up soon, and unharmed. I've enjoyed our conversation, but unless there's something else, I really must get back to this exhilarating paperwork." He nodded toward a series of open ledgers taking up a corner of his desk with a halfhearted grin.

"Actually, there is one more thing," Barrow said, reaching into his jacket. He paused a few seconds longer than might have been strictly necessary before casually taking the half-full phial of eldersight from his pocket and placing it on the desk. "Tell me, Mr. MacGowan, are you familiar with an organization called the Nightshade Cabal?"

7

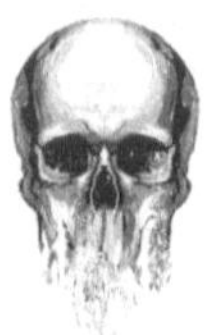

IF ONLY FOR THE BRIEFEST OF MOMENTS, BARROW SAW the practiced smile fall from Lawrence MacGowan's face as the racketeer silently regarded the phial in front of him.

He knew putting the eldersight down in front of MacGowan had been a gamble. If the illicit compound was once again being imported from abroad, the scoundrel was likely to know something about it. He very well might have even been involved. *That might also explain why Malleus is skulking about downstairs*, Barrow thought. If eldersight was making its way to the streets, the Triune Congress would certainly want to know where the drug was coming from.

"I take it you know what this is?"

MacGowan quickly regained his composure. Clearing his throat, he turned a steely gaze on Barrow. "I believe it's that drug you wizards are so fond of. Eldersight, isn't it?"

"I hate that word, *wizard*," Barrow said distastefully. "But yes, this is eldersight. This phial contains about half a dosage. Few spellcasters use it, really, and not just because it's exceedingly difficult to obtain. The visions it can induce make it popular among foreseers and shamans and the like, but the psychoactive effects of the drug can persist for days."

"Yes, yes, and if regular folk like me use it the delirium can be permanent," MacGowan finished for him, his patience clearly wearing thin. "All of which is very interesting, I'm sure, but I fail to see what concern it is of mine."

"The Wheelhouse is known as the place to seek out a great many exotic indulgences," Barrow pointed out.

MacGowan leaned back in his seat, steepling his fingers. "It may be that, but until this moment I hadn't seen a phial of eldersight in several years. Nor had I even heard about the vile stuff once again being trafficked through Halifax."

Barrow thought MacGowan looked troubled by the admission, as though he were bothered that something so significant might be happening in the city's underbelly without his knowing about it. He hoped that having caught the scoundrel off his guard so, what he said next might truly rattle him. "I had wondered, Mr. MacGowan, if you might know how this came to be in Emily Skye's possession."

Like a gambler laying down an unexpected high card when the dealer thought he held the winning hand, the gambit worked. MacGowan's jaw dropped and hung there for a moment before he recovered. "*Emily Skye* had this?" he finally sputtered. "Mr. Barrow, you must be mistaken."

Barrow shook his head. "It's no mistake. I found the phial myself this very afternoon, hidden in a desk drawer in her room."

MacGowan picked up the small glass phial and turned it over in his hand, watching the thick indigo liquid within slowly drain from one end to the other. "And you think this might have something to do with the Nightshade Cabal?"

"Miss Skye's sister had reason to believe the Cabal might have been involved in her disappearance."

"What would they want with a girl of seventeen, though?" MacGowan asked, his eyes still on the eldersight.

So, he doesn't know about Emily's preternatural abilities after all, Barrow thought. He decided against telling him about her talents. The old prejudices were slowly fading, but even so, few occultists practiced their craft as openly as he did. With Emily Skye's own mother exiling her to the nuns at Saint Patrick's convent, he could hardly fault the girl for wanting to keep hers hidden.

Experience let him believe he could trust Inspector Eddings with the girl's secret, but he was far less sure about Lawrence MacGowan. Rather than answer the man directly, he tried to redirect the conversation. "How much do you know about the Nightshade Cabal?"

"Very little, really," MacGowan shrugged, leaning back in his seat once more. He sipped at his brandy. "I don't have much in the way of dealings with spellcasters, but in my line of business, I do hear things. I know the Cabal is made up of what you call necromancers, going about performing sacrifices to raise demons and that sort of thing." He paused, a look of horror overtaking his habitually staid expression. "You don't think that Miss Skye...?"

Barrow shook his head. "Human sacrifice is extreme, even among the most fanatical of Cabal adepts. No, whatever their reason for snatching the girl might've been, I believe they needed her alive."

MacGowan's thick moustache twitched as he exhaled. "I sincerely hope you're right, Mr. Barrow."

So do I, Barrow thought, but left the sentiment unspoken. Even among necromancers, only the very fringe still performed human sacrifice. There were easier, less risky rituals to achieve most of the vile ends they sought. But Barrow knew as well as anyone that the blood rituals held a unique sort of power. Some followers of the dark paths took their practice a step further, believing the blood of the young held more vitality, making it better fuel for their dark sacraments.

There was a sort of twisted logic to that notion that Barrow almost had to admit he appreciated, but the idea that Emily Skye may have ended up splayed open at the end of some necromancer's knife sent ice running through his veins.

With no small effort, he pushed those black thoughts aside. Getting caught up in gloomy what-ifs and grisly speculation wasn't any use to anyone. The only way to help Miss Skye was to work on the assumption that she was still alive and hale, wherever she might be.

"I don't know for certain that the Cabal is bringing eldersight into Halifax," Barrow said, again steering the conversation. "It could be the sort of activity it would be tangled up in, though. If I can track down the source of the drug she had in her possession, it may in turn provide a clue to Miss Skye's whereabouts. Can you think of anyone who might be working with the Cabal in this?"

MacGowan's smile twisted into a contemptuous sneer. "You may want to have a word with Harold Penfold about that bit of business."

Barrow marked the name in his notebook. "And who is Mr. Penfold?"

"A customs clerk who has set himself up as a broker of 'exotic indulgences,' to use your own phrasing, Mr. Barrow. The whelp used to work for me under the table, helping some of the more dubious shipments make their way through the clearinghouse quietly, until he realized one fine day that he could rake in more profit by setting up on his own." He upended his glass, swallowing the last of the brandy in one heroic gulp. "The man has been a thorn in my side ever since. He owns a small warehouse near Pier 12."

"I'll look into it, but if you're just playing me against a rival, Mr. MacGowan..." Barrow cautioned.

MacGowan leaned back and spread his hands wide, a wolfish grin on his face. "I'd swear to you I'm not, but you're not likely to believe me. Then again, I'll not pretend that anything that hurts Penhold doesn't also help me. It may just be that we could be of use to each other here, Mr. Barrow."

Now it was Barrow's turn to display a practiced smile. As a rule, he fought shy of consorting with devils in his occult workings; he wasn't about to start trading with them in his ordinary goings-on. Fishing around in his pocket, he produced a calling card, which he offered to MacGowan.

"As I say, I'll look into it," he said, still smiling. "If you think of anything else that might help me find Miss Skye, please let me know."

It was past midnight when Barrow left the Wheelhouse, heading for his apartment on Gottingen Street. The streetcars had long since stopped running for the night, leaving him with little option but to cross the city on foot. He was not normally one to grudge a lengthy walk, but it was late and it had been a very long day indeed. There being no help for it, he turned up his collar and set off.

A heavy fog had settled along the waterfront, bringing with it a clamminess that felt as though it could be the very essence of damp itself called forth into the mortal plane. He smiled at the thought, wondering what a dampness elemental might actually look like, and what cause he might ever have to summon up such a thing.

In contrast to the rowdy scene he had just departed, the foggy night outside seemed still and silent. The lamplighters had long since tended their task and retired for the evening.

The gaslights lining each side of the narrow, twisting street did what they could to brighten the way, but they were spaced too far apart for their wan light to keep the night at bay. Each glowing nimbus offered little more than a marker to guide him along his path, but in the stygian fog their diffuse illumination barely reached the cobbles beneath Barrow's feet.

He paid the lamplight little mind as he became lost in his own thoughts. He had hoped Lawrence MacGowan might have been able to offer more in the way of help in locating Emily Skye. Even so, he reminded himself, the visit hadn't been a total waste. MacGowan had at least provided an avenue to explore the source of the eldersight the girl had somehow gotten ahold of. It wasn't much, but it was more than he had to go on an hour earlier; he would have to follow up the lead with a visit to Harold Penhold's warehouse in the morning.

The thundering engine of an oncoming steamcarriage shattered his concentration and the serenity of the night simultaneously. He had to shield his eyes as the steamcar's single brilliant headlamp cut through the eddying fog, the shaft of light listing from left to right and back again as the driver tracked the bends in the winding street.

The vehicle roared past, too fast for Barrow to catch a glimpse of the occupants in the passenger compartment. Sparks and flaming bits of coal spilled out of the speeding steamcar's firebox, scattering across the cobblestones as the vehicle careened around a corner and off into the night, its rubber tires screeching in protest as the driver pushed the engine to its limits.

Barrow sighed, watching the glowing embers fade as they cooled on the cobbles. Even though steamcarriages were still few in number, the newspapers were full of letters and opinion pieces calling on the mayor to limit the hours in which the new vehicles could be operated within the city. Barrow wasn't keen on any policy that impeded the wider adoption of new technologies, though he could see how the deafening racket the steamcars often produced might be considered a nuisance. Some models were, of course, louder than others, but punishing all steamcarriage owners for the sake of the inconsiderate few who operated noisy machines struck Barrow as particularly unfair. He wondered if there might be a way to make the deafening engines run more quietly.

And just when do you think you might have the time to pursue that grand notion? he thought bitterly as the dying embers winked away one by one, their ruddy glow swallowed up by the fog. He drew his coat tighter against the chill and turned to continue along his way.

Distracted as he was, Barrow didn't notice the figure that had sidled up to him until he had almost tripped over her. He staggered aside and clutched wildly at a lamppost, but managed to keep his feet under him. The woman he had nearly bowled over hooted excitedly as she deftly skipped out of his path, grabbing at her wide-brimmed oilskin hat before it could fall from her head.

The fog wasn't so thick that he couldn't make out her flushed face in the pallid gaslight, but it would've made no difference. He knew her by sound of her laugh and by the heavy smell of damp wool and corn whiskey that clung to her like a miasma.

"Good evening, Miss Ruby," he said politely as he straightened himself out. Bowing slightly, he touched the brim of his bowler, in part to ensure it had stayed atop his head as he stumbled.

"*Miss Ruby*, is it now? Sure an' it's not Mad Ruby, the Duchess of Spring Garden?" she cackled, her wild laughter like something out of a child's storybook. "That's what everyone else calls me, so it is, but never Isaac Barrow! I swear you're the only spellcaster left in the whole of the British Empire with a civil tongue in his head, so yeh are!" She flapped her arms and spun around in a circle, then leaned in towards him, as if to scrutinize him more closely. "So what would you, young Isaac? Have you come searching in the night for a reading, then?"

Barrow couldn't help but smile. He felt a great deal of sympathy for Mad Ruby. True enough, she was as batty as they came, but she was a gifted seer nonetheless. Red-faced and stooped, she looked like nothing much more than a pile of rags and scraps, given the ability to walk upright. A fondness for the drink had blunted the edge of her talent through the years, and her ramshackle appearance kept her out of the more decorous drawing rooms in Halifax. Still, among those who knew the truth of such things, she had garnered a well-earned reputation for accurate prophecy. Barrow often wondered what marvels Mad Ruby might have been capable of, had life only dealt her a more even hand.

"It's past midnight, Miss Ruby," he shrugged. "I was only heading for home, and searching after nothing more interesting than my bed."

"So you may think, so you may think," she said, wagging a gnarled, calloused finger in his face. "What we believe is so and what truly is, now, these things are not always the same. You should know as well as anyone that such a coincidence as this is rarely an accidental thing, young Isaac."

That much, at least, Barrow had to admit might be true enough. He hadn't gone looking for a seer, but nevertheless, he had found one while walking the streets with a question on his mind. More than one, at that. He wasn't sure he agreed with her assertion that coincidences didn't just happen—he would've been content to write off their chance meeting as just that—but in the moment the empathy he felt for Mad Ruby got the better of him.

"Very well then," he said, pressing a dime into her hand.

"Ah, payment in advance," she said, examining the proffered coin as if to ensure it wasn't fourrée. "I would've insisted on such before rolling the bones, of course. There's too many folks who don't like what they've been told and then change their minds about paying the scot, but by then it's too late!" She turned and shuffled towards an alcove at the side of a building, motioning to Barrow to follow.

"What'll it be, then?" she asked. "The bones, the stones, or the cards?"

Barrow thought for a moment before he answered. Among Mad Ruby's methods of divination, he held the least regard for the tarot; there was too much room for personal interpretation in the card's meaning for his liking, and too many ways for the seer to game the deck itself before the first card was drawn. At least with graven runestones or inscribed bones, there was the element of random chance in casting them on the ground before the one reading them set to interpreting how they fell in relation to each other.

"I'll cast the stones."

"Ah, a dance with Wotan!" Mad Ruby whooped, reaching into the folds of her disheveled layers and drawing out a small leather sack, cinched tight with a glinting silver cord. She loosed the cord and emptied the contents into Barrow's cupped hands.

She plucked two unmarked stones from the pile in his hands, one nearly perfectly round and the other more oblong.

Barrow immediately felt the power within the remaining runestones. Each of the flat stones was engraved with a different runic symbol. None of them were much bigger than the knuckle of his thumb, and each was a different type of stone, which Barrow knew was somehow tied to the ancient runic sign that had been cut into it.

"Close your hands and hold the stones tightly, and think hard on whatever it is that you seek," Mad Ruby said, kneeling to draw a chalk circle on the stoop and placing the unmarked oblong stone in the center. She returned the round stone to the leather pouch and tucked it away. Her reedy voice was serious now, all mirth and folly pushed far aside. "When you feel it's right, drop the stones in the circle, and don't be telling me what it is you're after. I need to read the lay of the runes with an unbiased eye, as you well know!"

Barrow nodded and kneeled beside the chalk circle. He closed his eyes, turning his attention to the power he held in his hands. He had no idea how long ago this set of runes had been crafted, whether by Mad Ruby or someone else, but the power coursing through them was ancient indeed.

The transmundane energy within the runestones seemed to ring in time with the beat of his heart, and the sounds of the night around him suddenly seemed to be coming from very far away. Soon, he heard nothing at all but the ancient song of the runes. He concentrated on Emily Skye, calling forth the image of the photograph Meredith had given him. He held the picture in his mind's eye for several moments until, swearing loudly, he flung the stones to the ground.

"What happened?" Mad Ruby demanded.

Barrow was waving one hand in the air. "The stones," he replied with a wince. "They suddenly became blisteringly hot in my hand!"

Mad Ruby's expression was one of grave concern. She bent to examine the runestones, carefully turning over those which had landed with their symbols facing down. Remarkably, only two of the thirteen had fallen outside of the chalk circle. "Well, they're cool enough to touch now," she said without looking up, "but I'll tell you this much before I even look at the runes; I don't care for the omen."

"I didn't think the stones burning through the flesh of my hand was a *good* sign," Barrow said derisively. The stinging had started to abate as soon as he had thrown down the stones, though it still smarted. He examined his palm, hoping there would be no lasting harm. The skin was an angry shade of pink, but he didn't think it would blister.

"Don't mock, young Isaac," Mad Ruby chided, again wagging a knobby finger in his face. "The stones have their own power, just the same as you and I, and they're trying to get your attention the only way they know how! What they have to tell you this night must be important indeed." She turned her attention to the runes, clucking and humming softly to herself as she studied their positioning.

Several breathless minutes passed, Barrow, biting his tongue as he waited for Mad Ruby to interpret the lay of the runes. Finally, impatience getting the better of him, he could wait no longer. "Well, what do they say?"

She cast him a withering look for his pique, but began her divination. "These two being outside of the circle is a bad sign," she said, pointing to the two stones that had fallen outside of the circle. Each bore a similar triangular marking. "These are the symbols for *home* and *family*, and they're not a direct part of the telling, I'm afraid."

"Why would that be an ill omen?" Barrow asked. He knew rather little about the runes, but he was eager to understand more of their meaning.

"These are the symbols of safety, young Isaac. Security. By falling where they have, they're telling me that whatever it is you're seeking after will lead you into peril, should you find and follow after it."

Barrow nodded, wondering briefly how finding Emily Skye could cause trouble. *If finding her actually leads back to the Nightshade Cabal...* He let the thought go unfinished. "What about the runes inside the circle?" he asked, turning his attention to rest of the stones.

"These two near the center of the circle represent male and female figures." She pointed to the oblong stone she had placed in the center of the circle. "Them falling so close to the questioner's stone tells me the pairing is central to whatever is to come, whoever they might be. Have you recently become involved with a young lady, perhaps?" Her grin struck him as lewd.

"Not as such, but I'm on the trail of a missing girl," Barrow said. "A woman visited my office this morning to seek my help in finding her sister. I was thinking of the girl when the stones became too hot to hold in my hand."

"I have to think you and this girl, you're the ones at the center, then." Mad Ruby fell silent for a long moment as she pondered the runes. "I fear you'll know little relief at finding her, even if she is alive."

"How do you mean?" Barrow asked.

"Every other sign within the circle marks uncertainty and upheaval, and the way they've landed spells out danger. More's the point, the direst of the ill signs are all directed at this central pairing. The dagger sign," she pointed at the stone, the runic symbol engraved upon it like a child's drawing of a sword, "is aimed straight at your heart, here.

"I don't know how, but finding the girl is but the first step along a dark path indeed," she continued, shaking her head sadly. She looked up at him, fear in her wild eyes. "All that is in the stones is doom. Doom for Isaac Barrow!"

8

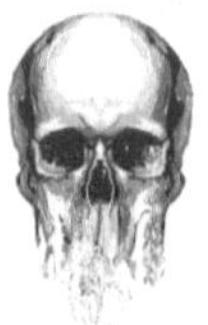

Barrow slept much later than he had intended. Mad Ruby's frightful foretelling had kept him from sleep well into the small hours of the morning. When sleep had finally taken him, it was a fitful slumber as terrible nightmares kept him tossing through what little was left of the night. Not usually one to remember his dreams on waking, he rose from his bed late in the morning.

The foul dreams had been full of unseen horrors hounding him as he made his way through impenetrable darkness. He had no way of knowing where he was, only a vague sense of an immense, oppressive weight overhead, ready to close down on him without warning. The path ahead was as caliginous as the way behind, and he despaired that he had no way of knowing which way he was heading. His feet dragged as though through mud while his unseen pursuers drew inexorably nearer. In the strange sense of time that dreams sometimes have, he felt he had been walking for days.

Stumbling back to the waking world was a murky affair. It didn't help matters that he hadn't set an alarm for the morning. A clock sat on his bedside table, but he rarely wound it unless he had a morning appointment. With the irregular hours he often kept when working on his research, he took steps to ensure his sleep went uninterrupted when he finally did return home to his bed. He had covered over the windows in his bedchamber with several layers of heavy brown butcher's paper some years ago, blotting out as much of the morning (or midday) sun as possible. The trick worked a little too well sometimes.

He screwed his eyes shut against the light as he wrapped his housecoat around his shoulders and shuffled out into the sitting room. The window panes unencumbered by brown paper or much of anything else, the midmorning sun streamed freely through flimsy curtains. Dust motes, some of them quite large indeed, danced lazily through the shafts of light as if in mockery of Barrow's deficient housekeeping. *I don't know why I even keep an apartment when I'm so rarely here*, he mused sardonically, not for the first time.

The apartment was on the small side, but large enough to have its own simple galley kitchen tucked off to the side. He rarely made use of the icebox, letting it sit empty most of the time, but he considered the twin-burner gas stove essential for making coffee if nothing else. He filled the percolator and lit a burner under it, then puttered around, bleary-eyed, while he waited for the coffee to boil.

A hefty stack of newspapers sat on the floor near a wing-back chair. He regarded these with a mix of scorn and regret. From a young age, Barrow had made a point of reading each day's newspaper from the first headline to the final classified advertisement. More often than not in the last several years, though, he found himself so caught up in either his own research, or aiding Inspector Eddings with some investigation or another, that days passed without his setting foot in the apartment, much less reading the daily news.

At first, he had saved the unread papers with the intention of reading them all in their entirety when the time to do so presented itself. It hadn't taken long for the futility of the exercise became apparent, but his stubborn side compelled him to let the stacks of unread papers grow. Eventually, though, he had simply given up, unhappily resigning himself to his own ignorance. Though it galled him to do so, he routinely relegated an entire week's worth of newspapers to the dustbin, unread.

"Who has the bloody time anyway?" he muttered as he scooped up the past week's stack and headed for the hallway, taking the rear staircase down to the building's alleyway entrance.

He glanced at the headline on the top of the pile, a fluff piece about the Trans-Canadian Railway, finally due to begin construction later in the year. The ambitious project had been delayed by false starts and broken promises, plagued by scandal after scandal, the worst of these bringing down Prime Minister Macdonald's ruling Conservative government some years earlier.

Macdonald's political career had somehow been able to recover, though, and had hammered the railway through the halls of Parliament. Barrow didn't have much respect for the man himself, but even he had to admit the prime minister had an iron resolve and a way of getting what he wanted.

The trash bins behind the building were all but empty. Barrow absently counted off the days, deciding the binmen must've been by for their weekly collection earlier that morning. He looked up at his bedchamber's papered-over windows, directly above, and shook his head. He must've been truly exhausted to sleep through the clatter and shouting that usually ensued just twenty yards below on trash day.

With a grunt, he swung open the bin's heavy steel lid and

deposited his bundle of newspapers, then let the lid drop shut with a grinding screech. He winced at the noise and gave a thought to greasing the grimy, rusted hinges. *Maybe later,* he thought with a shrug as he headed for the door. *It's hardly my job, but I have to listen to the racket, and it's not as though anyone else is likely to do anything about it.*

"Mr. Barrow?" called a small voice from somewhere behind him.

Turning on his heel he spotted a small boy, about nine years old, hurrying down the alley in his direction. Barrow recognized him instantly as Will Fergus, one of the Collywobble Boys. "Hello, Will," Barrow greeted the lad as he drew near, thinking it odd to find Will here without any of his chums around. The Collywobble Boys tended to travel in packs, especially when they were looking for mischief in the neighbourhood's back alleyways. "How are you this morning?"

One look at the boy's face, though, told him that Will wasn't out for a lark. He looked worried and frightened, his eyes tracked with red. "It's my brother, Mr. Barrow. He never came home yesterday," the lad said, his voice wavering. "I thought you might be able to help me find him." Tears spilled down the boy's cheeks as he choked back a sob.

No wonder he came alone, Barrow thought as he dropped to one knee and put a comforting hand on the sobbing boy's shoulder. *He didn't want his friends to see him bawling.* "Have you had anything to eat this morning, Will?"

Will snorted dramatically and wiped his nose on his sleeve. He shook his head.

"Come on upstairs, then," Barrow said, smiling. "I haven't eaten yet either. Let's see if we can't find something for breakfast, and then we'll figure out what we can do for your brother."

Something for breakfast ended up being bread and an old

jar of strawberry jam. The loaf had gone a bit hard and crumbly, and the jam had turned thick and sticky, but none of that kept Will from devouring several slices without complaint. Barrow fixed the boy a cup of hot tea to go along with the food, and sat across from him with his coffee as he cut a slice off the loaf for himself.

"So why don't you tell me what's the matter?" he asked when Will finally finished eating.

"It's my brother, Ian," Will said, wiping some stray jam from around his mouth with his sleeve. "He didn't come home from work yesterday. He's got a job gutting fish at one of the canneries down by the docks."

"Do you know which one?"

Will nodded. "The big one. Star of the Sea," he said.

Barrow flipped open one of his notebooks and made a note of that. "How old is Ian?"

"Sixteen, since April. Our birthdays are only a week apart."

Barrow nodded. "I don't suppose you have a photograph of him?"

The boy's incredulous expression answered that question. *Of course you wouldn't*, Barrow thought. *Not many around this ragged neighborhood who can afford frivolities like photography.* "Well then, what does Ian look like?"

"About like me, only seven years older and about as many inches taller," Will said, reaching a hand above his head to show what he meant. "An' he's got red hair, like dad used to have, before he went gray." Again, he wiped his sleeve across his nose, which was still running, albeit less so.

Barrow's pencil paused in its wandering on the page. "Red hair, you say?"

Will nodded once more. "'Red like the fires of hell,' mum always says."

Barrow's mind flitted back to the previous afternoon at

Emily Skye's room in Mrs. Winslow's boardinghouse, and the startled lad in the hallway who had bolted and leapt from the third-floor window. Barrow had only glimpsed him for less than a second and, with his oversized tweed cap pulled low, he hadn't gotten a good look at the boy's face before he had fled. It wasn't until the boy had leapt to the neighboring rooftop that he spotted his short-cropped red hair. Could that have been Ian Fergus?

He rubbed at his tired eyes. It would have been quite the coincidence to stumble upon Will's missing brother at Emily Skye's boardinghouse, he thought, but he had encountered things far more bizarre than mere coincidence before.

Mad Ruby's words from the night before echoed in his thoughts. *Such a coincidence as this is rarely an accidental thing, young Isaac,* she had admonished.

He jotted the notion down in his notebook, punctuated with a large question mark. He was unwilling to dismiss anything at this point.

"Did your brother have a sweetheart, by any chance? Any girls he had been courting?"

Lawrence MacGowan hadn't believed Emily Skye had been involved with any young suitors, but what employer knows all the comings and goings of his staff?

Will scrunched up his grubby face at the suggestion and shook his head vigorously from side to side, drawing a chuckle from Barrow. He was young enough that girls were still considered the enemy. *Give him a few years and he won't be making those faces,* Barrow thought with a grin. He decided not to discount the possibility that there was a connection between Ian Fergus and the disappearance of Emily Skye. Little brothers, after all, did not always know everything.

"You'll help me look for him?" Will asked, pulling a few tarnished pennies from his pocket. "I'll pay you."

Barrow smiled and closed Will's fingers around the small handful of coins. Ian Fergus was of an age where staying out all night was not an uncommon pastime. In all likelihood, the young fellow had been out carousing and would return home soon of his own accord. Still, Ian's little brother was worried, and Barrow wanted to set the boy's fears at ease if he could.

"I'll do what I can," he promised.

AFTER SENDING THE BOY ON HIS WAY, BARROW HEADED for his workshop. He muttered a word of thanks when he found no one waiting at the door to his streetside office this time; he had enough to contend with as it was.

Was there any connection between Ian Fergus and Emily Skye? Besides the two of them being about the same age, he simply didn't know if there was anything linking the two disappearances. He had little more than a hunch to go on, and he still had to follow up on Harold Penhold as the possible source of Miss Skye's phial of eldersight, for which he only had Lawrence MacGowan's debatable guidance as proof.

Too many what-ifs, he thought. At least with Henry Feele's autotype memory cylinder clacking out letters all through the night, he hoped he would have some solid evidence to support his hunch in that particular case.

He locked the door to the street behind him, drawing the blinds and ensuring the sign hanging in the window was turned to read *CLOSED* to any passersby. Descending the iron staircase to his underground workshop, he always felt mingled relief and anticipation—relief to finally be away from the distractions and hustle of everyday life that kept him from his research, and anticipation as he looked forward to the marvelous inventions that he would create.

He always left one lamp burning low. Without any windows, there was no daylight down here. He turned it up, then went about lighting the others before he set to the task at hand.

The ticker reel had run out at some point in the night, the printer spooling its output unceremoniously onto the floor in one tangled heap. Barrow found one end of the long paper strip and set to the chore of straightening it out, cursing himself for not rigging something up to keep the tickertape from becoming a Gordian knot as the machine had spit it out.

The ticker was not nearly as advanced a printing machine as the autotype unit the memory cylinder had come from. It only keyed letters, lacking the capacity for punctuation, and it didn't leave spaces between words as it printed, making its output difficult to read. The first few feet of ticker-tape it had hammered out were complete gibberish, letters printed onto the paper strip apparently at random, but as Barrow scanned through the length of the tape he found that words soon started to form, just as Henry Feele had described. Working between several yards of thin paper tape and a fresh block pad, Barrow transcribed the ticker's output carefully, parsing the words and adding the appropriate punctuation marks as he went. With growing horror, he watched those words come together to form thoughts, spelling out sentences.

I can't see anything. Why can't I see? I hear nothing. My legs. Dear God above, what has happened? Why can I not feel my arms and legs?

Barrow prided himself on his ability to stand back from a situation and regard it objectively with a keen, analytical mind. He knew his detached nature made personal relationships a chore, but he considered the trait invaluable when it came to solving mechanical or alchemical problems. This, however, was almost too much to bear.

Alice. Where is Alice? Who will take care of my little girl?

The final line he transcribed chilled him to the core.

If I have died this can only be Hell.

He slowly set down his pencil and pushed himself back from the desk, one hand moving of its own accord to cover his mouth.

The tickertape spooled several yards more, but Barrow couldn't bring himself to read another word of it. Any lingering doubt had been vanquished—as he had surmised, Henry Feele's memory cylinder contained human brain tissue. But he had not for a moment thought the victim it came from might still be aware on any level.

To be fully cognizant, but wholly disconnected from body and senses...

He shuddered. The very thought set his mind reeling.

This can only be Hell, indeed.

9

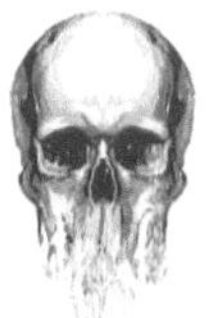

THE MEMORY CYLINDER SAT TO ONE SIDE OF THE LONG
workbench, cradled now on a pillow taken from the threadbare green chaise in the corner. He had carefully disconnected the piece from the tickertape printer, unsure what to
do next. The component could not be returned to service in
Henry Feele's autotype machine, that much was obvious. At
least in that capacity, Barrow figured he could modify a standard memory cylinder to replace it easily enough.

That still left him with evidence of an apparent murder
on his hands. He looked to the clock on the wall and swore
under his breath. Late as he had slept, the afternoon had
quickly slipped away. It was surely too late to catch Inspector
Eddings at the station. He gave a moment's thought to calling
on the inspector at home. Eddings had just yesterday invited
him to visit, Barrow reminded himself, but he ultimately
decided bringing word of a murder to his friend's home in the
middle of the dinner hour might not fall within the bound-
aries of propriety. Indeed, even if Inspector Eddings didn't
object to the macabre interruption, his wife, Jayne, was likely
to pitch a fit.

No, the matter would have to wait for the morning. He decided instead to follow up on the advice Lawrence MacGowan had provided regarding Harold Penhold. He packed a few things into his valise—various small tools, and a folding leather case containing phials of basic spellcraft ingredients—pausing as his hand came to the elementally-enhanced Webley revolver he had carried the night before.

The handgun had been suffused with the power of a captured storm elemental. Instead of firing lead bullets, it loosed a blast of electricity that could incapacitate a foe. That was the theory, at least. The weapon, like too many of Barrow's other ideas, remained untested.

Still, the den of a rogue like Harold Penhold was all too likely to be a dangerous spot. He holstered the Webley.

Located in the thoroughly disreputable northeast end of the wharfside—rougher even than the tenements of Gottingen Street—Penhold's warehouse turned out to be a ramshackle eyesore unfit for much of anything but a home for vermin. Few of the grid windows had all of their panes intact, and many were boarded over entirely. The peaked roof bowed precariously downward at the center. Looking up at the sad edifice, Barrow wondered how the place had been spared the wrecker's hammer.

The place didn't just look abandoned—there was nothing to suggest the place was in use at all. A warehouse or brokerage ought to have at least someone coming or going in the early evening, Barrow thought, but there were no signs indicating anyone was about. Nonetheless, he decided it wouldn't do to go blundering in through the front door, instead making his way around the north side to head for the rear of the building.

He was appalled at the state of the crumbling brickwork as he navigated the narrow alleyway between the warehouse and the next building over. No effort had been made to forestall the ravages of time on the structure. Fragments of masonry lay where they had fallen on the ground. Some of the larger pieces of mortar and brick were being swallowed up by thick moss, so darkly green as to be almost black, which crept up the walls where the sun never reached. The creeping moss reminded Barrow of mold growing on a neglected loaf of bread.

There was a single wooden door near the rear of the warehouse, set into an alcove of a style distinctly different from the rest of the building. Instead of crumbling old brick, the nook was built of solid granite blocks, which looked to be even older still. Barrow could tell the door itself had once been green, but most of the ancient paint had cracked and peeled away years ago, the boards underneath graying with age and exposure.

With a stroke of luck, the rusted knob offered little protest as it turned in his hand. The sagging door dragged heavily across the stone floor inside, opening only about halfway before stubbornly wedging itself in place. No matter, the gap was more than enough for Barrow to squeeze himself across the threshold, shouldering the door closed behind him.

The darkness inside was almost absolute. Feeling about, he couldn't find any lamps or torches on the walls. "Damn it all," he muttered under his breath, drawing a small waxed paper packet from one of the pouches at his belt. He shook some fine white powder into his palm. "*Accendo*," he whispered, gently blowing on the powder.

It glowed softly in response to the command. Absorbing the vitality in Barrow's breath, it began to swirl in his palm as if caught up in a tiny cyclone, then suddenly leapt into the air. The cloud of dust whipped around itself in midair, flared brilliantly for a moment, then finally took form as a glowing nimbus of diffused light. The pale blue illumination it cast was less than that of a gas lamp, but brighter than a candle.

Roughly the size of an apple and utterly weightless, the nimbus bobbed and weaved about in the air, trilling softly to itself like some carefree songbird. "Oh, stop that," Barrow snarked at it. It squeaked sadly and dipped down an inch, its radiance fading just a shade. Barrow sighed and muttered an insincere apology. The nimbus was an incredibly useful conjuration, but something about their cheery capering always irked him.

He was, however, instantly glad to have summoned it. By its pallid light he could see that he was just a few paces from the top of a narrow, steep stairway. There was no railing, nothing to have broken the fall he would've taken had his foot left the top step into total darkness.

"Let's go," he said, setting off down the stairs. The nimbus led the way, keeping pace while always staying about two yards ahead of him.

The narrow stairs descended much further than Barrow thought practical for any basement, and deposited him at the mouth of an equally narrow corridor. The walls were made up of the same granite blocks as the entrance, though time had not worn at the stone down here. There were empty torch sconces mounted in the walls, little more than hammered iron rings fastened to the stone with heavy bolts. Soot streaked the wall above each of these, but there was nothing to suggest they had been used in ages.

Urging the nimbus to its brightest radiance, he still couldn't make out just how far the corridor stretched. It seemed to run the entire length of the warehouse and then keep going.

A suspicion began to dawn on him; he knew of a series of tunnels and passageways beneath the city, the oldest dating to pre-colonial times, when the Halifax Harbour was still little more than a French outpost by the name of Chebucto. Many of these subterranean passageways had caved in ages ago. Others were forgotten entirely—it wasn't as though anyone had kept detailed maps over the years.

A handful of the old tunnels were still in use, whether for transport or as storage or repurposed as part of the city's growing sewer system. Others were used by smugglers trafficking illicit goods.

Just the sort of thing a man like Penhold would need, Barrow mused.

The passage he followed had clearly been maintained. There was very little dust on the well-worn stone floor. Rather than the musty, stale air one might expect, a faint breeze carried the scent of tobacco and exotic spices from somewhere down the line.

He followed the passage for about a half-hour, eventually coming to a point where another staircase, every bit as steep and narrow as the first, branched off from the main passage. He peered down the path he had been following, but the end —if there was one—was no more visible from here than it had been when he had started.

Curiosity won out. With a shrug, he decided to take the stairs and see where he had ended up.

Another stubborn door opened into the basement of some building, half-lit by gaslight and a row of small windows set high in the cement walls. It seemed to be the lower level of another warehouse, this one in far better repair than the first. He whispered a command to the nimbus, and it winked out of existence with a satisfied-sounding *pweep.* Barrow rolled his eyes.

Several rows of stacked shipping crates, barrels, bales of goods, and other freight and supplies made the basement into a labyrinth. Heavy wooden beams overhead supported the main floor, and Barrow could hear the muffled sounds of work going on above.

He heard voices drawing near. At least two men were

heading in his direction, chatting with the casual care of friends who thought themselves alone. Barrow ducked behind a stack of crates.

"I don't like Mr. Penhold dealing with all of this wizarding hokery-pokery," one of the men said, his voice deep and gravelly. Their heavy footfalls had ceased, placing them just on the other side of the stack of crates Barrow crouched behind.

"What difference does it make?" his fellow answered. "As long as he's paying you, what do you care where the money comes from?"

Barrow heard a match being struck as one of the men lit a cigarette. He peered between two crates. The pair of thick-muscled dockhands looked like rough customers. One of them carried a heavy crowbar, but other than that neither of them looked to be armed. He still decided it wouldn't be wise to risk getting into a scrap with them.

"I don't mind taking coin for moving opium and weapons and the like," the first fellow said while his friend sucked in smoke. "I don't even mind creeping through the rat tunnels all the bloody time. But I sure as hell didn't sign on for working with any damned wizards, Harry. It's downright ungodly, is what it is, and it's going to bring us nothing but trouble. It's not enough that Oriental with the tattoos is always around, now we've got that fellow with the eyes, too? He gives me the creeps."

"Can you afford to pick and choose which jobs you take, Jake?" Harry asked, passing the lit cigarette to his cohort. "Just shut up and take the money."

Jake set the crowbar down on top of an unmarked barrel as he took the cigarette. He took a deep draw of smoke into his lungs and held it there. "Oh, I'll take Penhold's money," he said, finally exhaling as he handed the cigarette back to Harry. "But don't think I'll like it."

"I'm not in love with the idea either, but Penhold's laying out twice what anyone else is paying. Whatever we're moving for 'em, this Cabal must be paying him a fortune. I'm telling you, take the coin and go see Ginny up at Madame Rushton's," Harry said, taking a last puff before stubbing out the cigarette on the side of one of the crates and tucking the unsmoked half back into his tobacco pouch. "She's lively, that one is, and she's got a pair on her that'll make you cry." Both men laughed at the lewd comment. "Come on, let's get back upstairs. We're not even supposed to be down here."

They kept talking, their voices fading as they turned a corner. He couldn't make out the conversation, but the bursts of unwholesome laughter that punctuated the discussion were enough for Barrow to speculate about the ribald subject matter.

Barrow waited a few minutes longer before he moved on. What he had overheard confirmed Harold Penhold's partnership with the Nightshade Cabal. Just how much eldersight their enterprise was bringing into the city remained to be seen.

Stepping out from behind the crates, he noticed Jake had forgotten his crowbar. Taking up the tool, he surveyed what he could see of the cluttered basement. With no sign that anyone else was about, he set to opening the nearest crate. The wood was aged and dry, and splintered when he tried to force the crowbar between the slats, but he managed to get the crate open, only to find nothing more interesting than several bolts of old sailcloth, which had long since been ravaged by moths and mice.

Examining several other crates and barrels, he concluded that the basement level held nothing of interest. He had been down here for an hour or more, and the only activity he had seen was Harry and Jake taking their clandestine cigarette break. Meanwhile, the sounds of work going on above had died away.

Barrow looked at his pocket watch, noting the late hour. "Must be past quitting time for thieves and thugs," he muttered under his breath.

There was a large cable lift at the far end of the room, powered by pulleys and counterweights to move heavy freight between floors, beside which he found an iron staircase. Rather than raise a racket by starting up the lift machinery, he crept up the stairs; it wouldn't do to alert anyone who might still be milling about upstairs of his impending arrival.

With Jake's crowbar gripped in one hand and his Webley revolver in the other, Barrow sidled through the door at the top of the stairs. Like any warehouse, the main level was essentially one large room with rows of heavy shelving.

Large windows let him see that it was nearly sundown. Doubtless, the lamplighters would already be making their rounds through the streets. Penhold's men, though, were nowhere to be seen. Barrow counted himself lucky for once and holstered the Webley. He kept to the shadows where he could as he made his way through the warehouse; just because he didn't see any danger didn't mean there was none about.

Harold Penhold had indeed been busy since splitting off from Lawrence MacGowan's enterprise. The man was also nothing if not organized. Barrow found several shipments containing opium poppies and resin, each labeled with a buyer's name. The narcotic was not prohibited in Canada, as it was in a handful of other nations, but its import was subject to heavy taxation. Barrow speculated that Penhold had ways of dodging those tariffs.

Opium smuggling was a serious crime, and Barrow noted that he would have to pass word along to Inspector Eddings, but that wasn't why he was here. He continued his search for the eldersight, certain it had to be here somewhere. Even a single phial would be enough.

Turning a corner, he discovered a single crate with an unusual shape. Oblong and flared on the long sides, it resembled a casket more than anything else. German text and an unfamiliar sigil bearing a stag's head had been burned into the unfinished wood with a branding iron. He frowned as he failed to interpret the writing, wishing he had paid more attention to his language studies as a youth.

He worked the crowbar under the lid and put his weight against it. The nails holding the crate shut protested, but the lid finally came free.

Hoping to find numerous phials of eldersight, Barrow was dumbfounded to instead discover an assemblage of mechanical parts that resembled nothing so much as a metallic, but vaguely human, skeleton. It appeared to be the stripped-down chassis of an automaton, though it clearly belonged to a model far more advanced than any Barrow had ever encountered. Though there was a space for the unit's head in the crate, that piece was unaccounted for. There was a notable impression still visible in the packing straw where it had once rested.

Like the missing head, the machine's limbs were detached from its torso at the hips and shoulders. These, at least, were present in the crate. Barrow picked up one of the arms to examine it more closely, marveling at the precise engineering that had gone into its construction.

It wasn't just that the chassis was more refined and fabricated from lighter materials than any he had ever seen; where even the most expensive consumer units on the market had little more than rudimentary claws, capable of grasping simple objects, this machine's hands boasted articulated digits. Each hinged brass knuckle was built around a series of miniaturized hydraulic pistons. He didn't know if it would possess quite the same level of dexterity as a human hand, but it would surely come close.

Barrow looked once more to the empty space the automaton's head had occupied, wishing he could get a look at the control module that would drive the assembled machine. With a sigh, he returned the arm to its spot in the crate and set the lid back in place.

Barrow was certain by now that he was alone in the warehouse, but he didn't dare nail the crate shut. Harold Penhold or one of his men would surely notice someone had tampered with it, but by then he would be far away. He looked again to the windows, seeing that the sun had set, and decided to head for home.

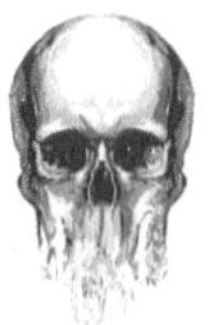

10

THE STREETS WERE QUIET AND GROWING DARKER AS Barrow hurried along. This part of the city was not utmost on the lamplighters' list of priorities. Cast in gloom and shadow, Barrow didn't see who clubbed him in the head and dragged him into the mouth of the alleyway by the collar of his overcoat. He was spun against the side of the nearest building, his left shoulder connecting heavily with the wall as his cheek scraped against the rough brickwork. His bowler went flying.

Reeling, he staggered and tried to turn to face his attacker, instead tripping over a pile of trash and falling to his knees. *I think I've just torn the knees out of my best trousers,* he thought, instantly admonishing himself for dwelling on such a trivial thing while being assaulted in a filthy, stinking alley.

Finding his feet and bracing himself against the wall, he turned and saw the Chinese mystic, Lai Jūn, partially shrouded in the eddying fog. "You've been poking your nose into the Nightshade Cabal's business, Mr. Barrow." He spoke each word deliberately. His English was thickly accented. "My employers have tasked me with ensuring your investigation goes no further. I owe you as well for interrupting my performance earlier this week."

Already bloodied and off-balance, Barrow found himself on the defensive. Hardly a prizefighter under the best of circumstances, he tried to stall. "Do you realize how twisted the Nightshade Cabal is?" he gasped. "The horrors it works to bring to this world?"

Lai Jūn shrugged that away. "The Cabal paid my passage to this land," he said. "For that, I owe it still. I have been assured that putting you to rest will settle my debt." He crouched slightly, making ready to strike again. "The matter is, as you say here, not personal."

Barrow didn't try to debate further. Reaching into his coat, he drew out the Webley. He managed to fire off one shot, hastily aimed and wildly off-target, before the weapon was knocked out of his hand. It fell to the cobbles with a clatter as the bolt of energy it released ricocheted harmlessly off a wall, leaving only the smell of ozone in the air and a scorch mark on the bricks. *So much for that*, he thought.

He wasn't quite quick enough to dodge the next punch, as Lai Jūn landed a glancing blow to his left ear. Fire surged there but, even under attack, the analytical part of Barrow's mind told him he had been lucky; had he taken it full in the face, he surely would've been knocked unconscious.

Barrow lashed out with a punch of his own, a wild, uncontrolled swing. Lai Jūn easily skipped back out of reach, then kicked Barrow in the ribs, pushing the technomancer back a few paces. He stumbled, but managed to keep his feet under him this time.

The kick hadn't had much force behind it. The technomancer had the impression Lai Jūn could've collapsed his ribcage and ended the melée had he truly wanted to put a swift end to him.

He was being toyed with.

Barrow wracked his scattered wits, trying to come up with any advantage. When it came to fighting skills, he knew he was no match for Lai Jūn. He ran through the mental inventory of what he carried with him, struggling to think of anything he might be able to use to overcome or at least distract his foe long enough to allow him to escape. Other than the dropped Webley, currently out of reach, nothing came to mind.

As Barrow regained his balance and brought up his clenched fists, desperate to defend himself, Lai Jūn stripped off his shirt and cast the garment aside. Barrow hadn't been close enough to make out each of the mystic's bestial tattoos when Lai Jūn had stood on the stage of the Theatre Royale. Right now he wished dearly he were at least as far away as he had been that night. There was a large, banded cobra on the mystic's left shoulder, and a screeching hawk in midflight on his left. A ferocious tiger—the same one he had brought to life on the stage—stalked across his chest, and the snaking Chinese dragon ran the length of one side of his torso.

Curiously, a brilliantly blue koi was emblazoned on the opposite side. The seemingly benign fish struck Barrow as being oddly out of place among the other fierce beasts.

As beautiful as the tattoos were, Barrow had little time to admire the artistry that had gone into creating them. Lai Jūn pressed two fingers to the cobra tattoo, chanting a few phrases as he did so. The image began to glow softly, the illumination pulsing in a rhythm which reminded Barrow of a beating heart.

Gawping, Barrow watched the glowing cobra steadily grow as it peeled away from Lai Jūn's body, until it was twice the man's height. He had seen the magic before, but from a safe distance. Being faced with the conjuration in an alley was another thing entirely. The serpent swayed from side to side as it grew to an impossible size, its wicked tongue flicking from its mouth.

At Lai Jūn's barked command, the wraith-like projection lunged at Barrow with a vicious *hiss!*

Had he hesitated just a half-second more, it surely would've marked the end of Isaac Barrow's investigative career. Instinct took over, and he leapt out of the ethereal serpent's path, landing hard on his bruised shoulder in a pile of wet garbage. Sparks flew as the beast's gleaming fangs clashed against the brick wall.

Acrid smoke rose from where a few drops of the cobra's venom trickled down the masonry, filling the air with a chemical reek. If the poison could burn into solid brick, Barrow didn't want to think about what it could do to his flesh.

The cobra recovered from its missed lunge and came around for another strike. Barrow heaved and managed to roll out of the creature's path, dodging once more. Knowing he couldn't avoid the snake's attacks indefinitely, he swatted feebly at the side of the thing's head as it twisted past, connecting without much force. To his surprise, the beast was solid and had scales that felt like those of an earthly serpent, though its hide was as cold as ice.

So, the projections have corporeal form after all, Barrow thought. *That means they ought to be subject to physical harm, if I can just get my hands on some kind of weapon.*

He hazarded a glance at Lai Jūn as he scrambled to his feet, noting that the mystic was panting, out of breath. Sweat streamed down his face, plastering his black hair to his scalp. Creating and maintaining the projection took a lot out of him, Barrow realized, to say nothing of what went into controlling the beast once he had brought it fully into being.

The serpent's tail whipped around and caught Barrow in the side of the head like a switch, knocking any ideas he might have had from his mind as he cried out in pain. He dropped to his knees once more. He saw red, tasted copper. The cobra slithered above him, pushing him to the ground with its oversized bulk. He could feel ropey muscles moving under its skin as it reared its head back and fanned its hood, gently swaying from side to side as its forked tongue flicked out from between wickedly fanged jaws. The beast seemed to be smiling as it readied itself for the kill.

A metallic report rang out like a bell. With a startled cry of pain, Lai Jūn pitched forward and sprawled on his belly. The monstrous cobra convulsed and fell, twitching to ground as if a string holding it up had been cut. The weight of it knocked the wind from Barrow's lungs, keeping him pinned to the ground even as the snake began to dissolve into a puddle of stinking gray ectoplasm.

Barrow wasted little time thinking about his good luck. He gasped as he struggled to kneel, every breath a battle to drag air into his lungs.

Behind Lai Jūn's prone body stood the red-haired youth he had seen at Mrs. Winslow's boardinghouse, dressed in the same patched dungarees and heavy boots. The lad must've gone back to retrieve his oversized cap, which had fallen to the ground when he had leapt from the third-floor window. A small spatter of Lai Jūn's blood smeared the end of the length of steel pipe in his hand.

No, Barrow observed now upon second glance as his head started to clear. *Not in* his *hand...*

"*Emily Skye?!*"

"Aye, and I'll get your name later," the girl said, casting the pipe aside with a loud metallic clatter. She came over to help Barrow to his feet. "For now, though, you'd best get yourself up out of the muck and run!"

Confused, but relieved to be alive at all following Lai Jūn's assault, Barrow did just that, pausing only to snatch up his Webley and bowler before following the girl down the trash-strewn laneway. He reminded himself once more that he would have to learn what he could about the mystic's tattoo magic, but once again, more pressing mysteries confronted him at the moment.

He followed the young Miss Skye for several blocks as she darted down alleys, hopped over fences, and swung under railings. At one point, faced with a particularly high sandstone wall, she climbed up a tenement block's fire escape and dropped over the wall to the ground on the other side. Barrow had no idea where he was being led, but the girl seemed to have a path in mind.

Finally, the alleyway they followed came to a dead end. She dropped to her knees and pulled a key on a long chain from her pocket. Unlocking and pulling open a coal chute door, she motioned for Barrow to squeeze through the small opening.

Barrow was out of breath. He hadn't quite recovered from being winded when the cobra's weight had come crashing down on his chest, nor was he in the habit of running through alleyways in the middle of the night. "The coal chute?" he stammered.

"Aye, but don't worry about the dust," she quipped. "You already look a fine mess."

It was true. He was dripping wet and bloodied, stank of garbage and rotting ectoplasm, and, as he had feared, had indeed torn out the knees of his trousers in the scuffle. Too wearied to argue, he did as he was told and awkwardly squeezed through the cast iron mouth of the coal chute, landing in an ungraceful heap at the bottom of the slide.

Coming down behind him, Emily Skye landed neatly on her feet. Streaks of black coal dust marked her face and clothing, but she paid it no mind. She checked the door to the coal chute, making sure it had locked fast as she had snapped it shut behind her.

Satisfied, she turned to Barrow. "Now then," she said, "how is it you seem to know who I am, sir, when I haven't the faintest notion of who you might be?"

"My name is Isaac Barrow, and I suppose you could say I'm a sort of investigator. I recognized you from your photograph, though I must say it's a passing resemblance at this point," he said, producing the picture from inside his jacket. "Your sister, Meredith, asked me to find you."

"Merrie?" She seemed surprised. "But I sent her a letter telling her what I was up to."

"It would seem that letter never reached her," Barrow said. "She was very worried about your disappearance."

Hopping up to sit on a barrel, Emily tried to wipe some of the coal dust from her face, but only smeared it further across her cheek. "You'll tell her I'm alright, won't you, Mr. Barrow?"

"You can tell her yourself, when I deliver you to her door."

Emily examined his face closely, but didn't answer that directly. "Have we met before, Mr. Barrow?"

"The other day, at Mrs. Winslow's boardinghouse," he said. "But only briefly. You might recall you resorted to self-defenestration rather than speak to me."

Her eyes widened, but she said nothing.

"Why did you run, Miss Skye? I meant you no harm."

"I thought you might've been with the Nightshade Cabal. You'll forgive me for not waiting around to see what a strange man all dressed in black is after, rifling through my bloomers and all." She shot him an accusatory look.

Barrow felt his face go red. He hoped the filth and the dim lighting would conceal his embarrassment. "I can assure you I am not, and never have been, an associate of the Nightshade Cabal."

"Sure an' I wish I could say the same," she said. He

believed she meant it. "I tell you true, I wish I'd never made the acquaintance. They're all up to something nasty."

"They usually are."

"That's true enough, but this is especially bad. People have been going missing from the streets. Poor folks, mostly, the sorts as no one would notice or care are gone missing."

Barrow frowned. "Victims for the blood rites?"

"I don't think it's any of that," the girl said. "There's something else going on. Maybe something worse."

"There's little more abhorrent in this world than necromancy," Barrow said, limping across the room to sit on a wooden crate. "How did you come to know the Cabal?"

She eyed him critically, as though deciding whether or not to trust him. "If you've spoken with Merrie, you know part of the story already," she finally said. "I ran away from home the year before last when Mum found out I was a speller."

"Spellcaster," he corrected.

"Either way," she said. "You find out how many true friends you have when something like that comes out, Mr. Barrow."

He nodded and urged her to go on.

"Well, I was living rough, making my way by stealing, mostly, before I got the job at MacGowan's. To make a long story short, I met a man there who turned out to be a spellcaster an' all." She sighed. "He knew with one look that I was the same as he, and he took me under his wing. He had a whole gang of us going, five in all, using spells and sneaking about to steal bigger and bigger things for him, and he fed and sheltered us like some Fagin of spellers."

Barrow was impressed at the reference. "What was his name?"

"I only ever knew him as Cooper," Emily said. "Anyway, Cooper wasn't a necromancer, but he had connections in what he called the wizarding underworld, and a job came up where he wanted us to steal the heart of a mummy from the museum. It was odd, since we always only stole money or things that could be sold."

"What did he want with a mummy's heart?"

"Nothing at all. That, it turned out, was to be on behalf of the Nightshade Cabal."

"I see," Barrow said. The pieces fit.

"We didn't do it," Emily went on. "The whole thing fell apart, which is a story for another time, but after it did, Cooper took the lot of us to meet his benefactor in the Cabal in the tunnels under the city. It wasn't the first time he'd taken us down there. Only when we arrived this time, there was a ritual being done in one of the big chambers." She paused. "The man Cooper knew was the one being put to the knife."

"He was killed for Cooper's failure?"

She nodded. "I think so. Mr. Barrow, I had never heard of such things before seeing that with my own eyes. We fled and managed to escape, and I decided to leave Cooper's employ that very night. After he drank himself to sleep, I filled a bag with whatever I could grab and left." She cast her eyes to the floor. "I still regret leaving the others with him, but I simply couldn't stay a minute longer."

Barrow was silent for a moment, unsure how to respond to the story. "Where are we, Miss Skye?" he finally asked.

"In a basement," she shrugged.

"I had guessed as much," he said dryly.

"I don't know where we are," she said simply, looking around. "Popping open the coal chute seemed the best way to get out of the dead end in the alleyway."

"You don't know which building we're in? Then how is it you had the key for the coal chute?"

"Magic key," she said, holding it up for him to see. "It

won't open every door in town, but I find it does the job more often than not. I nicked it from some drunken thief who had swilled himself senseless at the Wheelhouse one night. Thought it might come in handy some day." She giggled. "I daresay the thief I stole it from paid handsomely to have it made in the first place."

"Doubtlessly so, unless he stole it from someone else." Barrow normally would've admonished the girl for stealing a magical artifact; there were too many ways to track something like that and turn it against her. At the moment, though, he had more pressing concerns. "Shall we head up these stairs here and see just where you've led us?"

Climbing the stairs, they found themselves in the stockroom of a large shop. It was well past closing time, and thankfully even the after-hours cleaning staff had long since gone home for the night. Explaining how they had come to be in the store's basement would've been difficult, to say the least, especially given the ragged state they were both in.

They headed out to the street. Barrow looked around, trying to get his bearings as Emily used her magic key to lock the door behind them. The gas streetlamps at the corner brightened the night with their waxy yellow light. At nearly midnight, the street was deserted, save for a horse-drawn hansom heading away from them, far down the block. The clatter of the wheels and the horse's hooves on the cobbles were the only sounds to be heard.

"I know this place," Barrow said. "We're near the north end of Hollis Street. My workshop is not far from here, actually. There's a scrub sink with hot water, if you'd like to clean yourself up."

Emily cast a glance at his tattered, sodden trousers. His bloodied knees had started to scab over, the shredded fabric already becoming trapped in the sticky wounds like ants in tree resin. She laughed.

It took him a moment to figure out what the girl found so amusing. Looking down at himself, he let forth a short chuckle of his own.

"I suppose I could use a wash and a clean set of clothes myself," he admitted.

❦

FEW PEOPLE HAD EVER VISITED BARROW'S UNDERGROUND workshop. Aside from Inspector Eddings, who was an infrequent visitor at best, he didn't entertain many social callers, and he certainly wasn't in the practice of bringing clients into his inner sanctum.

"Look at all the equipment you've got down here," Emily marveled, her eyes flitting from one wonder to the next. "And so many books!"

Barrow's chuckle held little amusement. "You see how many books there are," he said, hanging his jacket on a hook. "When I look at these shelves, I see how *few* line them. I see the measure of my own ignorance." He groaned quietly, wincing as he unbuttoned his soiled waistcoat. The night's excitement was starting to wear off, and the lumps he had taken at the hands of Lai Jūn were beginning to ache. He gingerly felt at his ribs through his shirt; nothing seemed to be broken, but he knew he would be hobbling like an old graybeard for at least the next week.

"I've never seen near as many," Emily said, still scanning the shelves. "Not outside the Citizens' Library, anyway."

"Not even in Lawrence MacGowan's office?" Barrow asked. "I thought his collection quite impressive."

She shot him a look as if he'd said something absurd. Seeing the confusion on his face, she softened. "Kitchen scuttle like me weren't invited up to his suite," Emily explained. "Sometimes one or two of the dancing girls would be brought up, but even that was usually only if MacGowan were trying to impress some businessman or councilor. The only time most of us ever saw him was when he'd come down to the main floor himself."

"Of course. Anyway, the scrub sink is back here," he said, drawing across a cloth screen to provide her at least some measure of privacy. "There's soap, and there ought to be plenty of hot water. I often work late, so the boiler is kept hot at all hours." He handed her a rough washcloth. One of his spare suits hung next to a cheval glass in the corner beside the sink. "I'm afraid I don't have any clean clothes you would fit in."

"That's okay," she said, taking the washcloth as she headed for the sink and ducked behind the curtain. The taps squeaked loudly as she twisted the handles. "How did you come to be brawling in that alley?"

"Apparently there's a price on my head," he called back. "It would seem our Chinese stage magician is an assassin in the employ of the Nightshade Cabal."

"You must've upset them something serious to have Lai Jūn sent after you. He's one of the Cabal's deadliest. His services don't come cheap."

"He wouldn't be cheap, not with magic like that," Barrow muttered, shuddering at the thought of how the spectral cobra had very nearly ended him. He examined his battered face in a small mirror, tentatively picking bits of gravel out of a scabbed cut above one eye. His bottom lip had split and was beginning to swell. Exhaustion and dried blood made the bruising where his cheek had connected with the wall look worse than it really was. At least, he hoped that was the case. None of the abrasions looked deep enough to require suturing.

Emily stepped out from behind the curtain, patting her face with the dry end of the washcloth. Her damp hair, hacked boyishly short, stuck up at odd angles from her scalp. Barrow shook his head. Between the unfeminine coif and her rugged attire of heavy boots and dungarees, he supposed it was no wonder he had mistaken her for a boy when he had caught a brief glance of her at the boardinghouse.

"Is there something amusing, Mr. Barrow?" she asked when she caught his smile.

"Just my own lacking powers of observation, Miss Skye," he said, gesturing to her masculine hair and clothing. "Why this ruse?"

"There aren't many reasons for an unattended young lady to be walking around at the docks," she shrugged, taking a seat on the threadbare green chaise, "and most of the ones that do exist tend to draw a lot of unwanted attention."

"I think I understand," Barrow said as he ducked behind the screen to scrub the grime and dried blood from his own face. The harsh soap and hot water stung his cuts as he washed, and the alcohol he swabbed on his wounds afterwards did so even more fiercely, but at least they wouldn't fester.

He stripped off his shirt and ragged trousers to wash his aching body. His shoulder had already turned a furious shade of purple, as had the skin covering his tender ribs. Both knees were torn and bloodied. He regarded his battered figure in the cheval glass and shook his head. *You're no pugilist, are you, Isaac?*

Leaving his ruined clothes in a heap on the floor, he put on the clean shirt and trousers from his spare suit, leaving the waistcoat and jacket hanging on the rack. He didn't even bother with a shirt collar; he had been through too much this night to worry about propriety.

"You can rest here for a few hours, Miss Skye," he said as he emerged from behind the curtain, buttoning his cuffs. "It's too late to do much of anything else tonight. I'll take you back to your sister in the morning."

There was no answer.

Emily Skye was already stretched out along the length of the chaise, fast asleep.

11

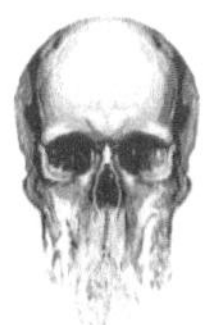

Barrow woke late once more, feeling even worse than he had when sleep had finally taken him. When Emily Skye had fallen asleep on the chaise, he had covered her with the only blanket he had on hand—a heavy woolen Hudson's Bay Company four-point—then dragged one of the wooden chairs from his office down to the workshop for himself. Sleeping upright in the chair with just his long overcoat for a coverlet would have made for an uncomfortable night under the best of circumstances; having just been thoroughly thrashed at the hands of Lai Jūn, the result was something near agony. He groaned softly as he rose to his feet, keenly aware of the weariness deep in his bones, and did his best to keep quiet so as not to disturb the girl.

He needn't have worried. She was already awake, reading one of his books: a rather dry volume on fluid mechanics. Barrow had found the text to be quite dull himself, but Emily seemed to be fully absorbed. In her other hand, she held a steaming glass beaker wrapped in a scrap of a towel.

He rubbed the sleep from his eyes, wincing as his knuckles rubbed at the bruising there. He wondered just how many shades of purple had bloomed on his face while he slept. "You made coffee?" he asked around a yawn.

Emily started, nearly letting the beaker slip from her hand. Engrossed as she was in her reading, she hadn't noticed Barrow stirring. "Yes, I hope you don't mind. I had to throw some coal in the stove there to get the heat up to boil the water," she said, nodding to the potbelly in the corner. A merry orange glow seeped out of the grate. "I couldn't find any cups, though. Would you care for some, Mr. Barrow?"

His answer came as a grunt, rather than anything that could properly be called words, but he certainly meant it in the affirmative. He took a beaker from a nearby shelf and handed it to her; he knew there were cups around here somewhere, but he couldn't be bothered to search them out.

Emily smiled and tipped the large, flat-bottomed flask she had used as a brewing urn, careful to keep too many of the ground beans from sluicing out along with the coffee. "I couldn't find any cream or sugar either," she apologized.

That scarcely mattered to Barrow at the moment. He preferred to take his coffee with a little cream, but in that instance, the taste was of much less import to him than the caffeine. Taking the beaker, he managed to mumble something that sounded like thanks. His split lip screamed in protest as it came into contact with the hot glass, but he managed to take a sip.

Certain people are blessed with boundless energy in the morning, requiring little time upon rising from their beds to shrug off the grog of sleep and get on with the business of the day. To Barrow's great annoyance, Emily Skye seemed to be one such individual. Seeing that he was notionally awake and at least somewhat ambulatory, the girl was flitting about and looking at everything in the underground workshop, questioning him intently about it all. He was halfway through the steaming coffee before he managed much more than two words in answer to any of her enquiries.

One contraption, in particular, seemed to have caught her interest. In his bleary state, it barely registered with Barrow that the girl was admiring one of his latest projects, a personal winged glider that could be worn on one's back. In size and shape, the machine was rather like a large alpinist's backpack, but the similarities ended there. The construct featured a pair of heavy, padded leather straps that looped over the shoulders. A shorter piece between the shoulder straps buckled across the chest, and there was a sturdy belt that cinched around the waist. Once secured into the harness with all of the fittings properly adjusted, the apparatus would cleave tightly to the operator's back.

The pack itself was rather flat and sleek, clad in brass. Barrow had polished this casing to a mirror-like gleam. What looked like several yards of heavy oiled canvas were folded neatly against each side, extending a few inches taller than the pack itself. Anyone not knowing better would think the wearer was transporting a pair of tent canvases.

A series of small levers were built into the straps of the harness. Too late, Barrow noticed Emily was fiddling with those controls.

"Don't touch the—"

He was cut off as she squeezed one set of levers together, activating the wing release mechanism. He dove out of the way as one of the glider's chiropteran wings sprung free of the ratcheting clasps that secured it in place, sending tools and papers and other bits and pieces scattering to the floor as it snapped to its full length, nearly eight feet to the outstretched tip. Oiled canvas stretched taut over skeletal brass framing, giving the wing its distinctly bat-like appearance.

Barrow held his bruised ribs as he rose from the floor. He

managed to reign in his ire with no small effort. "As I was saying, Miss Skye, *please don't touch the controls*," he said with a sharp intake of breath.

"Is it a flying machine? How splendid," Emily said, still marveling at the glider. She seemed oblivious to the chaos she had unleashed. "How does it work?"

Despite his anger, Barrow couldn't resist the chance to talk about one of his creations. The personal glider, though far from perfect, was one invention he was particularly proud to show off. "The operator puts his fingers into these control gauntlets fastened halfway along each wing," he explained, pointing out the leather glove that had been folded away inside the now outstretched wing. Clockwork contrivances built around each finger were connected to the glider's main harness by insulated wires. "These allow for a certain degree of control over each wing, independent of the other. As for how it stays aloft, many of the same aerodynamic principles that allow a bird to achieve flight work for this machine. It's based on a design from Leonardo da Vinci's notebooks. His schematics were very thorough, even if there's no evidence he ever built the machine himself." He smiled, proud of what he had accomplished. "Elemental bonding helps as well."

Emily looked up from the machine, a quizzical expression on her face. "Elemental bonding?"

"A thaumaturgic fusion of the mechanical and the supernatural," Barrow said, indicating a small silver ring inset in the center of the glider's harness, not much larger than a fifty-cent piece. "It's a relatively new alchemical process by which the function of a machine can be augmented by fusing the structure with a complimentary elemental or other minor spirit. You might improve a clock's accuracy by bonding it with a horological boggart, for example. In the case of the glider, I've employed a zephyr to overcome certain problems of aerodynamics."

"And the scorch marks here?" Emily asked, pointing to a discoloured section of oiled canvas. "What caused that?"

"An early misstep," he said evasively. "I haven't had the chance to patch the membrane yet, but the glider does fly. I have to admit, the controls aren't yet quite as responsive as I'd like, though, and landings can be, ah...well, troublesome."

Emily grinned at the awkward admission, drawing a cough from Barrow. "It's an impressive prototype nonetheless, Mr. Barrow. But look at the mess I've made!" She dropped to her knees and began gathering up the scattered pieces she had sent flying from Barrow's workbench.

Barrow grimaced as he knelt to assist her. Nothing seemed to have been broken in the accident, though the scattered papers he was gathering would take some time to set to rights. *This is exactly why I don't invite anyone down here,* he thought ruefully, then shook his head. As far as laboratory catastrophes went, this one had been relatively minor. Indeed, he had been the cause of far more disastrous calamities himself. At least nothing had caught fire this time.

He was sorting some papers when he looked over and noticed Emily kneeling on the floor, Henry Feele's outsized memory cylinder in her hands. The grayish gel within still glowed softly.

"I've seen these cylinders before," she said.

"Please be careful with that," Barrow said nervously as he stuffed a sheaf of pages into a folder. "It's from an autotype machine. That's an expensive piece of equipment, but becoming rather more common these days. Given the advantages over a standard typewriter, I expect in time we'll see an autotype in every place of business, and possibly even most homes. That particular cylinder, however, is a unique piece."

"I know it is," she said, still examining it closely. "I mean, I've seen others just like this. I wouldn't have expected to see one in your laboratory, however." She looked at him, a grave expression on her face.

Barrow was still rather distracted by the stack of loose pages in front of him. He didn't really notice what she had said, nor had he caught her apprehension. "It belongs to a client of mine, and I fear the investigation of that piece has turned up quite a grisly possibility." He paused then, seeming to realize what she had actually said. "Miss Skye, do you mean to say you've seen memory cells of this exceptional size?"

"Just so, Mr. Barrow, and quite a few of them, too. One of the times Cooper took me to the lair of the Nightshade Cabal, a necromancer we spoke to in the warrens was working on these. I don't believe he made the casing for them himself, mind you, but he was definitely making the stuff that was inside." She shuddered at the memory, but didn't go into detail. "He had made about ten or twelve of them, at least that I saw."

"Miss Skye, I need you to try to remember," Barrow said. "Where was it that you saw these cylinders?"

Emily frowned. "It's impossible to say, I'm afraid. The Cabal uses the old tunnels to move about unseen beneath the city, skittering about like a horde of rats."

Barrow nodded. What the girl was saying made sense. If a smuggler like Harold Penhold was making use of those clandestine tunnels, it was no surprise to hear the Cabal was using them as well.

"Well, that confirms part of my suspicions, while opening a new can of complications," he muttered, drawing a puzzled look from Emily. "Bad enough to have one necromancer at the heart of this mess, but the whole of the Nightshade Cabal is something else entirely. It would've been easier if there was just one murderous bastard to chase after. At least that's something I could have turned over to my friend who works with the Halifax Constabulary."

"Why can't you do that now?"

"Mortal authorities have no jurisdiction over crimes of the occult, Miss Skye," he answered. "If there's real necromancy or some other thaumaturgic process involved in making these memory cylinders, the crime falls outside their purview. There's a separate regulatory body who oversees such matters."

"The Triune Congress," she said. "I heard talk of it, and none of it very complimentary."

Barrow chuckled. "I can well imagine."

"It seems to me that simply because the crime itself is an occult offense, that's no reason your constable friend wouldn't have any advice to offer," Emily said, handing the memory cylinder to Barrow. "Perhaps you should pay him a visit and see what he can tell you?"

Barrow wasn't sure if he ought to be pleased or annoyed that Miss Skye's thoughts had followed his own so closely. "That is actually a great idea, Miss Skye," he said after a moment.

"Do you know what else is a great idea, Mr. Barrow?" she asked, a bright smile on her face. When he made no show of answering her question, she did so herself. "Breakfast!"

THE DINGY CAFÉ ON THE CORNER WAS MOSTLY EMPTY, though that was hardly an oddity for the place. Aside from the occasional workman briefly stopping in, they had the place to themselves. The surly cook had seemed mildly surprised to see Barrow at his counter a second time in as many days, to which Barrow could only shrug indifferently. He usually made a point of eating elsewhere, but this morning he didn't much care. As soon as Emily had mentioned food, he realized he was ravenously hungry.

Greasy slices of bacon and overcooked eggs were shoved in front of him on a chipped stoneware plate. The dishes didn't see much use in here; most of the café's customers took a sliced roll stuffed with bacon and egg wrapped in waxed paper they could eat while they walked to work.

Looking at the food in front of him, Barrow opened his mouth to call to the cook for tomato ketchup, thought better of it, and struggled to cut off a piece of the leathery bacon. With a sigh, he popped the meat into his mouth, instantly wishing he hadn't. Calling the stuff *inedible* paid the cook too high a compliment.

The stale coffee was no better. Barrow winced at the bitter taste and added a lump of sugar to his cup. He usually only took the smallest dribble of cream in his coffee, if he added anything at all. This stuff, though, demanded extreme measures. He wondered if the foul concoction had been brewed to celebrate William IV's coronation, or just Victoria's.

If Emily found the food objectionable, she made no mention of it. She offered little comment on much at all, tucking in as though it were her first proper meal in more than a week. For all Barrow knew, it was. Gulping the bitter coffee, she asked, "When can we go speak with the inspector?"

"*We* are not going to speak with anyone. You're going back to your sister," Barrow said firmly, stirring another lump of sugar into his own coffee.

"The bollocks I am," Emily said. At least, that was what Barrow *thought* she said; it was hard to hear her clearly around a mouthful of bread. Thankfully, she swallowed before continuing.

"I was on Lai Jūn's trail when you blundered into the

alley last night," Emily continued. "If you hadn't happened along when you did, I would've followed him back to their den." She paused to take a gulp of tea. "You'd likely be laying there dead in that alleyway right now, too."

Barrow didn't reply to that. He grimaced as though he'd bitten down on something that tasted worse than the eggs. "Someone would've found my body by now," he muttered under his breath. He hadn't meant her to hear that, but the satisfied grin that lit up her face was infuriating. "But how do you know Lai Jūn would've led you to the Cabal's hideout, Miss Skye? For all you know, the only reason he was out and about at all was to put a violent end to my investigation."

"And just where do you think he would've gone next?" she asked.

He mulled that over for a moment before answering. "I suppose he would've returned to them to report my demise," he said, "at which point you would have found their lair after all."

The girl said nothing, but her smile was mildly galling.

He threw his hands in the air. "All right, then! We'll work together on this, but damn me to the Abyss if I like it."

"You don't have to like it, Mr. Barrow," she said. Smiling, she popped another piece of bread into her mouth.

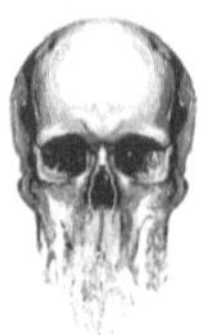

12

"Bloody hell, Barrow, you look like you've gone eighteen rounds with James Kelly," Inspector Eddings exclaimed, eyeing the battered technomancer incredulously from behind his broad desk.

Barrow and Miss Skye occupied the two seats opposite him. If the inspector's dim and dingy office had seemed small with two occupants, a third made it feel downright cramped. "I don't know who that is," Barrow said, shrugging off the inspector's observation.

"Of course you don't," Eddings sighed. "He's a bare-knuckle boxer, but I suppose that doesn't matter right now. What in blazes have you gotten yourself into?"

"I had a run-in with your stage magician," Barrow answered. When Eddings gave no hint that he followed, Barrow went on, "Lai Jūn, from the Theatre Royale the other night. I had the pleasure of making his close acquaintance in an alleyway last night."

Eddings whistled. "Those beasts he conjures up?"

Barrow nodded. "I can assure you he's dangerous enough

without them as well. As it turns out, he's also working with the Nightshade Cabal."

"Nasty business." As he did every time Barrow was in his office, the inspector offered the spellcaster a drink. As he did every time Eddings offered, Barrow politely declined. "Suit yourself," Eddings said, working the stopper from the bottle and pouring a measure of scotch into a glass. "How about you, Miss Skye?"

"No, thank you, Inspector Eddings."

"Bloody hell, not another one," Eddings muttered with resignation in his voice as he brought the glass to his lips. "All right, so Lai Jūn is sided with the Nightshade Cabal, and no doubt it sent him to put paid to you for poking your nose about in its affairs. Is that about the sum of it?"

"It would seem to be, yes," Barrow said.

"You have a knack for finding trouble, I'll give you that. So what was it that got you tangled up in Cabal business?"

"That's where the constabulary comes in," Barrow said, reaching into his valise and pulling out Henry Feele's memory cylinder. He placed it on the inspector's desk. "My experiment has concluded that the brain matter used in the cylinder's memory suspension medium is indeed human in origin."

Eddings nearly choked on his drink, spilling some down the front of his waistcoat. "Human? Are you quite certain?"

"Very. Moreover, Miss Skye believes the piece was crafted by one of the Nightshade Cabal's necromancers, or at least the storage medium contained within was."

The inspector had taken out his handkerchief and was dabbing the spilled scotch from his lapel. He eyed the damp handkerchief with some regret before tucking it away. "How the hell does that fit, though? Why would they be interested in making office machinery? I don't know as much about the

Cabal as I maybe ought to, but glorified typewriters hardly seem to be the sort of thing it'd typically pursue."

"That I don't know," Barrow admitted, his eyebrows drawing together.

"Perhaps they're not interested in making office machinery at all," Emily suggested.

"How do you mean?" Eddings asked.

"It's as you said, Inspector Eddings," she said. "It doesn't fit. Building a better autotype machine would hardly be of interest to even the most pragmatic member of the Cabal. The devotees are not exactly overly concerned with such matters of practicality. Could they be creating these memory cylinders for some other reason?"

"Okay, I'll bite," Eddings said. "What might that be, then?"

Barrow thought it over for a moment before he offered an answer. "Why do I perform half of the experiments I do, Jonathon?"

"Because you're a bloody lunatic who ought to be committed to the Hemlock Overlook Sanitarium?" A crooked smile split his face as he raised his glass in mock salute.

"To see if what I've dreamed up can be done," Barrow said, ignoring the bait.

"You think there's some unhinged necromancer out there turning people into typewriters, what? Just for the fun of it?"

"Necromancers are unhinged as a general rule," Barrow said, "but yes, that may be the short of it."

Eddings drummed his fingers on the desk as he thought that over. "You think there could be more of them out there?" he asked, pointing to the cylinder.

"I've seen them myself," Emily said. "A dozen at least, though the ones I saw were still empty."

"And that's not all, Jonathon," Barrow said. "You're no

doubt aware that eldersight has returned to the streets of Halifax?"

"I'd heard a few things, but nothing the constabulary has been able to substantiate."

"Consider this your confirmation," Barrow said, pulling the half-phial he had discovered in Emily's bureau from his pocket.

Emily shifted in her seat and shot him a look, but said nothing as he set the phial on the edge of the desk. The deep indigo contents aside, the glass phial looked rather like a miniature version of the memory cylinder when placed beside the larger glass tube. "The drug is extracted from plants that won't grow in our climate, so it has to be coming in from overseas."

"Aye, that's a toughie there," Eddings said with a frown. "We don't even know what the plant looks like. How are we supposed to stop it coming off the boat?"

Barrow leveled his friend a withering glance. "Can you really be that thick, Jonathon?"

Eddings blinked, but said nothing.

Barrow sighed and apologized, blaming his rancour on exhaustion and his various injuries before going on to explain. "For maximum yield, the essential oils have to be extracted from the leaves and bark before the plant dries out," he explained. "It's typically done by a process involving steam and compressing the plant fibers, although pressurized hydro-diffusion is becoming an increasingly popular method." Urged to move things along by the growing impa- tience evident on the inspector's face, Barrow continued. "I suppose none of that is really relevant by the time it gets to us, though. It would be processed overseas and shipped here in its concentrated form: a thick, oily, indigo-coloured resin with a rather acrid pungency."

"You seem to know a lot about processing narcotics,

Barrow. But then, you know a bloody lot about everything." Eddings took a drink. "As far as eldersight goes, where the Halifax Constabulary is concerned, the damned stuff doesn't officially exist."

"Foolishness," Barrow said.

"Can't argue that," Eddings nodded. "But on the book, that's the line I've got to give."

"And off the book?" Emily asked.

"Off the books, Miss Skye, the stuff is a bloody nightmare. I had hoped to be drawing my pension long before ever seeing it in Halifax again, but the Lord above weren't so kind. The constabulary doesn't have enough to deal with, with the sailors and soldiers washing up and drinking until all they can do is bash each other's heads in in the streets. We need opium dens and now eldersight mucking things up on top of all else?" He shook his head. "All right, you tell me, Barrow. Where is the cursed stuff coming from?"

"We believe the Nightshade Cabal is involved in that as well," Barrow said. "Miss Skye was following one of its members last night, and came very near to uncovering the base of operations for that particular venture."

"Is that right?" Eddings asked. When she nodded, he went on. "If you'd found the place, you'd've said as much instead of coming to me with a great bunch of questions I can't begin to answer. What happened to throw you off the trail?"

"Is that really important?" Barrow interjected. Eddings waved him to silence.

"I was forced to abandon my pursuit to come to the aid of Mr. Barrow," Emily answered with a nod in the techno-mancer's direction. "He'd just been assaulted in an alleyway, you see, and I fear the outcome would've been quite dire, had I not stepped in when I did."

Eddings raised an eyebrow, but left it at that.

Barrow allowed himself a small sigh of relief. He didn't want to explain to his friend the details of how he had been rescued by this waif of a girl.

"The man I was following wasn't anyone important," Emily continued. "Not even a member, just hired muscle. The Cabal keeps several hideaways, you see, and I was hoping he would lead me to one."

"And what would you have done, had you found the place?" Eddings asked her. "Begging your pardon for saying as much, Miss Skye, but I don't see one young girl against the Cabal as being the best odds."

Barrow nodded his agreement.

Emily had no ready answer. "I suppose I hadn't thought things through quite so far ahead," she said after a moment's consideration. "I suppose I could have tried to locate the Triune Magister and give him the information."

"The Triune Magister would be just as likely to throw you into the gaol as listen to anything you had to tell him," Barrow pointed out. "Malleus isn't the most flexible sort of man. As far as he's concerned, if you've had any dealings with the Cabal at all, you're an irredeemable wretch and deserve to be horsewhipped."

Eddings rolled his eyes at the mention of the Triune Congress and poured himself another drink. "Keeping the law isn't difficult enough on its own, you wizards with your own bloody police force out there mucking about."

"Mortal law isn't even remotely suited to deal with crimes of the occult, Jonathon," Barrow reminded his friend. "Do you really want your constables chasing after dybbuks and werewolves in the night?"

"Oh, I know the Triune has its part to play, Barrow. It doesn't mean I have to like it when its authority oversteps my own, though."

To that Barrow could only nod. He understood his

friend's frustrations, having had his own squabbles with the Triune Congress over the years. Malleus had made no secret of the displeasure the Triune's overseers held regarding Barrow's frequent consultations with the Halifax Constabulary, to say nothing of selling his talents to industry. As far as they were concerned, practice of the arcane arts should remain clandestine.

For his part, Barrow thought that foolish. Such secrecy bred only fear. It was also the kind of outdated thinking that allowed obscene elements like the Nightshade Cabal to operate in the shadows.

Eddings drained his glass. "At any rate, our constables have their hands too full lately with boring old mundane matters to be out there chasing werewolves or vampires or the like."

"There aren't any vampires in Halifax, Jonathon," Barrow said dismissively.

"Well, I couldn't remember what the other thing was that you said a moment ago," Eddings said. Barrow opened his mouth to reply, but the inspector put up a hand to cut him off. "As I was saying, we've got our hands full with what looks to be a full-on sequential murderer."

That got Barrow's attention. "Sequential murders?"

The inspector frowned. "It's bloody peculiar, Barrow. We've had four bodies turn up, all slain in the same way, and each exactly two weeks apart."

"How were they killed?"

Eddings shifted in his seat and glanced over to Emily. "Are you sure we ought to discuss this in front of the young lady?"

Before Barrow could answer, Emily did. "Inspector Eddings, I've witnessed the blood rites of the Nightshade Cabal performed firsthand," she said. "Can you say the same?"

"I fought in the Crimea, Miss Skye," Eddings answered indignantly. "I've been elbow-deep in my best mate's guts, trying to keep him alive until the medics could get there to sew him back up. Whatever nonsense it is that the Cabal gets up to, I've seen more than my share of horrors in my day."

Emily smiled sweetly. "I'm certain you have, Inspector. I never meant to imply otherwise. Regardless, my point was that I think I can handle whatever nightmares you've had come through the morgue."

Barrow was impressed at the girl's response, and even more so by the mollifying effect her words had on the blusterous inspector. Eddings was known almost as much for his stormy disposition as he was for his bravery and cunning. "Miss Skye has shown she's quite capable, Jonathon. She may even be able to offer some advice if you can tell us a bit about these murders. How these four people were killed, for a start."

The inspector remained silent for a moment, then nodded. "That's what's so odd. Every one of them, shot in the same spot, right at the base of the skull with a small-caliber bullet. No exit wounds."

Barrow shrugged. "A bullet of sufficiently small caliber might easily lodge itself within the brainpan," he offered. "A shot from a Derringer, for example. The bullet that killed President Lincoln remained in his skull."

"Ah, but there's the part that's giving us trouble," Eddings said, smiling despite the gruesome topic at hand. Even in a matter such as this, the inspector seemed to take some measure of enjoyment in disproving one of Barrow's theories. "None of the four we've found so far had any size bullet anywhere inside of 'em."

Now it was Barrow's turn to frown. "No exit wound, and no bullet to be found in the body," he said, thinking it over. "That's a riddle indeed."

"Could the killer have removed the bullets himself?" Emily offered.

"We thought of that too, Miss Skye," Eddings said, "but the coroner says the wounds are far too clean for anyone to have been mucking about like that. Besides which, what reason would anyone have to do such a thing?"

"That's right, it would be tricky enough surgery to remove a bullet if the killer cut his victim's head down the middle," Barrow agreed offhandedly. "But extracting the slug through the entry wound would be another matter entirely. Even the narrowest forceps would tear the brain tissue..." he trailed off, lost in distant thought.

A few moments passed in silence. When it didn't seem that Barrow was going to continue, Eddings cleared his throat, loudly.

"The brain tissue," Barrow repeated quietly, more to himself than anyone else before turning his attention back to the inspector. "Jonathon, would it be possible to examine the most recent victim's body?"

Inspector Eddings was visibly taken back by his friend's odd request, but only missed a beat before answering. "Impossible, I'm afraid. The poor woman's already a week in the ground."

Barrow brought his fist down on Eddings's desk, hard enough to startle both Emily and his old friend. "Damn it all!" he thundered.

"You know something, don't you, Barrow?"

"I've a theory, that's all," Barrow said, leaving it at that. "If—all the gods forbid—another victim is found, I'll need to see the body straight away."

"I make no promises," Eddings said, "but I'll do what I can. Dr. Brookfield won't be eager to have you poking about in his morgue."

Barrow made a slightly exasperated sound, drawing a

questioning look from Emily. "The chief coroner and I…let's just say we don't always see eye to eye," he said evasively.

"Imagine that," Emily said innocently. "And you being such an agreeable sort and all!"

Eddings snorted in laughter. When Barrow answered Emily's barb with nothing but a withering glare, the inspector outright guffawed.

"This one'll keep you on your toes, Barrow," he said when he regained his composure. "Whatever's going on with the eldersight and the memory cylinders, you'll get to the bottom of it. You're a damned good investigator. Miles better than any of the lot I've got here at the station house, and they're the best there is. It's a bloody shame you never signed on with the constabulary. You'd've made detective in no time."

Barrow chuckled softly at the notion, one his friend had expressed countless times over the years they had known each other. "I don't think that would've worked quite so well, Jonathon. My investigative methods are more effective when I'm not so…" he paused, searching for the right word, "…not so encumbered by the legal process."

Eddings laughed. "It's true, Miss Skye," he said to Emily, "I don't know how he comes up with the half of what he does. I'm just bloody glad he's on my side more often than not."

"What else do you know about the victims? Is there anything to connect them to each other?"

"The last three were John Does. We don't know much at all about them, I'm afraid," Eddings said. "The first was a patient from Hemlock Overlook by the name of Jenny Perkins. She was reported as escaped, and her body was found three days later in an alleyway up in Africville."

Barrow's eyes were wide. "She escaped from the sanitarium?"

"Their security is hardly ironclad, as it turns out. We went up there and questioned her doctors, and it seems she could very nearly have walked right out the front door whenever it suited her. Only the most dangerous patients are ever kept in restraints."

Barrow was silent as he considered all that Eddings had just told him. "I'd like to speak to those doctors myself," he finally said.

The look of surprise on the inspector's face quickly shifted to one of understanding as he followed Barrow's line of thought. "You think there's a connection between the Jenny Perkins case and this business with the Cabal."

"I'm not ruling out any possibilities right now, Jonathon," he said, rising to his feet. "I need to see to transportation. Miss Skye will need to get a message to her sister." He handed Eddings the calling card Meredith had given him. Though their meeting had been just a few days previous, it felt like weeks had passed. "Have one of your constables deliver the note to Meredith Skye at this address."

Eddings stared at him in disbelief. "My men are police constables, Barrow, not bloody couriers!"

"That's precisely why I ask, Jonathon. The Cabal may have intercepted Miss Skye's last letter to her sister. Hopefully one of your men will have better luck in delivering this one safely."

The inspector nodded, but still looked displeased.

"I would appreciate it very much, Inspector Eddings," Emily spoke up, a sweet smile on her face. "Meredith must simply be beside herself, and I would like her to know I'm safe under the protection of Mr. Barrow."

Eddings threw his hands in the air. "A pox take you both," he said, though the rancour had gone out of his voice. He handed Emily a pad, pen, and ink. "Very well, jot down whatever you need to tell her and I'll have Constable McAllister run it over this afternoon. It's about all that great galoot is good for, anyway."

Barrow jammed his bowler onto his head and headed off down the corridor, leaving Inspector Eddings and Miss Skye alone in the office.

"A moment, please, Miss Skye," Eddings said as she finished up her note. "If you're going to be aiding Mr. Barrow with his investigation, I'd consider it a personal favour if you would treat the matter with the utmost of care."

"However do you mean?"

"I meant what I said before about how clever Barrow is. He's not just clever, he's bloody brilliant, but he also tends to get wrapped up in his own head at times. Having someone along to balance him out ought to do him a world of good. He hasn't worked with anyone quite so closely since the Atherton affair."

Emily had no response to that. The name meant nothing to her.

"Mr. Barrow had taken on an apprentice a few years ago," Eddings explained, "a bright young fellow by the name of Ethan Atherton. He wouldn't've been much older than yourself, come to think of it. I think he rather thought of the lad as a younger brother."

"Was this Atherton a technomancer as well? Like Mr. Barrow?"

"Aye, that he was, Miss Skye," the inspector nodded. "I don't know that he was quite as talented as Barrow, mind you, but he always said that young Atherton had great potential."

"You say they were like brothers," she said. "Whatever became of him?"

Eddings drained his glass. At any other time, the sour look on his face might've said that he didn't care for the taste. "I fear I've said more than I should've, Miss Skye. It's really not my story to be telling."

13

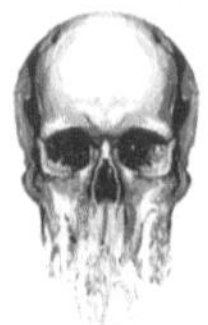

THE WORLD SPED BY AT AN ALARMING PACE AS THE thundering steamcarriage devoured the snaking country road. Though Hemlock Overlook Sanitarium was less than twenty miles from the north end of the city, the rough track took many twists as it wound its way first past the slums of Africville where the body of Jenny Perkins had turned up, then along the shore of Bedford Basin before finally turning inland toward the asylum's remote location on the northern slopes of Hemlock Ravine. Wincing at the expense, Barrow had hired the steamcarriage and driver at a cost of two dollars. The fare wasn't much more than a horse carriage, but he grudged spending it all the same. There was simply no quicker option available.

He found himself wincing now for a different reason. Speeding along the rutted surface of the rural track, the steamcar rattled and lurched and kicked up so much dust he wondered if the machine might scatter itself (to say nothing of its passengers) to pieces across the roadway at any moment. Clouds of thick black coal smoke belched from the engine's roaring firebox, turning the veil of dust in the steamcar's wake utterly opaque.

The vehicle managed to hold together despite the beating it was taking. Thankfully, the mild weather also held; among their few drawbacks, steamcarriages were notorious for getting mired in mud that would not trouble a team of horses.

The interior of the hired steamcar's passenger cabin was much like that of a horse-drawn hansom, with two bench seats set facing each other. Barrow could only speculate the steam-cars owned by the wealthy elite were more lavishly appointed than the rather utilitarian job he had been able to hire. No doubt the seats in those vehicles, at least, offered more in the way of cushioning, if not more robust safety features. His left hand desperately clutched a loop of leather hanging from the roof of the vehicle, the only concession the builders had made towards the wellbeing of passengers. The handhold helped, but he still wished there was something to secure his body to the seat itself. *Some sort of harness or lap belt, perhaps?*

With his free hand, he scribbled a reminder to look into the idea in his notebook, assuming he survived the trip. He swore under his breath as the steamcar hit off another bump, snapping the lead point on his pencil and gouging the page in the process.

He looked across the cabin to the young Miss Skye. Like him, she held fast to one of the leather loops as the wildly juddering steamcar did its best to toss her from her seat. While he was sure all colour had drained from his face, he was astonished to see Emily wore a gleeful grin as she bounced back and forth. *She's actually enjoying this.*

With the deafening noise coming from the steamcarriage's engine, conversation was impossible. Barrow had tried to shout a few inquiries towards Emily at the outset, but if she even understood his questions, her replies were utterly drowned out by the racket. He had quickly given up, turning his attention instead to his leatherbound notebook.

He breathed a sigh of relief as the vehicle finally slowed, pulling off the bumpy road onto the grounds of the sanitarium. A long gravel drive bridged the gap between the imposing iron gates and the sanitarium's entry, and offered a surface more suited to the vehicle. He admired the machine, but it was certainly meant to be driven on roads paved with flat stone or cobbles. The infrastructure, as was so often the case, lagged behind the technology.

Barrow emerged from the passenger cabin first, stepping gingerly down to the gravel as one might step onto the quay after several weeks at sea. The trip had taken scarcely more than an hour, and just over half of that had been on the jarring country track, but solid ground felt shaky under his feet all the same. He hoped he would feel steadier after a few moments.

He turned to help Emily out of the steamcarriage, but saw he needn't have bothered. The girl was quite handily pulling herself out through the vehicle's small doorway, giggling as she stumbled into the daylight. Her scuffed boots landed on the gravel drive with a crunch as she whooped excitedly, windmilling her arms to keep her balance.

Barrow took a moment to adjust his tie and set his rumpled jacket and trousers to rights, then set his bowler back in its proper place atop his head. He reached past Emily to retrieve his valise from inside the vehicle, then looked up at the sanitarium's imposing façade.

Hemlock Overlook was only a few decades old, he knew, but had been built in a much older style echoing Gothic architecture. Tall windows with pointed arches ranged the front side of the wide gray stone building, the two wings of which extended a hundred yards or more to either side of the portcullis, with a high-peaked rooftop and an ostentatious belfry towering above all. The effect made the building seem taller than it truly was. A semicircular veranda circumscribed by a marble railing atop ornate balusters ensconced the entry.

The sheer scale of Hemlock Overlook Sanitarium put Barrow in mind of the Technomancer's Collegium. Situated on a large parcel of land atop a breathtaking ravine and surrounded by an ancient grove of the majestic evergreen trees that gave the estate its name, the sanitarium seemed as much a primordial element as its lush surroundings. A carpet of thick moss crept up from the ground, tracking its course along the mortar between the stones. It looked rather as though the building had taken root and grown from within the earth itself.

Somewhat awed by the impressive edifice, Barrow looked down first at his own attire, then over to Emily. She must have caught something in his glance. "Is something the matter, Mr. Barrow?"

"I rather think we ought to have stopped to get you a change of clothes, is all," he said, looking her up and down. "I hadn't considered it until just now, but between the dungarees and the hatchet job you've made of your hair, you look like some feral thing I picked up on the side of the road."

She replied with a mock curtsy. "I dress for my own comfort, Mr. Barrow, and no one else's. If what I choose to wear upsets polite folk, they're free to put their eyes elsewhere and waste no time doing it, thank you very much."

Barrow opened his mouth to deliver a lecture about the importance of propriety, but thought better of it. Standing in the shadow of the sanitarium, he realized, it was neither the time nor the place for such a conversation. Instead, he tipped his bowler in thanks to the driver, a young fellow named Declan McMurray. "I wouldn't have thought it possible to make the trip so quickly, short of being fired out of a cannon into a waiting cargo net," he said, only half in jest, "but here we are, alive and hale. My thanks, Mr. McMurray." He pressed a coin into the driver's gloved hand. *More money spent*, he mused with some annoyance, but he believed in rewarding a job well done. The jostling ride hadn't been the driver's fault, after all; the young man had handled the vehicle more than capably over the uneven terrain, even if he had laid it a little heavy on the coal pedal.

McMurray, for his part, seemed unfazed by the rough ride they had endured. "Sure enough, I should be the one thanking you, sir!" he said cheerily as the proffered coin disappeared quickly into the pocket of his baggy woolen trousers. He removed his cap and goggles and pulled off the mask he wore to cover his mouth and nose on the road. The steamcar's passenger cabin was enclosed, but the driver's seat was out in the open with little but a pane of glass to shield him from the elements. Dust and grit and soot from the engine streaked the exposed parts of McMurray's face, but he smiled broadly despite the filth. "It's not often I've the chance to take her for a drive outside the city. Nice to open her up like that!"

Barrow glanced towards the sanitarium doors, wondering idly if he ought to have the young man committed. "We'll try not to be terribly long."

"Take all the time you need, sir. The car has kerosene headlamps, so we can travel on even after the sun goes down. We'd have to slow her down a fair bit in the dark, of course."

"Of course," Barrow echoed, thinking that might not be the worst fate. He wondered if the lingering ache he felt in his rump would bruise. *As if more bruising would matter at this point*, he thought ruefully. At any rate, he didn't expect young McMurray to be short of amusement while he waited for them to finish their business inside; a few of the sanitarium's greenskeepers had heard the noisy steamcarriage pull up the drive and were already ambling over to have a proper look at the vehicle. Barrow was sure they would be full of questions for the driver; steamcarriages were still an uncommon enough sight in the city, let alone out here in the countryside. No doubt the young man would relish the chance to indulge the gawkers and show off the machine. He had already pulled out a cloth and was working on shining the headlamp glass.

One fellow, though, held back from the group. Sallow and sickly looking, he gawped at the huddle from several yards away. He held a rake in his hands, but his grip on the tool was slack. He more dragged it than carried it as he shuffled his feet.

I shouldn't be too surprised to see some sort of invalid at the sanitarium, Barrow thought, though the man seemed rather out of place next to the rest of the able-bodied greenskeepers. He shrugged it off and turned to Emily. "Are you quite ready yet, Miss Skye?"

She shot him an annoyed look, but said nothing as she fell in behind him as he headed for the door. A fat black salamander seeking the shade of a low shrub eyed them lazily as they approached the entry. Two rows of brilliant yellow spots tracked down the amphibian's back to the tip of its twitching tail. The ancients had thought the slippery beasts were fire elementals given physical form. Thaumaturgic studies in recent years suggested that wasn't so, but the superstition persisted and salamanders remained a favorite choice of bonded familiar for ritual magicians. Barrow thought that was all nonsense, of course, but he nonetheless gave the small creature a wide berth. Certain superstitions ran deeply indeed.

The foyer was vast, lit only by the waning sun streaming through the tall windows, and all but deserted. Barrow spotted gas lamps mounted along the walls, and assumed they would be lit nearer to dusk. Potted lilies of countless varieties filled the space, orange pollen hanging in the air like a miasma. One of the greenskeepers was tending to the lilies, and ignored Barrow and Miss Skye entirely. The air was sweet with the flowers' perfume, but it seemed to Barrow that there was something unwholesome underneath the scent.

"Where are the staff? You would think there would at least be an admissions clerk over there," Emily said, pointing to a large, unoccupied desk that spanned much of the east wall.

"It does seem off, doesn't it?" Barrow agreed. "Well, we probably wouldn't learn much from gabbing with Jenny Perkins' physicians anyway," he said, looking around the foyer. He watched as the solitary greenskeeper shuffled off towards a corridor, leaving them alone in the space.

"We can't just go wandering around the place, though," Emily said. "We're bound to run into someone sooner or later, and how would we explain what we were doing in a spot we never should've been in the first place?"

"Miss Skye, you could scarcely be more right about that. I have just the thing," Barrow said as he pulled Emily aside into a small alcove. He rummaged around in his valise and handed her a small talisman on a thin silver chain. Not much wider across than a penny, the silver disc had a tiny green gemstone set in the center, and was inscribed on both sides with various runes and other symbols. "Here, wear this around your neck."

She took the piece, eyeing it with suspicion. "What is it?"

"I never came up with a name for it," he said, producing a matching talisman for himself. "Frankly, I had all but forgotten about them until the accident you caused with the glider in my laboratory. I found them while cleaning up the mess." He held up a hand to forestall her retort. "Anyway, these amulets are something I created a while ago, one of my first experiments using the elemental bonding process. They should keep us from being spotted."

Emily's skepticism was clear on her face. "And just how is a necklace going to do that?"

"Have you ever thought you saw something out of the corner of your eye, but when you turned to look at it, there was nothing there?" he asked. "But you still had the feeling that something was there, just outside the edge of your vision. Something the eye *knew* was there, but just couldn't grasp."

"Of course," she answered. "Doesn't that happen to everybody?"

He nodded. "It's called a Slimmerjak."

"Slimmerjak," Emily repeated the unfamiliar term. "And just what is a Slimmerjak?"

"No one really knows, exactly," Barrow answered with a shrug. "They're not quite the same thing as ghosts, but they don't have any physical substance to them, either. Personally, I think they defy the eye because they exist in a reality that only partially overlaps with our own, or maybe they're somehow just out of synch with our conception of time. I suppose it doesn't really matter right now. Slimmerjak are everywhere, though, and easy enough to capture if you know how."

"So these amulets have the essence of a Slimmerjak fused to them," Emily concluded, "which, what? Makes the wearer invisible?"

"They won't make us invisible, as such, simply...difficult to notice for a time. The effect should last for close to an hour, not much more. If someone knows we're there, though, they'll be able to see through the glamour."

"You have a gadget for every situation, don't you, Mr. Barrow?"

Barrow felt his cheeks flush at the girl's praise. "Ah, not quite, Miss Skye," he said awkwardly. Compliments, even small ones such as this, often discomfited him. "To be honest, I had no idea if or when I would ever have the opportunity to use these. They'd be helpful for thieves or other rogues, I suppose, but as a rule, I don't spend enough time sneaking into and out of places to ever need such a thing."

They both slipped the silver chains over their heads. Barrow's vision went blurry for a moment as the glamour took effect, and he heard Emily exhale sharply. "My apologies. I suppose I should have warned you about that," he said. "The transition can be quite jarring if you're not expecting it. Are you all right?"

"A little dizzy," she said, but she nodded a moment later. "I think I'll be fine in a moment."

"The vertigo should pass quickly," he reassured her.

She nodded.

Barrow clapped his hands and rubbed his palms together, a grin on his face. "Come along, then, Miss Skye. Let's have a look around!"

14

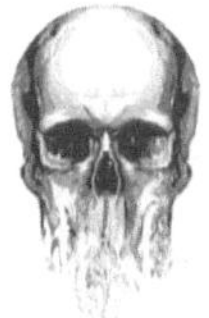

"THIS PLACE IS RATHER HORRID, WOULDN'T YOU SAY, MR. Barrow?"

Barrow nodded absently as he peered around a corner. The west wing of the sanitarium had held little of interest. Proceeding to the east wing had not turned up much of note, either.

"My mother almost had me committed here last fall."

"Yes, your sister mentioned something to that effect when we met earlier in the week." He tried a door, but found it locked. Security seemed to be tighter on this side of the sanitarium, with more of the patient's rooms bolted. Looking through the window, he spied a young fellow with his arms bound tightly to his chest, rocking back and forth on the edge of a bed with a threadbare coverlet. He felt a moment's pity for the man, but pressed on down the corridor.

Emily seemed more preoccupied with the sanitarium itself than its patients, looking from the ceiling's flaking plaster to the worn tiled floor and back again as she followed along. "Coming here would surely have been worse than death," she said quietly, picking at some paint peeling from the wall beside a doorframe. "Beside this, life at the nunnery looks decidedly less dreadful."

"Nuns aren't so bad as all that," Barrow said. "I spent some years with the sisters at Saint Joseph's orphanage as a lad myself."

"Is that so, Mr. Barrow?" Emily seemed surprised.

Barrow shrugged. He felt no shame in his humble origins, even if he rarely spoke of them. "It's true, Miss Skye. I started out as a foundling."

"And you know nothing of who your parents were?"

He eyed her for a long moment before he replied. "The sisters told me that my mother had come to them in the night, carrying me in her arms with little more than the blanket I was wrapped in. She was young, they said. Not much older than yourself, come to think of it, and weeping with fright." He chuckled. "I realize it sounds like something out of a penny dreadful, but there you have it. The curious tale of Isaac Barrow."

It wasn't a story he had told many people, but he felt the need to be open with the young woman who stood before him. Like her, he had found himself cast adrift in the world and in possession of abilities he couldn't understand, abilities which many found abhorrent. Emily had come close to the darker aspects those abilities courted; if he was going to help her find a better path, he realized, he would have to be honest with her.

Whatever reaction he might have expected from her, the look of pity on her face made him distinctly uncomfortable. The sentiment was not one he was accustomed to seeing aimed in his direction. He coughed, and turned his attention back to the corridor. "Shall we continue along, then?"

They walked to the end of the hallway in silence, coming to a large double door. Like the small doors in the east wing, this, too, was locked. "Miss Skye, do you happen to have that magic key of yours handy?"

She smiled and reached a hand deep into the pocket of her grubby dungarees, producing the key in question. She slid it into the keyhole and gave it a twist.

Nothing happened.

"That's peculiar," she said, removing the key and eyeing it critically.

"Indeed," Barrow said quietly, bending down to look into the keyhole.

"You know something."

"I suspect something," he answered. "It looks like a simple enough lock mechanism, but unless I miss my guess, someone has placed a ward on this door. There's only one key that will open this lock."

"So what do we do?" Emily asked. "Try some other door?"

"What would be the fun in that, Miss Skye? No, we'll be going through here."

"But you just said there's only one key that'll unlock this door," she said, looking confused. "Unless I've overlooked something, we don't have that key."

Barrow flashed her a lopsided smile. "There's more than one way to open a locked door, even if the door in question happens to be a warded one," he said. Taking a knee, he opened his valise and started rummaging through the contents. "The plate over the keyhole is iron, but the workings inside are sure to be steel and brass, maybe some nickel."

Emily's expression was skeptical. "So you're going to pick the lock?"

"I've never been much good at that," Barrow admitted, shaking his head. He pulled a handful of small phials and something wrapped in waxed paper from his valise and leapt to his feet. "No, Miss Skye, we're going to freeze the lock!"

"You're going to freeze the lock," she repeated, deadpan.

"Just so!" he said, mixing a few compounds together in a small silver dish he had set on the floor. He unfolded the waxed paper packet and sprinkled some powder into the swirling liquid mixture.

Pulling on a leather glove, he carefully picked up the dish and poured the contents into the keyhole. Frost crystals instantly spread out across the metal, accompanied by a sound, not unlike that of fresh-fallen snow being trod underfoot, until the entire faceplate was crusted with ice.

"Now what?" Emily asked.

Barrow knelt to put the silver dish back into his valise, taking care not to let it come into contact with any of the case's other contents. None of the freezing solution remained on the dish, but the metal was still colder than any earthly ice. "Now, Miss Skye," he said as he pulled out a small hammer, which he handed to her. "If you would be so kind as to do the honours, let's see what someone went to great pains to keep secret."

Emily took the hammer with a grin, then stepped up to the door as Barrow moved aside. She swung her arm upward and brought it down with surprising force, connecting with the frozen metal. The lock cylinder crumbled under the blow, the pieces falling to the floor like shrapnel. Emily giggled with glee.

The room beyond turned out to be some sort of recovery ward, with a row of ten beds ranged along one wall, each positioned under a tall window. The morning sun would shine brilliantly here, but in the late afternoon, the room felt rather dim and cold. A matching row of ten beds lined the opposite wall for a total of twenty in the ward. In all, nine of the beds were occupied, though none of the patients stirred when they entered the room.

"Are they all dead?" Emily asked, her eyes wide as she looked down the row of motionless patients.

"They're not dead," Barrow said, loudly snapping his fingers in front of one man's face. The man gave no response, dully staring straight ahead. A spot of spittle crusted the corner of his slack lips.

"Well if they're not dead, why are they all just lying there like that?"

"They're breathing, at least, but there's not much else going on." He walked to the next bed, snapping his fingers in front of that patient, again drawing no reaction. He tried the same to rouse a third, this one a young woman. He may as well have saved himself the effort. "It's as if they're not aware of us at all."

"They're not," came a deep, accented voice from behind them. Turning, Barrow recognized the speaker as Johan Morgentaler, the fellow he had briefly met some days ago in Higgins's shop. Morgentaler now wore a long white coat over his dark suit, and strode to where they stood at an unhurried pace. His steely eyes, as before, seemed to see through to Barrow's soul. "A keen observation, Mr. Barrow. Your reputation for cleverness is well-earned." He nodded to the woman beside Barrow. "But now, what does it mean?"

Barrow turned his attention back to the patient. She appeared to be somewhere in her thirties, but her mawkish appearance made reckoning her age any nearer than that impossible. Her uncombed brown hair hung lank from her scalp, looking oily and unwashed, and her skin had the loose dull hue typically reserved for the dead. Only the shallow rasp of her breathing and the occasional lethargic blink of her glassy eyes gave any indication of life at all. He picked up and squeezed the woman's hand, then pulled back the blankets at the end of her bed and brushed the sole of one barefoot with the tip of his finger. As when he had snapped his fingers, there was no reaction, no sign she felt anything at all.

"It's a catatonic state of some kind."

"Correct."

"Brought on by some illness?"

"No," Morgentaler said. His smile was thin as the blade of a knife and struck Barrow as rather less than sincere.

"An injury, then?" he asked, doubtful. He thought it highly unlikely that nine patients would find themselves in such a state, even if they suffered similar injuries.

Morgentaler confirmed it. "No," he said once more. The tight smile on his face spread.

He's enjoying this, Barrow noted as he leaned in closer to the woman, examining her lifeless eyes intently. He noted some light discoloration of the whites, an almost imperceptible lilac tinge. He smelled her breath as she exhaled, stale and warm, but there was something else there. Something familiar and sickly sweet.

"An opiate," he said after a long moment.

Morgentaler's grin grew predatory, entirely without mirth. "Very good," he confirmed. "That's one part of it, yes."

"You've given them eldersight," Barrow said, incredulous. "But then, these people should be raving like..."

"Like lunatics?" Morgentaler finished for him. Barrow nodded. "A microdose of the drug can actually have a calming effect, when administered in concert with a minor frontal lobotomy."

Incredulity gave way to horror on Barrow's face.

"Yes, Mr. Barrow. It's a procedure I first learned of in Bern some years ago," Morgentaler explained. "A doctor at the university was lecturing on the beneficial effects of what he called psychosurgery on the imbalanced brain. Of course, it was only a theoretical possibility at the time, but I think you'll find I've made great progress here."

"This is progress, Doctor?" Emily demanded, indicating the row of catatonic patients.

"As with any experimental treatment, some patients will inevitably respond better than others," he replied with a shrug. "Before you lie some of my less successful cases. My failures, if you will. They feel no discomfort, though I do regret not being able to better help them. If you could see the patients who have made full recoveries, though—those who are no longer plagued by the demons that have haunted them all their lives—I doubt you'd find my methods nearly half so loathsome."

"So-called surgeons used to simply trepan patients to let the 'demons' out of their skulls, Dr. Morgentaler. We've left such superstitions behind," Barrow replied, clearly agitated. Such anachronisms galled him, particularly when coming from someone who ought to know better. Emily placed a hand on his forearm to urge him to calm, but if he even noticed, he ignored the cautionary gesture. "We don't drill holes in people's skulls anymore, yet here you are cutting into the living flesh of the brain!"

"My techniques may seem cruel, I'll grant, but—"

"Your techniques go far beyond mere cruelty, Morgentaler," Barrow broke in. "What you're doing here redefines insane."

At that, Morgentaler had had enough. "I think we're about done here, Mr. Barrow," he said in a measured tone, his face stony as he clapped his hands together. The door behind him swung inward and two large men shouldered their way into the room. Both were dressed in grubby workman's attire, but neither carried a weapon.

"You're a resourceful sort, I'll give you that much. I doubt I would have thought of such a simple way to bypass a warded lock," Morgentaler continued, nodding to the shattered bits of metal by the two men's feet. The ice crusting the broken lock had melted, leaving a small puddle. "You do realize that I could have you arrested for trespassing, don't you?"

Barrow snorted laughter. "You'd have to explain what you're doing here to the authorities if you did that, Doctor."

Morgentaler simply shrugged. "Unlike yourself, I've done nothing illegal here."

That much, Barrow admitted, was true. "There's a line between the law and justice," he said. "Just because something is legal doesn't make it moral or just."

"Your lack of vision is disappointing." Rather than anger or malice, Morgentaler's face bore a look of resignation, even pity. "It's a shame you can't grasp the scope of what I'm trying to accomplish." He turned toward the door. "I would suggest you take your leave, Mr. Barrow, and I implore you not to dawdle. My men will ensure you and your companion don't wander into any other areas you ought not to be."

15

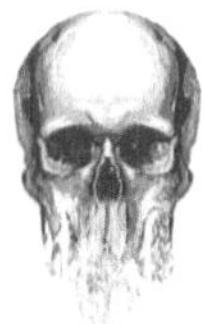

"The unmitigated hubris of that man, thinking he has the right to play God with people's lives!" Barrow thundered as the steamcarriage jolted along the rough road. The edges of twilight had crept in as they left the sanitarium, with a cloying evening fog rolling in from the nearby Bedford Basin. Declan McMurray had lit the steamcar's kerosene headlamps before they left the grounds, but as the young driver had prophesied, they had to slow their travel for the return to the city.

That suited Barrow just fine. His rump still smarted from the afternoon's journey, but even more to the point, the roar of the engine was more muted this time around as the young man demanded less of the vehicle, meaning conversation in the passenger cabin was possible, if not pleasant. He still had to keep reaching up to make sure his bowler stayed in its proper place atop his head as the car jounced and rattled over every bump. Eventually, he gave it up, placing the hat on the seat beside his valise.

"Can he do the things he says, though?" Emily asked

uneasily. Her carefree manner had been muted somewhat since they leaving Hemlock Overlook. "Can he really cure madness with surgery?"

"You saw the results of his *surgery*," Barrow spat the word.

The exchange was interrupted by a loud banging as McMurray rapped loudly on the hatch between the passenger cabin and the driver's coach box. Barrow reached across and slid the panel aside. "Is everything all right?" he asked the driver, leaning out and shouting to be heard.

"The car, she's fine," McMurray shouted back, "but I thought you ought to know we're maybe being followed, Mr. Barrow."

Barrow turned and leaned across the small passenger cabin, pulling aside the curtain on the steamcar's rear window. Sure enough, through the swirling dust and fog behind them, he could make out a dark carriage pulled by two horses maybe fifty feet behind them, keeping pace. He swore under his breath and stuck his head back through the front hatch. "How long have they been tailing us?"

McMurray shrugged. "Can't say for sure, but at least as far back as Africville. I noticed 'em back on Campbell Road and they've been with us since."

Barrow looked at the road in front of the steamcar. The headlamps were doing what they could to light the way, but the sun had now set and the fog was getting thicker. "Try to outpace him, Mr. McMurray," he said.

The driver nodded and adjusted his goggles as Barrow closed the hatch and settled back into his seat. The engine roared as McMurray pressed the accelerator and the steamcar picked up speed.

On a straight and narrow, the steamcar would have easily outpaced the conventional horse-drawn carriage. On the twisting country road after nightfall, however, the carriage was more or less a match for the newfangled vehicle. As the steamcar gathered speed, the driver behind them cracked the whip, urging his team from a trot to a gallop. Barrow swore.

A crack deadlier than that of the horseman's whip rang out. Barrow leapt across the small space to cover Emily as glass from one of the steamcarriage's side windows exploded into the passenger cabin, showering them both with glittering fragments.

"Well, if there was any doubt in the matter, I think it's safe to say we are indeed being pursued. Are you all right, Miss Skye?" he asked as he rolled to the side.

She nodded and used the sleeve of her jacket to brush some of the glass shards from the seat onto the floor.

Barrow reached into his jacket and drew out the elementally-enhanced Webley. *Not that this did me much good against Lai Jūn,* he considered as he checked the weapon. He pushed the thought away as he pulled aside the curtain on the back window once more, trying to get a proper look at their assailant. He was forced to duck down as he saw the flare of the villain's gun being fired a second time.

The shot went wide. The rogue, whoever he was, sat alone on the box seat of the carriage; trying to control his galloping horses while firing at a swiftly-moving target would be difficult for anyone, no matter how skilled a marksman.

Barrow crouched near the side door with the shattered window, Webley in hand. He twisted the release handle and swung the door outward. It opened toward the rear of the steamcar, but even so, he didn't think it would make much of shield; he doubted the panel was made of anything substantial enough to stop a bullet.

I must be utterly mad, he thought as he gripped one of the leather handhold straps and leaned out into the night to level the revolver at the pursuing carriage. The steamcar chose that moment to careen off a rut in the road, and Barrow had to fight to keep his grip on the thin leather strap.

He swore under his breath, steadied himself once more, and took aim. He squeezed the trigger, sending a bolt of blue-tinged energy hurtling from the barrel of the gun.

Like lightning, the shot arced wildly and crackled as it streaked through the night air. The driver of the carriage pulled the reins sideways, hard, sending his team off to the other side of the road to avoid the bolt. It tore past, narrowly missing the carriage, striking a tall tree behind them.

Barrow gaped as the tree exploded into a shower of blue flame and fell across the road, then looked to the gun in his hand. He had designed it to render a grown man unconscious, but aside from his tussle with Lai Jūn he had never had the opportunity to test the invention. Apparently, the weapon's payload was far deadlier than he had imagined.

He didn't have much time to think about it. He was tossed sideways back into the passenger cabin as the steamcar rounded a tight corner, barely keeping all four wheels on the roadway. Another shot rang out from behind them. Barrow's stomach lurched into his throat when he heard a pained howl.

He looked about the passenger cabin and spotted Emily in a heap on the floor. "Miss Skye, are you all right?" he called out, frantic.

She looked up at him. A small cut on her chin had barely started to bleed. "Tossed about some, but largely unharmed," she said, picking a tiny piece of glass from the abrasion and flicking it away.

The thunder of the engine died away and the steamcar began to slow. Barrow poked his head out through the hatch and caught some spatter of blood from the driver's seat.

Declan McMurray looked to him, one hand still limply clutching the steering wheel. His other shoulder was soaked with blood. "I'm afraid I've been hit, Mr. Barrow," the young man declared. He sounded puzzled by the statement, as though the very notion of being shot was preposterous.

He's going into shock, Barrow realized. "Try to keep the car going straight," he barked through the hatch. "I'll come out and take the controls."

"Are you utterly mad?" Emily demanded as he slid the hatch shut and made for the side door. "Have you ever driven one of these contraptions before?"

"I've observed their operation," he answered. It was not quite a lie. Before she could mount any further protest, he pressed the Webley into her hand. "Keep your head down, Miss Skye, and don't use this unless absolutely necessary."

Leaving the gawping girl behind, he once more pulled himself out through the steamcar's side door. A thin metal rail ran the length of the vehicle, hardly the sort of foothold he would've considered safe for such a mad stunt. There was little for his hand to grip along the vehicle's roof, but he scrabbled at what he could to keep his precarious balance. He only had to make it a few feet to reach the driver's box seat.

Trees whipped by, some dangerously close for comfort. Their branches threatened to sweep Barrow from the side of the speeding steamcar. McMurray had slowed a little when he had been shot, but not enough to make this an easy manoeuver.

Cra-ack! Another bullet pinged off the roof of the steamcar, careening harmlessly off into the night as Barrow hauled himself the last few inches and plopped into the driver's seat. McMurray had enough of his senses left about him to slide to the other end of the bench seat, but the lad looked to be on the verge of passing out. His face was ashen, his left shoulder dripping with blood. He was clearly in need of medical attention.

Of course, we'll have to lose this hooligan first, otherwise, we're all in the soup. Barrow grabbed the wildly oscillating steering wheel and got the steamcar back on a more or less straight course. Three unmarked pedals on the floor gave him a moment's pause, and McMurray was in no condition to tell him which of the three propelled the steamcarriage forward. *No help for it*, he thought as he jammed his foot down on the middle pedal.

Sparks flew from the wheel hubs as the steamcar's brakes locked in place, and Barrow had to struggle to keep his seat as the vehicle ground to a sudden halt. He heard Emily scream from within the passenger cabin, but the girl sounded more annoyed than afraid. He swore under his breath.

The carriage tailing them had narrowed the gap when McMurray had been forced to slow down. Now, caught short by the steamcar's sudden stop, the driver had to fight to keep his horses under control as they reared, whinnying and kicking madly at the air. Barrow heard the driver's whip crack several times as he struggled against the startled horses. The cruelty of that offended him; he believed treating beasts mildly got the best service from them. He hazarded a look over his shoulder and saw the villain's gun fall to the ground in the confusion.

He allowed himself a smile; it wasn't what he had intended to do, but his mistake had fouled his assailant all the same.

Barrow knew the chaos wouldn't buy him much time, but it was enough to figure out which of the three pedals was the accelerator and which allowed for the shifting of gears. He worked the pedals and the gearshift lever. The steamcar shuddered and the transmission gears made a terrible grinding noise, but the vehicle started to move once more.

Sure enough, the driver of the carriage had also managed to sort out his difficulties and had his panicked horses back under control. They pulled the carriage along close behind the steamcar, but without a weapon, the driver was less of an immediate threat as the two vehicles hurtled first through the outskirts of Halifax and then on into the city proper.

The carriage pulled up alongside the steamcar. The horses' eyes rolled in terror at the cacophony and flames coming from the steamcar's engine, but they feared the sting of the whip even more. Abandoning his own safety, the driver pulled hard on the reins, pitching his own carriage toward the steamcar. The two vehicles collided like galleons at sea, sending a hail of sparks and splintering wood into the air as madly speeding wheels ground against each other.

Barrow looked across to his would-be murderer. The cadaverous fellow sneered and shouted something vile, but he couldn't make out the words. He assumed it wasn't a cheery *how-do-you-do*, and kept on driving.

He shrieked in pain as the loathsome villain lashed out with the whip, tearing a strip of flesh from the back of his hand. The assassin was determined and resourceful, he had to admit. Holding onto the steering wheel with one hand, he grit his teeth and tried to think of some way out of this mad chase.

At the top of the hill, he spied salvation, or something like it. The spire of Saint Mary's Cathedral towered above all else.

The ghastly adversary hefted the whip once more, making ready to lash out again. Barrow jammed on the brake pedal, dropping behind the carriage as the surprised villain bellowed in rage. His horses kept their course and pulled far ahead of the steamcar.

Barrow pressed the accelerator pedal against the floor. The engine roared as flames belched from the exhaust pipes.

Knowing his desperate plan was utter madness, he coaxed everything he could from the vehicle as it gathered speed and thundered up the hill.

The enemy had managed to turn his carriage around in the road and was coming toward them, whipping his horses into a lathered frenzy. The maniac bore down directly at the oncoming steamcar.

Gritting his teeth, Barrow held the steamcar steady. The gap between the two speeding vehicles narrowed.

At the last possible moment, he pulled hard on the steering wheel, turning the steamcar toward Saint Mary's. The vehicle shuddered and nearly pitched over on its side as it took a sharp turn, its rubber tires screaming in protest against the cobbles as the carriage hurtled past.

Sparks flew as the steamcar's undercarriage scraped against granite as the vehicle bounded up the steps, then crashed through the wooden doors and sent a shower of splintering oak flying into the dimly-lit cathedral.

Barrow staggered from the sagging steamcar, dragging Declan McMurray with him even as Emily hauled herself through the side door, the Webley still clutched in her hand.

Despite the late hour, a handful of devout parishioners lingered in the cathedral, and a few of them came running to see what the commotion was. "This man needs help," Barrow barked to them, easing McMurray to the marble floor. He tore the sleeve from the driver's shirt and wadded up the fabric, then pressed it against the wound to staunch the flow of blood. "Don't just stand there gawping, fetch a doctor! Quickly now, he's been shot." Two men ran off. Barrow hoped at least one of them would return with aid.

Weary and battered, Barrow peered out through the ruined door into the street. The ruined carriage paused at the foot of the cathedral steps, but the corpselike driver kept his seat. In the yellowish light of the streetlamp, Barrow could see his would-be assassin's face—it was the same cadaverous-looking man who had been milling about outside Hemlock Overlook. He scowled before whipping his horses once more.

Barrow caught sight of someone inside the carriage as it rolled off, but couldn't see enough to tell who the passenger was. Hooves clattered on the cobbles as the scoundrels sped off into the night.

The steamcarriage was a total wreck. The front axel had broken, leaving the wheels sitting at an odd angle, and the steel-walled boiler had ruptured as the vehicle had crashed up the stairs. Boiling water gushed onto the floor by the gallon. Thankfully, the torrent doused the glowing coals from the firebox that had scattered from their own shattered casing. They hissed and sputtered, but on the granite floor, there was little chance of them setting the place alight.

"Mr. Barrow, you seem to have a talent for attracting the most determined of murderers," Emily said. Despite the rough ride, she appeared relatively unscathed other than the cut on her chin.

Before Barrow could reply to the barb, a thunderous voice boomed out from nearby. "What is the meaning of this?" A man dressed all in black strode into the narthex from a nearby antechamber.

"Begging forgiveness, Father," Barrow said. He hadn't set foot in a church in several years, but he still reverted to the formal address out of habit, surprising himself.

The holy man was surprised as well. "Isaac? Isaac Barrow?" He rubbed at his eyes as if in disbelief. "I might have known you would be at the heart of this ruckus."

It took Barrow a moment to recognize the fellow. When he did, his jaw hung slack. "Thomas Wall?"

"It's Deacon Wall these days," he said, kneeling beside Declan McMurray to examine the boy's wounds for himself.

"I'm not an ordained priest yet. Could your famed powers of observation be slipping in your dotage, Isaac?"

"I'm barely a year older than you are, Tom," Barrow exclaimed.

Emily coughed loudly, and looked from the kneeling technomancer to the deacon and back again. "I take it the pair of you know each other, then?"

"Forgive my rudeness," Barrow said as he looked up from where he knelt, fighting back the urge to layer that with bitter sarcasm. "Thomas Wall, may I introduce Miss Emily Skye."

The deacon inclined his head and smiled. "A pleasure, Miss Skye. Welcome to Saint Mary's," he said, his handsome face twisting with a sardonic grin. "And how is it you come to be in Mr. Barrow's company, crashing through our grand new door in the middle of the night? I can't say the circumstance is much of surprise, given his calamitous nature, but you're far too young and strike me as too well-mannered to be this scoundrel's sweetheart."

"Go howl, Thomas!" Barrow said. "I see taking the orders hasn't blunted your rapier wit any."

"And you're as stodgy as ever," Deacon Wall observed. Turning to Emily, he explained, "We grew up together. Orphans at Saint Joseph's first, then at school. I followed the path into the seminary while Isaac went off to that...what was the word? Collegeum, down in Massachusetts."

"You say that as if I had any damned choice in the matter," Barrow muttered. He knew that came out harsh, but at the moment he didn't much care.

"Things are changing within the church, Isaac," Deacon Wall said. "Our savior preached tolerance and acceptance, and the new generation—"

"The new generation thinks the old generation will die off tomorrow and leave them to change the world," Barrow broke in, then stopped himself, realizing he was all but echoing Malleus. While some of the other boys at their school had taunted him when his abilities began to become apparent, Thomas had never treated him any differently. He smiled thinly at the memory. "Spare me the sermon, Thomas," he said in gentler tones, and gestured to the ruined steamcarriage that sat in a heap nearby. "After the week I've had, I simply don't have the strength to debate it."

"I can scarcely imagine," the deacon said, looking over to the wreckage. "Who were those men?"

"I can't say for certain," Barrow answered, "though I have a few guesses."

"Why did they just up and leave, though?" Emily asked. "We're sitting ducks here."

"Superstitious types, perhaps?" Deacon Wall offered. "They didn't want to set foot on hallowed ground?"

"More likely they'd rather finish us off where there are no witnesses around," Barrow deadpanned. *Then again, that fellow driving the carriage did look decidedly corpselike,* he thought. *Maybe he couldn't set foot on hallowed ground.*

Deacon Wall clucked in disapproval. "You were ever the scoffer, Isaac."

Barrow ignored that and tentatively pulled the wad of bloody cloth away from Declan McMurray's shoulder to examine the wound. It looked as though the bullet had gone clean through the muscle without striking bone. That much at least was a little bit of luck. The bleeding had slowed, and the boy's breathing was shallow but steady. His pallid skin told that he had lost rather a lot of blood, but he didn't seem to be in immediate danger of bleeding to death. The lad needed a doctor all the same.

"You can leave the lad with me, Isaac. I'll ensure he gets the aid he needs," Deacon Wall said, seeming to follow his thoughts. "Though you may want to see a doctor yourself," he added, pointing to Barrow's right hand.

Barrow had scarcely noticed the wound where the assassin's whip had flayed the skin from his hand. Now he keenly felt the searing pain as he let the blood-soaked cloth fall to the floor. He nodded and turned to Emily. "Miss Skye, if you'll allow me to see you home, I do believe we'll call that an end to this night's adventures."

16

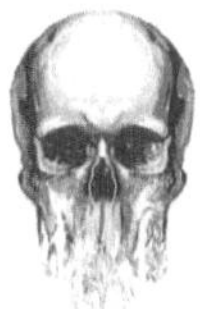

MEREDITH SKYE STIFLED HER OBVIOUS ANNOYANCE AT being woken after midnight when she saw the state of her sister and Isaac Barrow standing at her door. She opened her mouth but said nothing, instead sighing and shaking her head as she ushered them in. Her small apartment was scrupulously clean. Barrow had only met her once, but he would have been surprised to find it any other way, had he ever thought to see the place for himself.

Without a word, she filled a kettle and set it on the stove, then knelt to stoke the coals. Closing the grate, she stood and gestured towards Emily with the poker. "All right, then," she said, "what sort of madness do you call this, getting into God knows what kind of trouble and sending some hapless constable around with naught but a letter as an explanation?"

Barrow held his hat in his hands. "Miss Skye, I can assure you—"

"I'll deal with you in a moment, Mr. Barrow," Meredith cut in, keeping her fiery gaze locked on Emily.

Emily shrugged her shoulders and rolled her eyes. "We're fine, Merrie," she said in an impatient manner only a teenager can truly affect. "We were in a minor steamcarriage accident earlier this evening, but Mr. Barrow made sure I was safe."

Barrow had to cough to stifle surprised laughter at the masterful way Emily downplayed the evening's misadventure. By the sharp look Meredith shot in his direction, he suspected she saw through the subterfuge.

The elder sister sighed once more. "Whatever you've been up to, Emily, we can talk about it in the morning." She turned to Barrow. "And as for you, Mr. Barrow, I asked you to find my sister, not drag her all over creation and nearly get her killed."

"I assure you it wasn't my idea, and I care for the notion even less than you do," Barrow said shortly, letting his impatience get the better of him. "I'm hardly keen to have some troublesome youth following me around. Your sister, however, is hardly one to take no for answer, as I'm sure you know." He looked at Emily and smiled. "In truth, I must admit her aid has proven invaluable."

Before Meredith could speak to that, she was interrupted by the whistle of the kettle. "Here, go wash up," Meredith offered as she handed Barrow the kettle and a pitcher of cold water and pointed him toward the lavatory door. "There's a spare dressing gown hanging on the door. It may be a bit, mmm...short for you, but it'll be better than that ruined shirt."

Barrow thanked her as he closed the door behind him. He poured the steaming water into the basin with some of the cold, then set to unbuttoning his stained shirt. Working the fasteners proved to a minor ordeal; his hand throbbed where the assassin's whip had torn his skin. He finally got the shirt off and looked himself over in the mirror. His ribs remained mottled with dark bruises and stung as he prodded at them with two fingers, but they felt no worse than they had before the mad chase.

He splashed warm water on his face. The basin took on a

swirling pinkish hue as he lathered up the soap and set to scouring first his hands, then arms, sticky with Declan McMurray's drying blood. Even through the closed door, he could scarcely help overhear the sisters talking.

"Look at you, Emily," Meredith chided. "The atrocious clothing I've grown used to, but what on earth have you done to your hair? You look like some urchin boy from a Dickens tale. And this cut on your chin! You can't get tangled up in whatever mess Mr. Barrow has gotten himself into. I simply forbid it."

"Do you?" Emily replied, her voice acidic. "Mother forbade me a whole host of things after Father died, as you'll recall, and you've seen how well that worked out! Besides which, I'm already well tangled up in the matter, so it's too late now."

Meredith sighed heavily. "I know I can't stop you, little sister, but I do worry."

"I know you do, and I love you for it," Emily replied gently, "but I'm old enough now to take care of myself. Besides, Mr. Barrow will watch out for me."

"Aye, and who will watch over Mr. Barrow?" Meredith teased. Both ladies laughed.

Barrow felt his cheeks heat; the barb held enough truth to sting. The decrepit reflection staring back from the small mirror was barely recognizable. He sometimes went days without sleep while working on his experiments, but that sort of exhaustion was nothing compared to the weariness he now felt as he scrubbed Declan McMurray's blood from his hands.

And what of you, young Miss Skye? Will I be washing away your blood as well, before all is said and done?

He sighed and patted his face dry. No amount of scrubbing would remove the heavy lassitude that dragged at his eyes. Content that he had done all that he could, he wrapped the flimsy robe around his shoulders and cinched it at the waist, then walked back into the sitting room.

Emily looked him up and down. "Very nice, Mr. Barrow," she said with an impish grin. "The lilac trim really compliments your brown eyes." The ladies collapsed in a fit of giggles.

"I'm so pleased that you're amused," Barrow shot back, but his offended tone only served to make the sisters redouble their laughter. He waited for them to settle themselves before he went on. "If you're quite done, then, I really think I ought to be heading home myself."

Emily sobered, wiping a tear from her cheek. "Very well," she said, "shall I meet you at your workshop in the morning?"

Barrow looked to Meredith, halfway hoping she would raise some objection. If the elder sister had anything to say, she held her peace. If Meredith had thought better of trying to keep Emily on a tether, what chance did he have? "Very well," he said. "I'll see you at nine o'clock."

He pulled on his overcoat and popped his hat onto his head. With the hem of Meredith's decidedly feminine bathrobe hanging nearly to his knees, he realized he looked ridiculous. The hour was late, and the streets would be all but deserted, but he still hoped no one would see him as he set off for home.

Constable McCallister was waiting at the door to his streetside office when Barrow arrived the following morning. He carried no umbrella to hold off the light rain, but his heavy wool overcoat likely did a fine job of keeping the damp from reaching his uniform beneath. He huddled in the doorway all the same.

"Morning, Mr. Barrow," the big fellow said as he handed

Barrow an envelope. "I've got a message from Inspector Eddings."

"Thank you," Barrow said, glancing first at the envelope, then at the young constable. "Can I offer you anything? A cup of tea to warm up, perhaps?"

"Thank you, sir, but I have duties I must get back to." McCallister tapped the brim of his helmet and headed off at a clip.

Barrow watched after the big man as he hurried away. The dressing down he had received from Inspector Eddings earlier in the week was likely still fresh in McCallister's mind.

He was just as happy to have his offer of hospitality declined. The stove in the office would be cold, and truth be told, he didn't much care to take the time to first start the fire and then brew a pot of tea for the constable. Nevertheless, propriety demanded that he make the offer.

He collapsed his umbrella and tucked it awkwardly under one arm. With the letter from Inspector Eddings clutched in his injured hand, Barrow fumbled to get his key into the lock.

He barely had time to scan the page before Emily swung open the door and strolled into the office. Normally someone barging in without ringing the bell, or at least knocking at the door would've set his teeth on edge. Given what he had just read, he scarcely noticed.

"Good morning, Mr. Barrow," the girl chirped. "I trust you're well, and managed to get some sleep last night."

He waved the pleasantry aside. "We're in luck, Miss Skye," Barrow said, a grim edge in his voice contradicting his words as he folded the page back into its envelope and tucked it inside his jacket. "Inspector Eddings has sent word."

The girl had been removing her overcoat, but paused at hearing that. "Is that so?"

"It would seem our killer has struck again," he said, punctuating it with nothing more than a single nod. "Another body has been brought into the city morgue."

THEY MET INSPECTOR EDDINGS SOON AFTER AT THE Halifax Dispensary, where part of the basement did duty as the city's mortuary. Standing in the shadow of Citadel Hill, the squat brick building looked more like a large schoolhouse than a modern hospital, despite being established just a short quarter-century ago. The Dispensary's mission of providing treatment to those who otherwise would not be able to afford a doctor's care meant the small facility was always a hive of activity, but the staff always did its best to ensure no one was turned away.

They went around the side of the building, trudging a short distance along Prince Street as it sloped downwards, away from the Citadel. Had the morning been clear, they might have been able to see along to the harbour and across to Dartmouth, but the street ahead remained shrouded in fog.

Near the rear of the Dispensary building, Eddings led the way through a large yellow door into the basement level. Barrow had long thought it odd that the otherwise discreet entrance had been painted such a bright color, given the fact that it was used primarily for the conveyance of cadavers, but let it pass without comment.

"Inspector, you had mentioned that our Mr. Barrow and Dr. Brookfield don't get along so well," Emily said as they walked towards the entrance. "What is it about Mr. Barrow that offends the coroner so?"

"It's actually the other way around, Miss Skye," Eddings answered cheerily. "Barrow believes Dr. Brookfield to be rather unqualified for his position."

"Marcus Brookfield is as unskilled as he is unimaginative," Barrow said with a disdainful sniff. "The man still believes the flu is caused by miasmas."

The temperature noticeably dropped as they entered into a small reception area. Barrow knew from previous visits the morgue within would be chillier still. Being underground certainly helped in maintaining the cool temperature required for the morgue's operation, but there were unseen systems at play aiding the process. A cooling system of compressors and copper tubes pumped chilled water mixed with certain chemical compounds through the walls and under the floor, drawing heat out of the room through specialized vents lining the baseboards. The air chilling systems were prone to frequent breakdowns on hot days and terribly expensive to install. As such, they were only found in the richest of homes and in specialized facilities like the city morgue. The technology was fascinating, but as he did every time he visited, he set it aside with some resignation. He was here on more pressing business.

A short hallway led them to the door of the morgue itself. A line of hooks lined the wall, a crisp white linen apron hanging from each. "You may wish to wait out here in the hallway, Miss Skye," Eddings said as they paused at the entrance. "The morgue can hold some ghastly sights within."

"Haven't we been over this, Inspector?" she answered, reaching up to take an apron from the row of hooks.

The inspector tipped his hat in apology, then turned to Barrow and rolled his eyes.

"Shall we, then?" Barrow said, taking down an apron of his own and tying it around his middle. Clapping his hands together, he led the way through the arched door into the mortuary proper.

He may not have held much regard for Dr. Marcus Brookfield's skill as a physician, but Barrow couldn't fault the city's chief coroner on the state of his workspace. The large room was immaculate, the white tiled walls gleaming from their last deep scrubbing. The cold air carried the mingled scent of embalming chemicals and bleach. Sample jars and other supplies lined the shelves in perfect rows. Barrow was just as sure the medical instruments in their drawers below would be just as neatly arranged. It was the degree of order he aspired to maintain in his own often chaotic workshop.

Seemingly out of place in the state-of-the-art mortuary, Dr. Brookfield himself was decidedly of the old school. Easily in his sixties, if not older, his decades of experience were written in the lines of his once-handsome face. His hair had gone to white, and his hard eyes were entirely without mirth. Rather than the modern white smock most medical professionals wore, he still dressed in a short gray frock coat while he worked. The various shades of faded blood spattered here and there on the front of his coat told of how many times it had been laundered.

He regarded Barrow with palpable contempt, but his eyes widened in surprise when he saw Emily following behind. Eddings bringing a woman into the mortuary would've been rare enough, but seeing anyone as young as Miss Skye here was truly abnormal.

At the center of the room, the body lay covered by a white sheet. "What have you, Dr. Brookfield?" Barrow asked as he eyed the draped cadaver.

Brookfield's eyes slid to Inspector Eddings, wordlessly asking if he seriously had to indulge the technomancer. Eddings said nothing, but his unyielding gaze spoke volumes. With a resigned sigh, Brookfield answered. "The deceased is male, estimated to be between fifteen and twenty years of age." The coroner rattled the facts off impatiently, as if he hoped to get Barrow up to speed and out the door as quickly as possible. "Cause of death appears to be a single gunshot to the back of the head with a small caliber pistol at close range, though we have yet to perform an exploratory to find the bullet."

Barrow raised an eyebrow. "You're not expecting to find one, though, are you, Dr. Brookfield?"

"No," Brookfield said simply. "This is the sixth body to arrive on my table in twelve weeks with a wound like this. I assume Eddings told you about the others."

"He did," Barrow said.

"What was his name?" Emily asked.

"We don't know," Brookfield said. "He didn't have any identification on him when he was brought in. In fact, he was stripped to his undergarments. A pauper, no doubt, going by the rough area where he was found."

"That would fit the trend," Eddings put in.

"Well, then," Barrow said, reaching for the sheet covering the body, "shall we have a look?"

He gasped as he pulled back the sheet to uncover a mop of red hair, crusty with dried blood.

Eddings eyed him curiously. "Do you know the lad?"

Barrow had never met the boy on the slab, but he nodded even so. The dead youngster had the same fiery red hair and freckled cheeks as his younger brother. "I know his family," he said quietly. "His name is Ian Fergus."

Dr. Brookfield jotted that down in his notebook. Barrow needed a moment to recognize the expression on the coroner's face; he had never before seen the stoic man display the least bit of sympathy.

Barrow cleared his throat. "Now, shall we see if we can't figure out how our young friend here met his untimely end?"

"What do you mean? He was shot in the head at close range. You can see where the bullet entered, here," Dr. Brookfield said, gently lifting the lad's head and pointing to the small wound with his pencil. "It entered almost in the exact center of the squamous section of the occipital plate, just like all the others."

Barrow fished around inside his jacket, pulling out a small leather case, from which he removed a mechanical loupe. As he fit the piece to his eye, its telescoping lens clicked and whirred as it extended to increase magnification.

"Your examination, in this case, was as thorough as ever, Dr. Brookfield," he said after a few moments, his voice flat.

Brookfield seemed taken aback by the unexpected compliment. "I thank you, Mr. Barrow."

"Don't," Barrow said shortly. "This isn't a bullet wound, and I would wager London against an orange that none of the others were either."

"What do you mean, it's not a bullet wound?" Eddings asked.

"If Dr. Brookfield had examined the bone under magnification, he may have discovered the striations left behind by whatever bored into the boy's skull."

"*Bored?*" Brookfield sputtered, incredulity plain on his craggy face. "Come now, Mr. Barrow."

"Indeed," Barrow said seriously. "This wound was inflicted using a high-speed drill of some sort. Possibly driven by an electric motor, but I couldn't really say that definitively. By all means, have a closer look yourself," he added, handing the loupe to the coroner.

Brookfield took the tool without a word, though his expression was sour. He leaned in to more closely examine the dead boy's skull.

"Is that why there's been so little fracturing on the victims' skulls?" Eddings asked.

"Just so," Barrow confirmed. "It's also why you haven't found a bullet in a single one of the other victims."

"What do you mean?" Brookfield asked, handing the loupe to Inspector Eddings so he could have a closer look for himself. The coroner was still clearly skeptical, but willing enough to follow Barrow's line of reasoning if it might answer the rash of unsolved cases that had crossed his table of late.

"What I mean is, we're not looking for what entered this boy's skull to kill him, but rather what was removed. I'd need to do a full cranial exploratory to be sure, and that is by no means an operation I'm qualified to perform," Barrow said, probing the wound with some surgical instrument he had picked up, "but even with a cursory examination, I suspect that in each case we would find some amount of brain tissue missing. The long-term memory center of the hippocampus, to be specific."

"The autotype cylinders!" Emily exclaimed, clapping her hands together.

"Just so, Miss Skye." Barrow regarded her with growing respect. The girl was quick-witted, he had to give her that much.

Dr. Brookfield clearly hadn't followed the turn in the conversation. "I expect one of you is going to fill the rest of us in at some point," he said irritably. "Why not now?"

Barrow recounted the mystery of Henry Feele's errant autotype machine and the experiments he had conducted on the device's memory cylinder, as well as what he had discovered at Hemlock Overlook while looking into the death of Jenny Perkins. He hadn't been able to connect the woman's murder to the autotype cylinders yet, but he was sure the link was there, waiting to be discovered.

"It's a ghastly business," Eddings finally said when Barrow had finished. He had already heard Barrow's theory, but some of the colour had drained from his ruddy cheeks at hearing it once more. "It fits, though, if you're right about these not being gunshot wounds, which it looks like you are." He shook his head. "Necromancy! Pah!" He spat on the floor, much to Dr. Brookfield's chagrin. "If I get my hands on the madman behind all this, I'll make the bastard regret the day his father woke up with a stiff one in his knickers. And if the damned Triune Congress has a problem with that, they can bloody well sod off an' all!"

Dr. Brookfield had also gone rather pale as he listened to Barrow. More so than Inspector Eddings, the coroner had an appreciation for the medical science behind Barrow's hypothesis, as well as being able to speculate what it meant for the victim. "To have that awareness, but without corporeal form...without even a mouth to cry out?" He swallowed hard. "I can't begin to imagine a more horrible kind of living death."

"I can think of several, but that's neither here nor there," Barrow said, carefully packing the telescoping loupe back into its leather case. At the press of a button, the device had retracted in on itself until it was no larger than a closed pocket watch. "Jonathon, I'll need to see the spot where the body was discovered. I trust your detectives haven't mucked about too much with the scene?"

Eddings bristled at the implication, but nodded. "Aye, I knew you'd want to give it a thorough go-over with that blasted lens of yours," he said.

Barrow clapped his friend on the shoulder, then patted his jacket where he had safely tucked the device away. "We've discussed this, Inspector," he said, smiling. "There's nothing stopping you from giving one just like it to each of your constables."

"That may be so, Barrow," Eddings said, "but tell me this; just how much do you think the Halifax Police Commission has in the budget to pay you for making a hundred of the damnable things?"

"Ah, well," Barrow nodded, "I suppose there is that quibbling detail."

THE SALT TANG IN THE AIR GREW STRONGER AS THEY walked in silence towards the harbour, Barrow leading the way with Miss Skye following a step behind.

An ancient iron railing, its edges rounded with countless layers of thick green paint, ran the length of the quay, separating the street they walked along from a steep drop to the docks below. Barrow leaned against the rail, his hat in his hands, looking out over the wharves.

The fog had mostly lifted while they had been in the mortuary, and the waterfront was alive with activity. Ships of all sizes came and went, some belching smoke as their engines drove them forward, other nearly silent under sail. Longshoremen labored along the docks, shouting and singing and cursing as they loaded and unloaded cargo. Seagulls too numerous to count circled overhead, their mournful keening adding to the oceanfront orchestra.

A boy lay dead on the coroner's slab. The world carried on.

"It's my fault Ian Fergus is in Dr. Brookfield's cold chamber, Miss Skye," Barrow said quietly after a long moment, still watching the bustle below. "His brother came to me a few days ago, just as your sister did when you went missing, and I all but ignored his plea for help."

"You can't blame yourself for what happened to Ian Fergus," Emily said. "For all you know, he was dead before his brother asked for your help."

"Perhaps you're right." He stared straight ahead, unable to meet her gaze. "I suppose we'll know once Dr. Brookfield has determined the time of death."

"And either way, will getting maudlin about it bring him back?" Emily demanded. "Will your moping about help Jenny Perkins any?"

Barrow looked at his feet. "You shame me."

"Good," she said. "There's nout you can do for them that's already dead, Mr. Barrow, but you're the only one who can do something to make sure the same doesn't happen to anyone else."

He thought on that for a long moment before nodding. "You told me that you had seen crates packed full with those memory cylinders?"

Emily nodded. "Yes, but as I said, I've no idea which tunnels we traveled through to the warehouse."

"Do you know where you entered, though?"

The girl nodded once more. "I think I could find it again, yes," she said. "But what good does the starting point get you if you don't know the path through the maze?"

"We need some answers, Miss Skye. We need to find our way to that warehouse," Barrow said, popping his bowler onto his head. He turned to her and forced a thin smile. "And I think I know just how we might find it!"

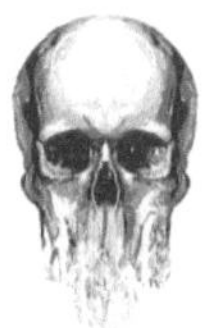

17

"WHAT ARE WE DOING OUT HERE?" EMILY ASKED, turning her collar up against the damp chill. Point Pleasant Park, scenic and crowded by day, was deserted as the clock neared midnight.

"There's to be a lunar eclipse tonight," Barrow said simply, as if that explained everything. Noting Emily's confused expression, he went on. "The divide between our world and the Otherwhere grows thin under an eclipse. If you want to capture a faerie, there's no better time."

Emily snickered. "Faeries aren't real, Mr. Barrow."

"Of course they are, Miss Skye," Barrow answered as he walked out into a clearing and set his valise on the dewy grass. Kneeling in the damp greenery, he opened the case and drew out a small ceramic saucer, a spoon, and a half-pint jam jar. "Haven't you read *A Midsummer Night's Dream*?"

"Of course I have," she scoffed. "But that was just a play."

Barrow looked up at her as he tried to work the jam jar's sealing band free. "Was *Julius Caesar* just a play, Miss Skye? Were *Antony and Cleopatra* some made-up madcap?"

"But those plays were histories, Mr. Barrow," the girl

protested. "Those ones were based on real people, and recounted true events."

"If you ever meet King Oberon, I'd suggest you keep such opinions to yourself. He would be wounded to hear you consider his plight less dire than that of poor Caesar."

Barrow grunted as he struggled to open the jar; the sticky stuff inside had sealed the lid tight as pitch, and his hand still ached from where the fiendish carriage driver's whip had torn his flesh the night before. "Aha!" he cried in triumph as the band finally twisted free. He plunged the spoon into the jar and plopped a healthy dollop onto the saucer. "Out, vile jelly! Where is thy lustre now?"

Emily rolled her eyes. "Assuming for the moment that faeries actually do exist, how do you expect this to capture one?"

"Ah, but this is just the bait. Faefolk can't resist sweets."

"Marmalade, though?" She made a face.

Barrow shrugged. "We're not trying to attract one of the nicer faefolk." He set the saucer on the grass, then rummaged around in the valise once more. "This is the trap, though," he said, opening his bandaged hand to show her five short silver nails. He pushed these into the earth, forming a pentagon around the plate and making certain their heads were well-hidden by the grass. "Come on," he said when he had finished, ushering Emily towards the cover of some nearby bushes.

"I can't lay down a proper containment circle," he explained in a hushed voice once they had settled in a spot where he could observe the baited trap. "Any faerie with half a brain would notice that from a mile away. But the silver nails will give me enough of a focal point to project a containment spell on the ground around the saucer. Most of the smaller faefolk aren't very strong when they're in our world, so it should hold whatever we catch."

"This all feels like madness, you know," Emily said, shifting her rump uneasily on the bumpy log she was using as a makeshift seat. "Faeries, murderous scientists, and all the rest."

"There are more things in heaven and earth, Miss Skye, than are dreamt of in your philosophy," Barrow answered, drawing another eye roll from the girl. "Old Will was on to something there. But tell me, given the odd things you've seen with your own eyes since discovering your sorcerous abilities, why do you find yourself skeptical of the fantastic things you haven't yet seen?"

Emily opened her mouth to answer, but instead fell silent. Her eyebrows came together as she thought it over. "I suppose because there's so little magic in the everyday," she finally replied. "Everything in the city is just so...normal. *Mundane.*"

"That's the right word for it," he agreed. "I think you'll find, though, the more open you allow yourself to be to everyday magic, the more of it you'll begin to see."

"How do you mean?"

"Many things that seem commonplace have magic in them, whether by nature or design, and people don't even realize it," Barrow explained. "They take for granted that simple seeds planted in the soil will sprout into new plants, but they never give a thought to how many miracles had to line up *just so* for that to happen in the first place."

Enough moonlight made its way through the leaves to let him see her eyebrow quirk upward. "You sound as though you're talking about the hand of God, Mr. Barrow."

"Maybe I am," he admitted, wondering if the serenity of his surroundings was perhaps bringing out his more philosophical side. "The older I get, the more I realize there are questions I'll never be able to answer, no matter how much I learn about the world around me. I don't know that I believe in God, as such, but I've seen too many inexplicable things to discredit the idea out of hand. Demons, werewolves, angry spirits: is the existence of God too outlandish an idea beside all that?" He peered across the still clearing, illuminated by the pale light of the moon. "Hush, now, Miss Skye," he whispered. "I think our trap is about to bear fruit."

The ferns that ringed the far edge of the clearing rustled. Barrow held his breath as he waited to see who—or what—he had lured in. *I'll feel rather foolish if my bait has drawn the notice of nothing more otherworldly than a curious squirrel,* he thought sardonically.

He was vindicated a moment later as a creature shaped more or less like a tiny man stepped out from between the ferns. Barely more than a foot and half tall with spindly arms that reached past his knees, the little fellow was hideously ugly and dressed in grubby clothes that put Barrow in mind of a coal miner. His skin was oily and mottled with red and indigo patches that looked like bruises. A curious blue cap sat atop his head, and coarse black hair stuck straight out from under it like the twisted bristles of a well-used paintbrush. Tiny leathery wings protruded from his shoulders; they didn't look like they would be able to carry the faerie into the air, but Barrow needed no reminding that looks were often deceiving when it came to the faefolk.

The little creature stood a few feet from the platter, eyeing the marmalade with suspicion. Licking his lips as his black eyes scanned the clearing, he seemed to be weighing appetite against reason, as if trying to decide if the risk was worth it.

Finally, temptation won out, and the faerie darted towards the bait. He dropped to his knees beside the saucer and greedily scooped tiny handfuls of the sticky marmalade into his mouth.

"*Captivitas!*" Barrow exclaimed as he burst from his leafy hiding place. A circle of blue light flared around the saucer.

The faerie cried out in surprise and rage and leapt high into the air, but was knocked back to the ground as he struck against the unseen barrier. "Let me out!" he demanded, his voice a snarling baritone that seemed too big to come from such a small body. "I'll tear the eyes from your skull and wear 'em around my neck!"

"Such threats hardly sell your case," Barrow said coolly. He knew the savage little creature would carry through with the violent promise, if given the chance. "You'll be in that circle until I decide to free you. Why don't you calm yourself so we can discuss that?"

The faerie eyed him with pure malice, but kept quiet.

"That's a fellow," Barrow said, dropping to one knee a few feet from the circle. "Shall we start with your name?"

"Hobnail," the creature said after a long moment. "Hobnail McSorely."

He knew it wasn't the faerie's true name. The names of faefolk are closely-guarded secrets, and not freely given to mortals. It mattered little.

"He doesn't look like a faerie to me," Emily said. She stood a few feet back from where Barrow knelt.

"I'm frightfully sorry to disappoint so fine a lady," Hobnail sneered.

"The storybooks have a lot of apologies to make," Barrow shrugged. "There are many different varieties of faefolk. Only a few look like tiny princesses with butterfly wings."

"And many of my kin are a good deal more fearsome than I," Hobnail interjected. "I would have the name of my captor."

"Call me Mr. Barrow."

Hobnail cast a sour look at him. "That's only part of your name!"

"I know about fae name magic," Barrow said. "You didn't give me your true name, and I'll not give you all of mine. Be glad you got as much as you did."

"You're not as moronic as you appear, Mr. Barrow," Hobnail said, eyeing Barrow now with something other than hatred. It wasn't quite respect, but it was a step in that direction. "Fine, then. What would you name as the price of my freedom? Riches? Power? You humans are all so dull." The little fellow looked past Barrow to Emily, his face twisting in a rictus grin. "Perhaps the undying love of the young lady there?"

"Nothing so base," Barrow said distastefully. "All I need is your help in tracking a magic echo, in a passageway Miss Skye here walked through several weeks ago."

"I'm not some snuffling bloodhound, Mr. Barrow," the faerie scoffed.

"But you can do it?" Barrow pressed. "You can follow after the trail left behind by a mortal practitioner?"

"Of course I can," Hobnail sneered. "The stink you mortals leave in your wake is bad enough, but the trail of magic energy you wizards leave behind is overpowering." He pinched his nose dramatically. "I could smell one of you coming from a mile away, any day of the week."

"If that's so, then how did you end up trapped here?" Emily put in.

Hobnail scowled at her. "A moment of weakness, lass. It has been far too long since I've had sweet marmalade left out in offering. Hardly any of you mortals leave tribute out for the fae at all anymore." He shook his tiny head. "I should've known it was a trick."

"But you didn't, and you fell into it, and here you are," Barrow said. "Are you willing to bargain?"

"Aye, fine," Hobnail said. "It's a small enough thing, I suppose, but you'll owe me a boon in return."

"That seems fair enough," Barrow said after a moment's consideration. "You'll want to hold that in abeyance, I assume?"

"Of course. One never knows when one might need a favour from some fool mortal," Hobnail said through a smirk. "Summon me at sundown tomorrow, wherever this echo trail of yours begins, and I'll do my best to lead you to whatever awaits at the other end. After that, you're on your own." His wicked, toothy grin split his face in a way no human visage could possibly imitate. "Of course, to get started, I'll need a drop of the girl's blood."

"Out of the question," Barrow said flatly. "Absolutely out of the question."

"Magic echoes fade, just the same as any scent. The trail you expect me to track for you is several weeks old," the detestable faerie pointed out. "I'll need a strong sample to get on the trail the girl walked. More than anything else, magic is in the blood, as you well know. There's no better medium for the chore."

The faerie was right, and Barrow knew it. The smug look on Hobnail's little face only added to his frustration.

Before he could answer, though, Emily stepped forward and placed a hand on his shoulder. "I'll do it," she said simply. "It's my blood we're discussing, so it ought to be my decision, Mr. Barrow. If it will help put an end to these killings, I'll do it."

Barrow started to protest, but the determination in her eyes stopped him cold. Instead, he turned on the faerie. "The bargain being struck is between you and I, Hobnail McSorely. Any forfeit owed to you will be paid by me, not Miss Skye. Her blood is no gift, and gives you no claim over her in any way, in this world or any realm of the Otherwhere, in this life or the next, or the one after that. Are we agreed?"

Hobnail mulled that over for a moment, as though

looking for some way to wring more advantage from the offer. The fact that he was trapped may have influenced his acquiescence. Finally, he sighed. "Very well, Mr. Barrow," he said. "But I warn you, you'd best not pull any tricks to get out of the deal when I come to collect."

Satisfied, Barrow nodded.

"Call on me at sundown tomorrow. You know how to do that, don't you?" He paused, waiting for Barrow to nod before he continued. "We'll see what I can do for you then. Now, let me out of this damned circle!"

INSPECTOR EDDINGS SHOWED UP EARLY THE NEXT morning, announcing his arrival with a sharp rapping of his walking stick on the glass set in Barrow's office door. Impatience was clear on the inspector's face as Barrow ushered him in off the street. He hung his hat and coat by the door, then settled into one of the chairs by the potbellied stove.

Barrow took the other seat. "What have you, Jonathon?" he asked around a yawn.

"And a good morning to you too, Barrow," Eddings said sarcastically, placing an oversized envelope on the small table between the two seats. "Your manners are slipping again. Anyway, I called in a few favours, and I've learned about all there is to know about this Morgentaler character. It isn't much, I'm afraid. Born to a wealthy family in Austria, he studied at the best schools in Europe. Up until two years ago, he worked alongside a Dr. Burckhardt at the University of Bern, in Switzerland."

"That wouldn't be Dr. Gottleib Burckhardt, by any chance?"

Eddings rolled his eyes and let out a sigh. "I suppose I shouldn't be surprised that you've heard of him, too."

"He's one of the leading researchers mapping out the mysteries of the human brain, Jonathon. The work he's doing is really quite extraordinary. His articles—"

"Yes, yes, I'm certain they'll change the world and all that," Eddings cut in impatiently, "But apparently our Morgentaler didn't share your high opinion of the man. It seems the two had a rather spectacular falling out."

"Do you know what they quarreled over?"

"Bloody hell, Barrow!" Exasperation flashed across the inspector's face once more. "I can only find out so much. It's not as if you asked me to pull the record of one of the local drunkards off Gottingen Street," he said, tapping the envelope on the table with two fingers. "It's a wonder I was able to suss out as much about the man as I did. Anyway, Morgentaler had been all but a ghost in the years since, until he took the position at Hemlock Overlook."

"Fair enough. I do appreciate you looking into this," Barrow said. "What else did you find? How long has he been in Halifax?"

"He arrived by steamship six months ago."

Barrow leaned back in his chair. "By steamship?"

Eddings nodded. "I thought that odd myself. He's a doctor, after all, and a man of means besides. Why would anyone travel by steamer when he could easily afford a first-class ticket on a fancy new airship?"

Barrow frowned as he mulled that over. Even the slowest airship could cross the Atlantic in five or six days, while the same voyage by steamer took weeks. Seafaring had come a long way over the last century, with new engines driving ships across great distances with no need for a sail. But the ships themselves remained cramped, damp, and often filthy. Only the relatively low cost of the fare made travel by sea even remotely appealing.

The inspector was right—it made no sense.

"There is one more thing," Eddings said, calling Barrow's attention away from steamships. "Morgentaler also had a young wife in Bern."

"Had?" Barrow asked. "Past tense?"

"It sounds like a nasty thing." A sorrowful look replaced the inspector's typically stony expression. "Maybe you can make better sense of it, but the way I read it here, it sounds like she suffered from a sort of spreading paralysis that started in her fingers and toes and was slowly working its way toward her heart. Her body was dying like a sick tree losing branches, but her mind was seemingly unaffected by the illness. She was watching it happen. The physicians at the university had never seen the like, the poor lass."

Barrow suppressed a shudder as he thought of the young woman, trapped in a body dying by slow increments. "What became of her?"

Eddings shrugged his shoulders. "No one knows. Morgentaler took her to his family's estate in Austria when he had his row with Burckhardt, and she hasn't been seen in the two years since. There's no record of her death, though."

Eddings pulled his watch out of his waistcoat, opened it to check the time, then snapped it shut. "I'd best be on my way. If I'm not at my desk by quarter-past eight, Constable McCallister is liable to panic and send out a search party." He stood and crossed the small room to retrieve his hat and coat. "You really should think about relocating to a better neighborhood, Barrow. This street catches too much of the spillover from Gottingen for my liking. Jayne worries about you as well."

"You've seen my workshop downstairs," Barrow said with a shrug. "Where else in the city could I afford as much space, and away from curious eyes?" He shook his head. "And you can tell your wife that I'm quite able to look after myself."

Eddings chuckled. "If I told Jayne about half the trouble

you've gotten yourself into lately, she'd demand I never leave your side." He smiled a warm, genuine smile as he shrugged his big shoulders into his heavy wool coat. "You're a good friend, and far from the most useless of men, but I've no notion of becoming your bodyguard."

"It has been an eventful week," Barrow admitted, his understatement drawing a guffaw from his friend. "Thank you, Jonathon. I'm in your debt."

"Call it payback for your help with the Osgood investigation last month. The scales between us have a way of finding their balance." Eddings popped his hat onto his head and headed for the door to the street, where he paused before heading out. "There's something else I ought to tell you though, Barrow. From what my contacts tell me, you're not the only one asking after Dr. Morgentaler."

18

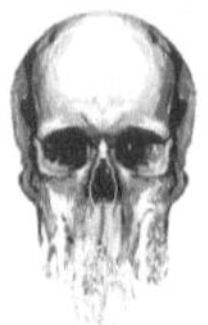

Barrow followed Miss Skye into the mouth of a darkened and dingy alleyway, not far from the same wharf-side street that was home to Lawrence MacGowan's Wheelhouse tavern. Dusk was still about a half-hour away, but this narrow passage likely never saw much of the sun even at its zenith. Thick moss and tiny mushrooms grew between the damp bricks of the buildings on either side, slowly working to reclaim this place for the very earth itself with an inexorable determination.

Strewn with trash and other refuse, smelling faintly of grease and excrement, it was, he observed, not much different from the alleyway in which he had first met the young woman following his tussle with Lai Jūn. *Then again*, he thought, *one alley is much like any other.*

"Are you quite certain this is the way?" he asked as he trailed behind. Instead of his black leather valise, he carried a large oiled canvas satchel, its one strap slung over his opposite shoulder. The bag felt rather clumsy as it swung against his hip, but it left his hands free. Not knowing what they would come up against when they entered the tunnels beneath the city, it was an easy trade-off to make.

He also carried a short staff in one hand, longer than a walking stick and carved from ash. Unlike the ancient and powerful staff Malleus carried, this was a fairly benign item Barrow had crafted himself several years earlier in his first year at the Technomancer's Collegeum. He had painstakingly drilled out the core and inserted a length of pure silver rod, and rather than some puissant gemstone inset at the pommel was a simple blown glass globe. Though not infused with any supernatural or elemental force, the staff was a useful instrument and, if necessary, even a powerful weapon in its own way.

Emily eyed it with some bemusement. "For someone who hates being called a wizard, you do look the part with that in your hand."

He shot her a withering look but left the barb unanswered, which only seemed to amuse her all the more. He sighed.

They came to what looked to be a cellar door behind a building, a simple wooden hatch near the ground that no one would ever give a second glance. Much of the paint had long since flaked away from the wooden slats of the door, which had dried out and grayed over the years. A rusty length of chain was threaded through iron pull rings on each side of the door, aside from that Barrow saw no lock of any sort. "This is the place," Emily announced, kneeling to pull the chain aside. "We're in luck! They haven't done anything at all to secure the entrance."

"Wait, Miss Skye," Barrow said sharply, eyeing the door with suspicion. "There might be no padlock on the chain, but the Cabal may have set other wards in place over the entrance. I would have, were it along the route to my own hideaway. Here, let me show you." He knelt beside her and laid a hand on the weathered wood, and motioned for her to do the same.

"What am I feeling for?" she asked as she set her hand next to his.

"It'll be a subtle thing, if it's there at all," he explained. "Something like a vibration deep within the wood itself. Depending on what type of ward is in place, it may feel as slight as a babe's breath, or a swirling torrent of ragged energy."

She held her hand against the hatch for nearly a minute, focusing intently where her hand pressed against the wood. "I don't feel anything," she finally said with some frustration in her voice.

Barrow smiled. "That's because there's nothing there to sense," he said with a shrug. "Sloppy, but that's the Cabal for you." He pulled the rusty chain through the iron rings with the raspy sound of metal against aged metal, then looked up to the sky as he let the chain fall to the ground. "It's almost sundown now, wouldn't you say?"

Once you have a faerie's attention, summoning him is a fairly simple thing. Barrow set the same saucer he had used the night before with another large dollop of marmalade on the ground, then sprinkled dried petals from several varieties of flowers around it. "Hobnail McSorely, the sun is now setting," he called out. "Accept this offering, and come forth!"

Nothing happened. Barrow wondered if Hobnail McSorely would answer his call. Faeries were notoriously contrary by nature, and even with a bargain in place, there was no guarantee the little creature would hold up his end of the deal.

He started to think about what other methods, if any, he might use to track the path through the maze of subterranean tunnels. But with a flash of light and the green smell of some ancient, dewy forest, Hobnail appeared, the scowl on his little face as surly as ever.

"Well, Barrow, here I am," he said, folding his arms across his tiny chest. He wrinkled his nose as he looked around the alleyway. "And a more befouled and utterly *human* place you could not have called me to! It never fails to depress me when I see what you loutish brutes have done to your world. I almost didn't come."

"I'm glad you did," Barrow said, doing his best to sound stern. "A bargain spoken is a bargain made, and I wasn't eager to try to bind you to your word against your will."

Hobnail's stubby wings twitched. "I'd like to see you try," he said as he stooped to pick up the saucer Barrow had set out. He swept the glob of marmalade into his mouth with one hand. "Let's get going," he said, licking his sticky fingers with an impossibly long tongue.

"A moment before we proceed," Barrow said, pulling a waxed paper packet from his satchel. He unscrewed the glass globe from the end of the staff and emptied the packet of powder into it.

"What's that, then?" Emily asked, watching him intently.

"This will light our way once we're in the tunnels."

"Is it magic?"

Barrow shook his head. "I do have ways of conjuring a magical light source, but we're on the trail of a necromancer, Miss Skye, and possibly the whole of the Nightshade Cabal. Its acolytes may not be the most skilled of magicians, but it still wouldn't be wise to announce our presence with a spell for something so simple as light," he said as he pulled a matchbox from a pocket inside his jacket. "This is just good science, a chemical compound of my own design. It's mostly magnesium, with some other elements in the mix. Magnesium burns brighter than anything else, but quickly. The other elements act to slow the burning. The effect is brighter than lamp oil, and should give us several hours of light." He struck a match, set the powder alight, and screwed the globe back in place. The stuff was slow to catch, but soon burned with a bright, steady luminescence. "There we go!"

He pulled open the wooden hatch, revealing a set of rickety steps leading down into the darkness. There was no railing of any description, and each step sagged slightly under his weight as he descended, but held. Emily followed a few paces behind, while Hobnail McSorely fluttered along at the rear, borne aloft by his tiny wings.

Barrow was glad he had lit the torch before starting down. Otherwise, here at the bottom of the steps, the darkness would have been absolute. He set the staff against the wall, making sure it wouldn't fall over, and breathed in the cool, damp air. It smelled faintly of wet stone and old dust.

"This must be the place," Hobnail said, still hanging in midair. "I can smell the magic echoes in the air already. Plenty of you mortal wizards have been through here."

"Will you be able to pick out one trail from the many?"

"If you quit jabbering and give me a drop of the girl's blood as promised, I can."

Barrow drew a silver hatpin from his satchel and took Emily by the hand. "I'm afraid I don't have much practice at this."

"Let's just get it over with," she answered, setting her jaw. "If you know a jab is coming, sometimes it'll hurt less, but it doesn't mean I want to spend all day waiting for it."

Barrow nodded and, without another word, pushed the sharp end of the pin into the fleshy part of her fingertip. She winced, but didn't pull her hand away. A drop of blood, crimson in the light of the torch, welled up on her skin. He held out a thimble to catch the blood as it fell, then handed her a small gauze pad. "Here, wrap this around your finger for a few moments," he said, then he turned to the faerie and handed over the thimble.

"I hope you realize I find this utterly revolting," Hobnail said, wrinkling his nose. He stuck his nose into the thimble and inhaled deeply. "Ugh, human stink!"

Emily looked offended, but before she could say anything, Barrow interjected. "Have you got the echo, then?"

"Aye, I've got it," Hobnail said. "Try to keep up."

Hobnail kept a steady pace as he led the way down the corridor, never flying past the reach of the light cast by Barrow's staff. The brickwork of the tunnel walls caught the light, too, giving back swooping shadows that played tricks on the eyes. Water trickled down the walls here and there, pooling in spots where the floor had worn down over the years. Something slick squelched underfoot. Barrow didn't look back to see what it was.

They walked on in silence for a long while, Hobnail guiding them as tunnels intersected and branched off from each other until Barrow had lost all sense of which direction they were headed. At one point they had to clamber over some fallen brick and stone that blocked the way. The cracked bricks they scrabbled past looked freshly-broken. Barrow wondered if the collapse had been an intentional attempt by someone to cut off the route.

As though signaling a step farther back in time, the regular brick eventually transitioned to walls of roughly cut stone. These granite blocks had been quarried and cut to a roughly uniform shape, but their irregularity and rough edges spoke to a definite lack of sophistication on the part of the masons who had labored on them. Barrow surmised these passages dated back to the earliest French occupation, if not earlier. "Does this look familiar?" he asked over his shoulder.

"This is the way we came," Emily answered with a nod. "I think there was another fork just up ahead."

When they came to that junction, Hobnail followed the path to the right. A hundred yards down that passage, however, they came to another pile of fallen stone and rubble. This collapse had done a far better job of sealing the tunnel, filling the space from floor to ceiling with debris.

Even little Hobnail could find no way to squeeze through the passage. "Well, the trail ends here," he said. "I'd say someone didn't want you following 'em past this point."

"It does look like a controlled demolition, with some additional material piled on for good measure," Barrow agreed.

"Couldn't you just..." Emily started, waggling her fingers absently at the pile of debris. "You know, magic this mess away somehow?"

"It doesn't work that way. You can't just blink a pile of stone out of existence. The best I could do is push it aside, but there's nowhere to push it to, and even if there were somewhere down here for me to move all of that stone to, forcing a displacement like that would leave me exhausted for several days." He shook his head. "We'll just have to find another way around."

"You won't be needing me, then," Hobnail said.

"These tunnels all connect," Barrow said. "We're going to have to take a few extra turns, but we'll still need you when we rejoin this passage further down." Hobnail opened his mouth to protest, but Barrow cut him off before he could speak. "If you take off back where you came from now, you'll forfeit on your end of the bargain. Would you be known as Hobnail Oath-breaker?"

The faerie glowered at him, but said nothing more. He followed along as Barrow led the way back to the last junction, drifting about half as high as he had when he had been out in front.

"What do we do if this tunnel is collapsed as well?" Emily asked as they headed down the left passage.

"Go back and try the next one?" Barrow said with a shrug. He could see the next question in her eyes—*And if that one is collapsed too, what then?* He had no good answer to that, and was glad she didn't ask.

As it turned out, he needn't have worried. The tunnel remained intact. The floor beneath their feet sloped almost imperceptibly downward as they walked and the air grew more humid. The rich smell of earth around them became stronger and stronger as they descended. Barrow thought he could feel a slight breeze coming from somewhere further along.

"What is that up ahead?" Emily asked. At the very far reach of Barrow's light, a looming, oblong shape, darker than the granite walls of the passageway came into view.

As they drew nearer, the shape revealed itself to be an iron door, hung on massive hinges. The surface was decorated with ornate castings of oak leaves and *fleurs-de-lis*.

"Unless I miss my guess, Miss Skye, what we're looking at here is the entrance to some forgotten catacomb."

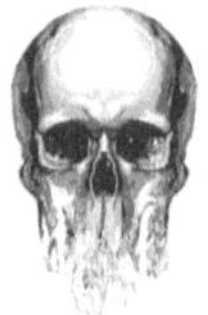

THE RASPY SOUND OF RUSTED METAL GRINDING AGAINST rusted metal pierced the silence as Barrow forced the iron door open. Though stiff, it swung more easily on its hinges than he had expected. He examined the dirt and dust on the floor, noting the arc the door had already made through the grime. Someone had been this way, and recently.

Emily's eyes were wide with disbelief. "We're on the trail of a necromancer—or *several* necromancers, for that matter—and you want to go traipsing through a room full of corpses?" she demanded. "You'll have to forgive what may seem a stupid question, Mr. Barrow, but isn't that a very *bad* idea?"

"Not at all," Barrow said simply. "A necromancer needs a fairly fresh corpse to work a reanimation spell to any real effect. The deceased human body quickly loses mobility as it starts to dry out, decay, and fall apart." He pointed to the graven *fleurs-de-lis* on the door. "Any corpse we'll come upon down here is from the days when the city above was still a French Acadian settlement. Centuries old, and long since withered away. Even if our necromancer could reanimate such a long-dead body, it wouldn't be able to move around much, if at all."

Emily had no reply, but her face was the picture of dubious skepticism. Hobnail also said nothing, which Barrow counted as a small miracle. The glowering faerie looked anything but pleased, though.

The chamber they entered was long and slightly wider than the tunnels they had traveled, smelling of damp decay and things long forgotten. The only sound to be heard was the faint but distinct trickling of water slowly working its way down through the stone above. The light cast by Barrow's staff did not come close to reaching the far end of the lengthy catacomb, but was easily bright enough to illuminate the nearby walls.

Along each wall were recessed niches, four to a column, many occupied by what little remained of those long-dead Acadians. In the half-darkness, they looked like something from the pages of a penny dreadful. Some were reduced to no more than bare skeletons wrapped in shrouds, all flesh picked clean ages ago. Others, though, had a bit more dried meat still clinging to their bones.

They could see the remnants of what might have once been colourful decorations around each niche, but any identifying marks that once adorned these resting places were illegible. Even in this place, sealed away and untouched by human hands for more than a century, time wore its slow effects upon the works of man.

Barrow swore under his breath as his foot found a puddle, not deep enough to soak his shoe through, but enough to dampen his sock. Some unseen rodents, startled by the human intrusion, chittered angrily and scampered away, startling Emily and Barrow both. Hobnail snickered.

"Imagine, all these bodies hidden away down here, while life in the city above goes on," Emily said. She sounded nervous, as though she'd rather remain silent but needed to distract herself from her grim surroundings.

"It's not that unusual, really," Barrow said. "Spring Garden sits atop an old burial ground that's much larger than the present graveyard, and Deadman's Island didn't get its name for no reason. We're never very far removed from those who went before us."

Emily shuddered at the thought. "How many of these catacombs are there?"

"I don't know of any others like this," Barrow answered. "I had no idea this one was here, actually. But the warrens beneath the city are said to be a fairly sprawling system, dating back hundreds of years."

He stopped then and raised a hand, urging the others to silence. From somewhere in the looming darkness ahead came a sound, soft at first, like the rustling of dried leaves in a lazy autumn breeze.

"What is that?" Emily whispered, the edge of panic in her voice.

Barrow had no answer. He listened to the darkness. The shuffling, scraping sound grew steadily louder, closer. Whatever it was, it was coming towards them.

Movement at the edge of the staff's light went from shifting shadow to solid form as a shambling, lurching figure emerged from the gloom. Shriveled and hunched, clad in hanging rags, the walking corpse was barely mobile. Little more than a raspy wheeze came from its fleshless throat as it struggled to reach a gnarled hand towards them. Two more withered cadavers trailed a pace behind, their movements just as awkward.

"I thought you said a necromancer couldn't animate such a long-dead corpse," Hobnail accused.

"It shouldn't be possible," Barrow replied, even as he

watched another pair of the walking dead fall in behind the first three.

"Then how do you explain that?" the faerie screeched, bobbing up and down in the air and pointing wildly. "They're behind us, too!"

"Both of you, get behind me, now!" Barrow barked, pulling something that looked like a coil of silver wire from his satchel. He threw the coil at the floor, hard. As it struck the stone, the wire unfurled, springing open and landing on the floor a few feet in front of them, a perfect circle precisely nine feet in diameter. "Get inside the circle!"

When all three stood within the ring of silver wire, Barrow chanted a handful of Latin phrases. The circle around their feet began to glow. "May the circle protect all within!" he declared, planting the butt end of his staff against the stone floor. At his command, the wire flashed brilliantly bright white for a moment. When it subsided, the trio were ensconced in a column of soft, shimmering light.

"We're safe inside the circle," Barrow said, a few drops of sweat beading on his brow, "but we can't stay here forever."

"Do you think?" Hobnail snarked. He jabbed an angry finger in Barrow's face. "You're going to get us all killed in this stinking place, you blundering jackanapes! I never should have followed you down here." Barrow steadfastly ignored him, which made Hobnail sputter indignantly and screech even more loudly.

The walking dead, numbering eight or nine now, were indeed approaching from both sides, reaching out almost plaintively towards them. Their feet dragged on the floor, their jaws hung slack. None had eyes or much else left to express anything resembling human emotion, but the way the ragged remnants of mealy flesh and lank hair hung from their skulls made them look more pitiable than anything else. The deplorable things were still a deadly threat, though, and sure to be relentless in a manner no reasoning beast could ever be.

"What will we do?" Emily asked.

Hobnail shrieked as a shambling corpse reached out a desiccated hand towards him.

The cadaver howled as its withered fingertips came in contact with the sorcerous column of light and burst into white flame. Barrow winced and set his teeth as he wrestled to keep the circle intact, feeling rather like he had had the wind knocked from his lungs. He could feel a bead of sweat trickle down between his shoulders, tickling his spine as it went.

The corpse fell to its knees, white flame licking its way up its arm. It struggled to crawl away as it was further engulfed, finally collapsing on the floor as it was reduced to little more than a pile of ash and charred bone.

"I'm surprised there was enough of him left to cry out like that," Barrow said as he watched the immolated corpse finally stop twitching. "His lungs and vocal cords should've rotted away to nothing long ago." He shrugged. "No matter. I suppose we've got more pressing concerns at the moment."

"Your composure is admirable, Mr. Barrow, or might be under less dire circumstances," Emily said, her own sangfroid seeming rather insincere. She didn't quite clutch at his sleeve, but her posture was tense and she stood nearer than might have been strictly necessary. Apparently, the cadaver's fiery demise hadn't fully reassured her.

Barrow could hardly fault her for that, though. Lacking any remnant of human reasoning, the remaining corpses took no heed from their fellow's end, and continued their slow advance toward the circle. The circle would hold them off as long as he could keep it going. But dealing with the one he had dispatched so far had felt like a punch in the gut, and he had no way of knowing how many more of the foul things lurked in the shadows.

Another sound from the darkness derailed that train of thought. A guttural, echoing laughter drew Barrow's attention to the far end of the catacomb. A dim red glow hung in the gloom there.

Barrow stared in disbelief as the scarlet radiance drew nearer. "Dear God. They wouldn't... they *couldn't!*"

"Who?" Emily asked, her features colored by the ruddy light. "Wouldn't they what?"

"The Cabal, Miss Skye," Barrow replied gravely. "The maniacs have raised a lich."

They saw it, then, as it emerged from the stygian darkness. The lich did not shamble with the ungainly limp of its undead legion, instead levitating a handsbreadth above the floor. A full head taller than the tallest of men, the lich wore long scarlet robes that may once have been magnificent, but now hung in streaming tatters from its grotesque form. It carried a staff topped with a large ram's skull, a maelstrom of baleful red flame raging within.

In place of the lich's eyes were two yawning pits of unending, burning darkness. Atop his head was a twisted horned crown, crusted with oversized, garish jewels. If they were regular gemstones, any one of them would've been worth a fortune. But these stones were imbued with ancient, ungodly power. Their value transcended all mortal notions of material wealth.

Leveling the ram's head staff at them, the lich shouted something in an ancient tongue, unspoken in the living world in millennia. A torrent of flame drawn from the deepest abyss erupted from the ram's skull towards them, engulfing Barrow's column of light entirely.

Barrow gripped his own staff tightly with both hands, holding it directly between his companions and the lich. Fire a deeper red than he had ever seen raged around them for a moment that felt like an eternity, but the protection circle held until it subsided.

"We need to perform a rite of banishment," Barrow said. "That thing must be sent back to whatever corner of Hell it was called from."

"How do we do that?" Emily asked.

"I'll need you to take over the protection circle," he said. He put up a hand to silence her as she opened her mouth to protest. "You can do this, Miss Skye! A protection circle is a simple thing, especially once it has already been created, but I can't maintain it and work the banishment at the same time."

Emily nodded and set her shoulders back, steeling herself. "What do I do?"

Barrow smiled. "You'll need to take my place. When I hand you the staff, you must focus your thoughts inward. Block out everything else and direct all of your energy through your palms and into the staff. You'll feel an almost magnetic force between yourself and the circle. The protection spell is already manifested; keep your mind focused and the spell will take care of the rest."

Hellfire from the lich's staff erupted around them once more. Hobnail screeched angrily, but Barrow couldn't tell if he was cursing at him or the lich. Again, the circle held back the attack.

"Place your hands above mine," Barrow instructed. "It'll feel as though the staff is being pulled every which way, but you must keep it steady. I won't release my grip until you're fully in command of the protection spell."

Planting her booted feet wide on the stone floor, Emily did as instructed. Her hands trembled. Her face froze, a visage of intense concentration and grim determination.

"I think you have it," Barrow said after a moment. "I'm going to release the spell to you now."

Emily's eyes remained intent on the staff, her jaw tight as she nodded once, almost imperceptibly. As Barrow let go of the staff, she gasped as the full force of the protection spell pulled at something deep within her. The staff wobbled violently and was very nearly wrenched from her hands, but she managed to hold on.

There was a bad moment there as the lich realized what was happening. Recognizing the protection spell was being passed from Barrow to Emily, the horrific thing reared back and hurled another blast of hellfire at them, hoping to strike at the precise moment their defense would be at its weakest. A flood of flame exploded around them, and the barrier of white light bowed inward. Emily cried out and rocked back on her heels, but kept her footing. The shield wavered, but held.

The lich howled in rage, its savage roar the sound of every child in the world simultaneously waking from a shared nightmare.

"That's the stuff!" Barrow encouraged her as he set about the banishment. From his satchel, he drew a rolled leather case, similar to one that would hold an army field surgeon's instruments. Instead of scalpels and specula, though, Barrow's case housed the workings for most basic magic, all premeasured and scrupulously organized by type and usage. He took out a crisp white linen handkerchief and laid it on the dusty floor.

This should be a full bolt of virgin cloth on a pristine wooden table, but we'll have to make do with what we've got, he thought to himself. A meticulous planner in all things, working slapdash field magic like this always made him uneasy. It didn't help that he so rarely needed to resort to field magic under such dire circumstances.

Onto the handkerchief, he meted out roughly equal amounts of dried herbs–-thyme, rosemary, powdered ginger root, and a few others. In the center of the square, he placed the nub of a short, stubby white candle.

He rummaged through the case and his satchel, patted down his jacket pockets, then swore. He had somehow lost his matches along the way. *Well, nothing else for it.* He narrowed his eyes, fixing on the candle and nothing else, and focused his thoughts. "*Flagro,*" he whispered.

Nothing happened for a few maddeningly long seconds, but then the candlewick flickered into light. He allowed himself a sigh of relief; if the minor flame spell had too much force behind it, he would've set the entire banishment ablaze.

"Now what?" Emily demanded, panic in her voice. The lich had crossed half the distance towards them. The remaining animated corpses, seemingly warier of the lich's hellfire eruptions than the protection circle, also milled around not far from where they stood.

"The candlelight serves as a substitute for sunlight in the spell," Barrow began. "It activates the—"

"Whatever it activates, just get on with it!" Emily snapped.

Barrow muttered something caustic about young people ignoring learning opportunities under his breath. Raising both hands above his head, he spoke in a booming voice, addressing the lich directly. "Beast of the abyss," he called out, leveling one hand to point at the lich, "I defy the one who has set you against us! Return to your abode of the damned, and plague the living world no more!"

The lich howled again in rage and despair as it found itself pulled from the air, crashing to its knees as the magic that held it aloft was suddenly canceled out. It struggled to its feet and tried to continue its advance towards them, but it was bound to the stone floor of the chamber. Holding its scepter in both hands, it readied to unleash another volley of hellfire.

Barrow shook his head, sadly. "It could've been easier for us both this way," he said, but if the beast was listening, it didn't seem to care. Barrow again raised both hands, preparing for his next incantation.

"Promise of the Rising Sun, enter this dark place and make your light known," Barrow chanted. At his words, the light of the candle grew impossibly bright. The shambling corpses turned to scurry away from its light as quickly as they could. "Cleanse this place of the evil within, and cast these horrors back to the darkness from whence they came!"

He threw a handful of powdered magnesium toward the candle's flame. As it flared, streaks of white light burst up from the floor around the lich's immobile feet. It looked as if the floor had been poked with a pin to let the light shine through.

Where the light struck the beast's body, black smoke rose from its skin. Tiny tongues of white flame licked at the creature's pallid flesh, its ragged silk robes burning away as it howled in fear and pain.

Hobbled by the white flame, the lich was reduced to a crawl as its legs were engulfed, but it continued its advance toward them. Less than ten feet separated the horror from the line of silver Barrow had set on the floor, and the lich kept coming.

Its legs charred ruins, it dragged itself along the stone floor by the elbows. Thin shafts of light continued to break through the cracks between the stones, piercing what remained of the lich's flesh. The horned crown fell to the floor, the gold and jewels shattering as though they were crafted of nothing more substantial than paste glass.

When it was within a few feet of the circle, one of the lich's arms caught flame. It dropped the ram's head staff as the arm and hand burned away to a stump. Barrow felt a pang of regret as he watched the white flames consume the staff, but the destruction of such a powerful relic was a regrettable necessity.

The lich reached out with its remaining hand, its fingertips sizzling as it made contact the column of light. With a look of pure malice on what was left of its face, it forced the hand through the barrier, skin and sinew unraveling as it broached the defensive spell.

That was too much for Emily to withstand. With a gasp, she fell backwards onto the stone floor, the protective light dissipating as she collapsed. Barrow cried out in alarm as he rushed to her side.

"I'm sorry, Mr. Barrow," she said between panicked breaths.

"You did fine," he said reassuringly, taking back the staff she still held. "You bought me the time I needed to do what I had to." He turned and looked at what was left of the lich, which was little more than its trunk and one arm. It was still a dire threat—the thing's very touch meant an instant and rather painful death.

Barrow looked to the glowing glass orb at the end of his staff, hoping enough of the slow-burning mixture of chemical compounds remained for his next move. He unscrewed the glass globe and emptied the contents onto the candle, repeating his earlier incantation.

The lich writhed and shrieked as more light from below pierced its body until it was fully engulfed in dazzling white flames. Its agonized cries ceased as it crumbled to ash on the floor. It might just have been the way the sound reverberated through the chamber, but to Barrow's ear, it endured much longer than any sound possibly could.

Even as the lich disintegrated, the light coming from between the cracks in the stone persisted, providing plenty of illumination for the time being. *I'll have to conjure a nimbus when we move on to the next chamber, after all,* Barrow thought.

Sweating, Barrow helped Emily back to her feet. They had nothing left to fear. As the lich had burned up, its undead horde had fallen to the floor where they stood, as dead as they had ever been.

"You said the necromancers couldn't raise the dead in the catacomb," Hobnail accused once more, swatting him on the shoulder. "Do you never tire of being wrong?"

"I wasn't wrong," Barrow snapped back. He gestured to the fallen bodies. "Not really. This was not the work of our necromancer, at least not directly. I never thought for a moment the Cabal would've evoked a lich."

"What was that thing?" Emily asked. Sweat streaked down her face.

"The thing is called a lich," Barrow repeated. "The fused being of a minor demon and a dead sorcerer, usually created when a necromancer messes with demonic forces beyond his ability to control. He ends up a soulless horror, cursed to forever walk the shadowy divide between life and death itself. Its powers over the dead extend far beyond those of simple necromancy."

"That sounds very bad."

"Oh, it certainly is that," Barrow said. "A lich is like any other demon summoned to the mortal plane. Incredibly useful as long as you can keep it under your thumb, but capable of unleashing unimagined horrors should it manage to break free." He performed a quick inventory to ensure his gear was intact. "Most demons who break free are happy enough to simply devour the idiot who summoned them and return to the netherworld from whence they came, but a lich set loose on earth would do his best to turn this world into a nightmare realm inhabited only by the walking dead."

The blood drained from Emily's face. "You let me work a protection spell against something that deadly?"

"The protection circle was already up," Barrow said, kneeling to gather up the wire ring. "All you did was keep it going." When that didn't seem to mollify her, he smiled and tried to redirect the conversation. "In a way, you know, this is good news for us."

Emily's jaw hung slack for a moment, incredulous. "An insane necromancer sends a death-obsessed half-demon after us, and you're grinning about it?" she demanded. The edge of anger in her voice softened to mere exasperation. "How is *that* possibly good news?"

"Simple," Barrow said with a shrug. "The Cabal collapsed an entire tunnel to direct us to this place, and raised a lich to put a stop to us. They're desperate, and frightened that we're on their trail." He started off past Emily, heading toward the far end of the catacomb as she stood stock-still, gawping in disbelief. "Either that," he continued, "or they've come even more unhinged than I could've imagined!"

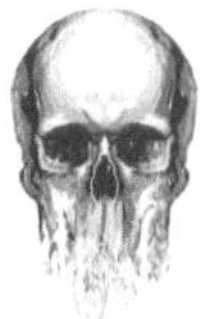

20

A DOORWAY AT THE FAR END OF THE CATACOMB LED TO yet another long, winding tunnel. Its arched ceiling seemed lower than the others they had followed, and the floor sloped steadily downward. No one said much as they followed the floating nimbus of light down the passage, the encounter with the lich weighing heavily on their minds.

Not wanting to frighten Miss Skye or Hobnail any more than they were already, Barrow had tried to sound nonchalant about the Cabal bringing the half-demon into the material plane. His feigned sangfroid seemed to steady his companions, but did little to calm his own jangled nerves. *What can I do against someone who could call forth such a horror?* Try as he might, he couldn't think of an answer to that.

The descending tunnel eventually brought them to another heavy wooden door, which opened onto a steel walkway suspended above a cavernous chamber. Looking over the railing, Barrow estimated it to be roughly thirty yards above the floor below. There was a light coming from somewhere below, so he muttered a few words to dim the nimbus.

"This appears to be a natural cavern," he said quietly as he examined the stone, speaking more for his own benefit than that of his companions. No mason's chisel had hacked away at the walls; the primordial ironstone was smooth to the touch and showed signs of being carved out by the unhurried trickle of groundwater over millennia. "Given how many twists and turns we took, it's impossible to say, but we may be directly beneath Citadel Hill."

The walkway clove to the cavern wall. Clearly a modern addition, the steel supports were secured with heavy anchor bolts driven into the ironstone. Here and there, Barrow could pick out much older wooden beams fixed to the wall, presumably the remnants of some previous structure.

The light from below swooped and danced along the walls, carrying muffled voices with it. Six figures far below huddled around a burning brazier. Under other circumstances, in another place, these might have been ordinary men enjoying the flame's warmth. The soft glow the flame cast might have been as inviting as any campfire. But with its supplicants cloaked in black robes trimmed with crimson, chanting in some ancient tongue, the arcane ritual was anything but a cheery campfire song. In the ruddy light, the men cast devilish shadows on the stone as they rose and fell in a lengthy series of genuflections.

Each rising crescendo of the ritual they performed was punctuated with a prostration. Whatever verses they droned were lost in the massive chamber's resounding echo, reduced to a reedy murmur by the time it reached Barrow's ears. As far as he could tell, no one among the assembly seemed to be leading the intonation.

"What are they doing?" Emily asked quietly, her eyes wide.

"Another summoning ritual, perhaps," Barrow answered, "though not one I recognize from the motions alone. For all I can tell from here, they might simply be praying to some forgotten god." He chuckled. "It could even be that they're working to keep control over the lich they raised, not realizing we've already dispatched the thing."

"Should we not...I don't know. Shouldn't we *do* something about them?"

"I'm open to suggestions."

"Couldn't you..." She waggled her fingers. "I don't know. Fire, or something?"

Barrow shook his head. "They're still men, Miss Skye. Misled and twisted in their thinking and in their actions, certainly, but men nonetheless. Even if I could from up here, I wouldn't kill them out of hand. You can't just go around murdering everyone who disagrees with you. You have to give them a chance to see the error of their ways. It's rather hard for a man to do that after you've set him ablaze."

"Sentimental human foolishness," Hobnail put in with a sneer. "They're trying to kill you, or have you already forgotten?"

Barrow shrugged. "Be that as it may, I've seen what happens when spells of bane backfire on those casting them." He once more thought back to Edward Osgood. "I sincerely hope I'm never so deep in the soup as to have to risk trying my hand at such nonsense. Even if you don't immolate yourself in the process, you run a very real risk of being consumed by the vile forces that make dark magic possible once you start dabbling in it. You're putting your very soul on the line."

He hoped the look he leveled at Miss Skye as he said this helped the point sink in. He didn't think he had to worry too much there; the girl might have been young and headstrong, but whatever else she was, she was clearly no fool. She seemed as appalled by the Cabal's depredations as he was, if not more so.

The look she returned held some reservation, as though

she thought he was right but remained far from happy about admitting it. "So what do we do, then?" she asked, folding her arms across her chest and cocking her head to one side.

"Absolutely nothing," Barrow said. "We'll let the Triune Congress know about this ritual chamber, of course, but for now we move on as quietly as we can, cross to the other side of this cavern, and leave these acolytes to their games."

"Hold up a moment," Hobnail said, pausing as he drifted along another narrow tunnel. He dropped to the floor, put his nose to the ground, and inhaled deeply. "Yes, that's it! I have the scent once more."

"Are you certain?" Barrow asked, looking back the way they had come. The passage leading from the ritual chamber had been joined by another a few hundred feet back, and the trio had continued along the way they had been headed rather than pursuing the adjoining branch.

"Of course I'm certain." Hobnail sneered, snorted noisily, and spat on the floor. "You know, Mr. Barrow, with all the trouble and danger you've put me through since we made our deal, I'm thinking I ought to have held out for two boons from you."

"Perhaps so," Barrow said impassively, folding his arms across his chest, "but that's the bargain we struck."

Hobnail muttered something under his breath as he set off along the way once more.

The tunnel sloped steadily upward, the incline enough to make Barrow's calves ache. He soon found himself short of breath. Shaking his head, he resolved in that moment, when this affair was all over and done with, to get into the habit of daily calisthenics.

Well, perhaps every second day, he told himself. *Who has time for all that every day?*

"Do you feel that?" Emily asked.

Thankful for the momentary rest, Barrow paused. Sure enough, he could feel a soft breeze coming from somewhere up ahead on his cheeks and hands. Tiny hairs on the back of his neck bristled. He breathed in, smelling a slight salty tang.

"We're near the surface," he said, "and near the waterfront as well, unless I miss my guess." A renewed vigour in his step, he set off toward the end of the passage.

21

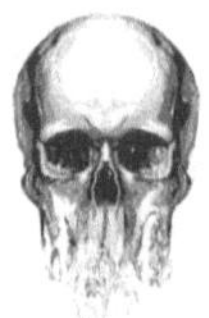

The hatch they emerged from opened into the basement of some warehouse, the room they stood in being nothing more remarkable than a disused storage space. Wooden shelves lining the walls sagged against each other, and splintered and rotting remnants of broken barrels were piled in one corner. Evident even against the grime, recent footprints tracked through the dust, telling Barrow the place was not as neglected as it appeared.

He poked his head out into the corridor, making sure there was no one around before calling the others forth. Compared to the subterranean labyrinth they had followed to get here, it seemed a fairly modern facility. The walls were made of interlocking concrete blocks, and gas lamps mounted every few feet provided ample illumination.

"I think this is the place," Emily said, looking around the rather nondescript corridor. "I tell you this, Mr. Barrow, when this is all said and done, I hope never to see the inside of another basement or tunnel."

"I can't disagree with you much there, Miss Skye," Barrow agreed, keeping to himself that he would rather have spent the last several hours in his own underground workshop. He didn't feel the need to nitpick on the point. "Are you sure, though? These places all look much the same, in my experience."

"I believe so," she said. "It smells the same, and I've definitely heard that sound before."

Barrow paused a moment to listen. He heard a low, irregular mechanical hum coming from somewhere further along the passage.

"If this is the end of the trail, then it's also the end of my part in this, and none too soon," Hobnail said, making a show of brushing some imaginary dust from his arms. "I've met my end of the bargain, Barrow, and I'll return at some point to collect on the boon you owe me."

"I'll look forward to our next meeting, Hobnail McSorely," Barrow said dryly. "Give my regards to Queen Titania the next time you're at Oberon's court."

With an obscene gesture, the faerie spun around in the air, and was gone.

Emily stared at the space he had occupied. "Well, how do you like that?"

"I can't say that I'm sad to see him go, but we wouldn't have made it this far without his help," Barrow said, checking his watch. It was just under an hour past midnight. He had lost all track of the time while in the tunnels. "Let's move on."

"The room with the crates of memory cylinders was upstairs," Emily said as they left the storage room and started down the corridor.

The rhythmic mechanical noise grew louder as they crept along the passage. At first, Barrow assumed it was something in the building's heating and cooling system, but the tone and tempo were off. It gnawed at his curiosity.

Before too long, the corridor came to an end. To the left, a set of stairs went up to the ground level. There was also a mechanical lift, large enough to carry several pallets of heavy freight. On the right-hand side was a large wooden sliding door, the wide oak slats framed with iron. The noise was louder here than anywhere else.

With a glance toward the stairs, Barrow cupped his hand around his ear and leaned toward the door. "This won't take long, Miss Skye," he said.

"Don't you think we'd best move on, Mr. Barrow?" Emily asked, glancing over her shoulder. "Find what we came for, then get out of here before we're discovered?"

"A few minutes, just to see what's making that racket, then we'll head upstairs."

Emily rolled her eyes, but kept any protest to herself.

Gripping the handle, Barrow was pleased to find the large door unlocked. It was heavy, but well-greased casters carried it along the track with ease.

Their eyes soon adjusted to dim lighting in the large room, though the far corners remained cloaked in shadow. The unadorned hydrostone walls reminded him of his underground workshop, though this space was larger by far than his own hideaway. It was also a good deal colder. The hairs on the back of his neck stood up in the chill, and he could see his own breath as he exhaled.

Cool steam eddied about the chamber, clinging to the dusty concrete floor. An array of pipes ran up the walls and along the ceiling overhead, dripping condensation as they disappeared into the dark corners. The conduits struck Barrow as being a recent addition to the space, bracketed to the walls haphazardly. Many of those pipes also ran across the floor, feeding into the base of a raised octagonal dais at the center of the room.

Barrow stepped over a few of the pipes absently, drawn forward by the increasingly loud mechanical noise. He could tell now that it was coming from the platform. A web of hoses and heavy cabling spun out from the underside of the dais in all directions, connected to instrument panels placed throughout the immediate area. Every twenty seconds, a blast of air hissed from underneath the platform, sending the mist swirling across the floor.

Three steps brought him up onto the platform, face to face with the capsule. It was the only word that seemed appropriate for the odd, oblong object, made of riveted steel panels and fixed to the dais with heavy brackets. It was slightly larger than a casket, rounded on all edges, and was held closed with a series of substantial pneumatic swing clamps. The only other notable feature on the capsule's exterior was a large circular pane of glass, which looked like a ship's porthole, ringed with brass and set near one end of the top. It was obscured with condensation, but a faint light shone from within.

Barrow had a quick look at a few pressure gauges and reams of paper inscribed with what looked like seismic readouts. Without knowing the machine's purpose, though, the readings meant little to him.

"What is all this?" Emily asked as she came up beside him.

Between the humming noise and his fascination with the machinery, he hadn't noticed her following along as he had approached the capsule. "I don't know," he said, tentatively placing one hand on the porthole glass. It was cold to the touch, but not uncomfortably so. He examined the dampness that beaded on his fingertips. "Just water," he said quietly before wiping away more of the condensation. Peering into the capsule, he fought back a shudder.

The woman inside was beautiful. Flaxen hair lay about bare shoulders, and in the soft white light within the capsule, her skin was the colour of fresh cream. She looked as though she could have been sleeping peacefully, if not for her pallor.

She lay perfectly still, though, not even breathing. Barrow couldn't see any signs of physical injury.

Emily gasped when she looked over his shoulder and saw her. "Dear God," she said, reaching for the pneumatic clamps. "We've got to get her out of there."

"Wait!" Barrow exclaimed, grabbing her firmly by the wrist before she could twist the first clamp's handle.

Emily stared at him. "You just want to leave her in there?"

"We've got no idea who she is, but more to the point, we don't know why she's in there. I've never seen anything like this machine, Miss Skye, nothing even remotely like it." He shrugged. "Without knowing what it's doing to her, I don't dare open it up and pull her out. For all we know, if she even is alive, doing so could kill her."

Emily thought that over for a moment before nodding, ceding the point. "We've got to help her somehow, though," she persisted. "Whatever they've done to her, it's not right to leave her locked up inside some machine."

"I won't disagree there," Barrow said as he let go of her wrist. "And once we know just what we're dealing with here, we'll help her if we can. I promise you that. Come on, let's see if we can figure out what we're looking at here."

Barrow scratched at his chin as he studied the myriad instrument panels on the dais for a few minutes. Most of the gauges were unlabeled. He finally threw his hands up in defeat; none of them offered any clues to the contraption's purpose, nor the identity of the woman within.

Emily went around the far side of the platform to investigate another series of controls. Trusting her not to do anything rash, he stepped down from the dais. There was a bulky desk nearby, piled high with papers and other assorted bric-a-brac, and an oversized chair off to one side.

Had he been an odontophobe, he would have run

screaming from the room. Instead, he crossed over to have a closer look. The sadistic-looking chair was equipped with restraint straps for the patient's arms, legs, and chest. The headrest had its own restraints, but that wasn't the most unsettling thing about it. It was shaped like an inverted U, leaving easy access to where the spine met the base of the skull. Bloodstains on the concrete floor told of the gruesome deeds that had been performed on those unlucky enough to find themselves in the chair.

The instrument of those acts was also at hand. A segmented armature mounted on a swivel was bolted to one side of the chair. At its end was an electric drill, unlike anything Barrow had seen before. A series of rubber tubes fit one side of the casing, and there was a large pneumatic coupling mounted just behind the chuck. The drill also had an attached electric lamp and an eyepiece, presumably to give the operator a closer look at his subject. The entire assembly looked to have been custom fabricated.

Barrow flipped the switch on the electric light, half expecting nothing to happen. The filament began to glow almost immediately. Backed by a parabolic mirror, the illumination it cast was focused into a remarkably bright, narrow beam.

He smiled. Gas lamps remained the common standard for good reason; Edison's goal of making electric bulbs quickly and cheaply enough for everyday use was still far from becoming reality. His bulbs remained costly and hard to come by. Whoever had put this wicked assembly together had spared no expense.

Taking his own loupe from his pocket, he leaned in to more closely examine the drill's augur. Four inches in length, it terminated in a fine point. Under the loupe's magnification, he noted that the point was hollow.

"It would appear this is what they used to extract the

victims' brain matter," he said quietly. He spoke more for his own benefit than anything else; Emily was still on the far side of the dais. "This contraption would hardly be portable, though. They must have done the extractions here, and then dumped the bodies elsewhere."

He paused, looking over the chair itself once more. The leather restraining straps showed signs of use, scuffed and worn where the buckles would have held them fast as the victims...

As the victims fought against them while these maniacs drilled into their skulls. The realization made his stomach turn. *Dear God, they were alive through the whole ordeal.*

He grabbed the chair's arm to steady himself, and the drill armature swung off to the side, casting its narrow light into one dark corner of the room. Something metallic caught that light and reflected it back at him. He only saw it for a moment as the light danced across the darkness, but the thing was familiar.

Seizing the drill, he pointed the light on that spot once more, and felt a moment of confusion. Standing against the wall was the body of an automaton. As he walked towards it, he recognized it as the same advanced prototype unit he had discovered a few days ago in Harold Penhold's warehouse.

The unit's head was still absent from its body, but on a table, to one side of the machine he found several pieces of rubbery material, laid out like a set of fresh clothes. The stuff had a pinkish tan hue and varied in thickness from a quarter to nearly a half-inch. Picking up one of the pieces, he was struck by how much it felt like human skin. He instantly saw that the piece he held terminated in four slender fingers, cut off at the second knuckle.

Realization dawning, he pressed the rubbery piece against the metal fingers of the automaton's hand. It molded seamlessly to the chassis: a perfect fit. The result looked astonishingly lifelike and, he thought, decidedly feminine.

Suspicion began to dawn on him as he glanced from the capsule in the center of the room to the headless automaton and back, thinking all the while of Henry Feele's autotype memory cylinder and the murdered psychiatric patient, Jenny Perkins.

He bounded over to the desk beside the dais and snatched up a folder stuffed with pages, one of several stacked on the desk. His suspicions were more or less confirmed as he read the name on the folder's index tab, written in a steady hand:

Morgentaler, Annelise.

The same name was written on every folder in the stack. Before he could tell Emily what he had found, Barrow's attention was called to the far end of the room by a low metallic grinding noise. Compared to the capsule's rhythmic hum, this was a ragged cacophony. Two points of blue light appeared in the shadows, slowly moving together through the darkness as if scanning the room.

A massive automaton took shape as it emerged from the shadows. Unlike the streamlined unit that lay dormant nearby, this was no sleek, refined prototype. A hulking form, the machine was taller than Barrow by nearly two feet and similarly broad across the shoulders, its exterior cladding all rivets and heavy panels that clanged and scraped against each other as it moved. Wires and hoses hung from gaps in its armoured paneling, and a large canister of some sort swung from a bracket on the machine's left hip.

This was clearly a machine of pure, brute purpose. A machine of war.

The construct moved slowly at first, each gesture accompanied by a series of pneumatic hisses. Like a train building up a head of steam, though, it was soon barreling towards

Barrow, knocking aside anything in its path with great shrugs of its massive shoulders.

"Stay behind the platform, Miss Skye!" he bellowed as the automaton advanced, crossing the room with surprising speed and implacable purpose. The machine's unblinking blue eyes remained fixed on Barrow as the gap narrowed with each thundering step, its metal feet resounding heavily against the concrete.

Showing incredible strength, the machine shoved the heavy desk with one hand, sending it clattering across the room. Papers and instruments scattered to the floor. Barrow felt a momentary annoyance at that—he would need the information in those documents if he was going to help Annelise Morgentaler.

Of course, he had to survive the hulking automaton's onslaught first. The thing was upon him, and he scarcely had time to unholster the Webley before the machine crashed into him, ramming his chest with one big arm and sending him tumbling to the floor.

Carried forward by inertia, the automaton barreled into a standing metal cabinet packed with medical supplies. The cabinet crumpled as though it were made of nothing sturdier than waxed paper. Syringes, sample bottles, rolls of gauze, and a myriad of surgical instruments spilled across the floor.

Barrow managed to hold onto the Webley as he hit the concrete, feeling the weapon's elemental energy building as he rolled clear of the mess. He took aim carefully, knowing he wasn't likely to get a second shot off against the automaton.

Lightning arced from the barrel of the gun as he pulled the trigger, striking the automaton in the shoulder. The machine rocked back on its heels and windmilled its hefty arms to keep its balance, but did not fall. Barrow watched intently, wondering what mechanical workings kept the machine upright under such a blast of elemental force. The weapon, far exceeding its intended lethality, had felled a mature tree with ease.

He didn't have much time to ponder it, though. Relatively unfazed by the Webley's lightning blast, the machine stood over Barrow now. He tried to roll aside, but the automaton bent down and scooped him up, wrapping its massive arms around his middle.

His left arm was pinned uselessly between his chest and that of the automaton, and his weapon fell to the floor. That annoyed him less than it might have otherwise—the Webley would need a few minutes to rebuild its elemental charge before it would be able to fire anyway.

He smelled machine grease and steel and stale sweat, and instantly felt absurd for noticing his own lapsed hygiene at such a moment. The machine squeezed, hydraulics steadily closing its arms around Barrow's chest. His already tender ribs cried out in protest, and he heard at least one of the bones crack under the pressure.

Barrow desperately scrabbled at the thing's head with his free hand, hoping to at least distract it enough to worm out of its clutches, but the machine barely seemed to notice as he swatted at it. He managed to get the very tips of his fingers in between two panels and pulled at the metal plate with all the force he could muster from such an awkward position. The panel came away in his hand and clattered to the floor, but the stink that filled his nostrils was anything but mechanical.

Fighting back the bile rising in his throat, Barrow stared up in revulsion at sallow, pockmarked skin and a bestubbled jawline, marred with a row of bleeding puncture wounds. The skin of the cheeks around the circular eyepieces was scarred, crusted with dried blood and pus. Parched and cracking lips peeled back from yellowed teeth as the thing bellowed in pain. The sound was at once both mechanical and pitiably human.

He had little time to contemplate it before he was tossed aside like a ragdoll, falling against a web of cables and hoses that fed into the base of the dais. Several of the lines came free of their couplings, twisting across the floor like writhing serpents as whatever gasses they carried spewed into the room. Barrow groaned softly as he rolled to his knees, holding his injured ribs.

The machine—no, the *man-machine*—staggered, clutching at its exposed mouth. Dark blood seeped slowly between metal fingers. Though the wounds along the thing's jaw were fresh, the trickling ichor looked more congealed than fluid. Irrationally, Barrow thought of cherry jelly.

"Hey!" Emily called out from across the room. "Over here, you ugly mechanical bastard!" She had found a metal prisebar somewhere, which she wielded like a cricket bat. Her skin had paled, but her eyes burned furiously.

Turning towards her, the man-machine moved slowly. Each step it took towards her seemed to take a great deal of concentration.

Barrow shook his head to clear the cobwebs. *I can't let her try to fight that thing.*

Without another thought, he grabbed for one of the loose cables on the floor, an electrical line nearly as thick as his wrist. Taking care to hold onto the insulated sheathing, he staggered after the man-machine, sparks crackling from the hank of exposed wires at the end of the cable.

This is utter madness, he thought, each step sending a fresh wave of pain through his midsection. *I seem to be saying that rather a lot lately, though.*

Coming up behind the behemoth, Barrow took a half-second to choose just the right spot, then jammed the raw end of the cable into the man-machine's back, wedging it into a gap between two steel plates just above its left hip. He was thrown backward—whether by the small electrical explosion or by a spasmodic swing of the man-machine's arm, he couldn't say—landing once again in a heap near the base of the dais.

With another groan, he looked up to the towering man-machine. It had turned away from Miss Skye to set its steady gaze on him once more. Metal squealed against metal as it tried to take a step, then staggered and fell to one knee. Tendrils of black smoke rose from its chassis, filling the air with the stink of burning oil and flesh. Its left arm hung uselessly at its side. A severed hose dangled from the metal canister on its hip, dripping some viscous, milky-white fluid onto the floor.

A strangled, animal snarl came from its throat as it struggled back onto its feet. Instead of heading towards Barrow, though, the man-machine turned awkwardly and loped toward the doorway, dragging its left leg behind it. It reared back and smashed down on the door hardware with its good arm, sending the pieces scattering across the concrete floor. It heaved on the handle, sending the massive wood and iron door sliding along its track as though it weighed nothing at all. Then, without so much as a look over its massive metal shoulder, the man-machine was gone, leaving just the smell of burnt metal and the fading echo of its clanging footsteps hanging in the air.

Emily dropped the prisebar and hurried over to help Barrow as he struggled to his feet. "What on earth was that?"

Barrow shook his head. "I don't know, Miss Skye," he said, wincing. "Some horrid marriage of flesh and machine. I've never seen the like, nor even heard of such a thing." He had fallen hard, taking the brunt on his right shoulder. He pushed against it with the heel of his other hand. The pain was blinding, but the arm didn't seem to have come out of its socket. He muttered his thanks for that small miracle. "When this is all over and done with, I'm spending a week in bed," he declared. "Let's see if we can't find a bandage or something to wrap around my ribs."

They found several cloth bandages in the debris the man-machine had scattered across the floor, and Emily was helping him tie one off when they were distracted by a hissing squeal from the capsule on the dais. Triggered by some automatic system, the levers on the clamps holding the lid shut swung open. A rush of cold air carrying a chemical reek hit Barrow in the face as the lid of the capsule opened slightly. An alarm bell blared from one of the consoles nearby, its shrill tone reverberating through the room.

"Might we want to leave the area as well, Mr. Barrow?"

"Another grand suggestion, Miss Skye," Barrow agreed as he buttoned his shirt. With some difficulty, he shrugged back into his jacket, not even fretting at the freshly-torn shoulder seam. "Someone will no doubt be along soon to see what's the matter. Frankly, with the ruckus just now, I'm surprised no one has come to see yet." He clicked his tongue between his teeth in disapproval. "Rather a slipshod operation, this."

He picked up and holstered the Webley. "At any rate, I should think we would want to exit by a different way than our mechanical friend. I think I saw a staircase at the other end of the room. One moment, though." With a wince, he knelt to pick up the piece of the man-machine's faceplate he had torn from the thing's mask.

The piece was nearly featureless, fabricated from a single plate of steel and surprisingly lightweight for its size, with two small round vents set on either side. He wondered if the thing had to breathe. It was, he had to admit, a very impressive piece of precision metalwork.

His admiration for the piece was short-lived, though. Turning it over in his hand, he choked back a gasp. Gelatinous-looking blood beaded on the bifurcated ends of the rivets on the inside of the panel. "My God," he said, his voice near a whisper as he pulled his loupe from his pocket and set it to his eye. As the lens focused on the row of bent rivet shafts, he felt his stomach lurch once more. The sticky blood on the pins was flecked with bits of skin and white fragments of bone. "The fiends bolted it right into his flesh."

2 2

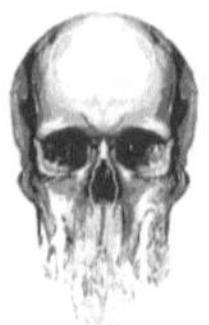

"She's Dr. Morgentaler's *wife?*"

Emily had stopped and turned so suddenly on the stairs that Barrow almost bowled into her. He straightened his tie and nodded. "Inspector Eddings was able to obtain some information on Johan Morgentaler. The doctor's wife had contracted an unknown illness that was slowly paralyzing her body while leaving her mind intact. He had become something of a recluse while he sought a cure, and no one had seen Annelise for several years. Everyone assumed she had died."

"But he had just locked her away inside that machine?"

"So it would seem," Barrow said. "I would need more time to study the machine to be certain, but I believe its purpose is to slow her metabolic processes to a point near death, prolonging her life until he could find a cure for her condition." He winced as a wave of pain from his ribs shot through his body. "In a way, it's rather ingenious. Quite a few mammals go into a state of hibernation and sleep right through the winter, and Dr. Morgentaler seems to have devised a machine to mimic that process."

226

"A hibernation chamber," Emily said, giving a name to the contraption.

Barrow couldn't help but smile at that. Somehow, having a name for the machine made the idea of it seem less farfetched. "Just so. I doubt she can survive in there indefinitely, though. Even with her metabolism dramatically slowed, the sickness is still ravaging her body. Its progression is only retarded, not fully halted. At most he's postponing the inevitable, and he has to know he's running out of time. Speaking of which, shall we continue along?"

They continued upward, taking care to make as little noise as possible. Barrow shook his head at that; if the ruckus he had made fighting the man-machine hadn't alerted the Cabal to their presence, nothing they did now was likely to draw its notice.

"The inspector always says there are two main motivations for murder," he said, "love, or money. All this time I've been under the assumption Dr. Morgentaler was trying to build a better memory cylinder, hoping to profit from the commercial applications of the technology. However, now I believe he was trying to find a way to transfer his dying bride's brain from her failing body into that of an automaton."

"All this because he couldn't bear to part with the woman he loves," Emily said. "It's almost rather romantic, wouldn't you say so, Mr. Barrow?"

"What it is, Miss Skye, is utter, grotesque madness, and a complete affront to the natural order of things," Barrow said, scarcely noticing the degree to which his vehemence startled the girl. "What he's trying to achieve would be miraculous if he were to bring his scheme to fruition, but his methods are an abomination. The fact remains that Dr. Morgentaler is murdering innocent people to perfect his process."

"And that...*thing* you fought down there. The mechanical man, that was, what? Some sort of guardian he built?"

"Perhaps." Barrow shrugged, instantly wishing he hadn't done so. He grit his teeth as a stabbing pain shot through his shoulder. He might not have dislocated it in his tussle with the man-machine, but it still ached fiercely. He frowned and shook his head. "Still too much guesswork going on here," he muttered in frustration. "Let's keep moving."

Emily led the way. Barrow wasn't eager to put the girl out front, but she had been here before and he hadn't. Despite the discoveries in the makeshift laboratory downstairs, he still wanted to see the stockpile of memory cylinders for himself, just to see how busy Dr. Morgentaler and the Cabal had been.

A door at the top of the stairs opened into the rear end of a large warehouse area. He could see now that the building was a large customs house. As freight arrived from overseas and was brought up from the docks, this was where import duties would be assessed and ultimately collected by their recipients. Row upon row of pallets and crates ran the length of the building, their contents awaiting inspection.

The perfect place for Morgentaler's operation, Barrow thought. *Supplies and equipment could be moved in and out of here without drawing any notice whatsoever. He must have the customs officers in his pocket.*

A large rat chittered angrily and scampered off into the shadows. The customs house was otherwise deserted. Barrow glanced up at dark windows, then at his pocket watch. There were still a few hours before the morning shift would arrive. Regardless, they hurried as they made their way along the corridor, uneager to spend more time here than was necessary.

"Down this way," Emily said, heading for another set of stairs. These lead to a mezzanine level, where a row of small offices looked out over the customs house.

A few of the doors along the corridor were open. The

sheer amount of paperwork stacked on some of the desks made Barrow cringe. When it came to his own work, he reveled in the minutiae, but this was another level entirely. He recognized the importance of accounting and inventory management, but was quite happy to leave such cheeseparing to someone else.

Emily strode towards a closed door at the very end of the corridor. There was little to set it aside from any of the others, but she seemed confident. Barrow sputtered and choked on a few words of caution as she grabbed the handle and swung the door open before he could say much of anything. Swearing under his breath, he followed her into the room.

The windowless room was darker than the corridor had been. The light seeping in from the hall helped, but not much. It took a few moments for his eyes to adjust to the gloom. A faint odour of raisins hung in the air.

That struck him as odd, but he paid it little mind as he scanned the room. It appeared to be another storage room, though what seemed to be stored here was mostly clutter and junk. He looked past the pile of broken chairs, boxes of unsorted papers, and an old desk piled with bits of this and that, picking out a large crate in one corner.

He picked up a prisebar and wedged it under the top of the crate. With what strength he was able to coax from his injured shoulder and ribs, he leaned into the bar and felt the wood come apart.

The crate was full of oversized memory cylinders like the one he had removed from Henry Feele's autotype machine. Packed in straw in two rows of eight, there had to be dozens of them stacked in the deep crate. However, these cylinders were empty, little more than glass tubes capped with copper enclosures at each end. They might almost have been beautiful in the simplicity of their design, were it not for their grisly purpose.

Barrow was musing over that when the door to the corridor behind them slammed shut. Despite the unmistakable sound of a bar and lock being secured from the other side, he ran toward the door and beat his fists against it. The futility of that quickly sunk in. He slumped against the door and slid to the floor.

"What do we do now?" Emily folded her arms across her chest. "Sit here and wait for someone to come along and put an end to us?"

Glaring up at her, Barrow rubbed at his temples. "That's really not helping, Miss Skye."

"Well, don't you have some explosives of some sort in your kit?"

"Why would I have explosives?"

"You seem to have everything else you could ever need," she shrugged. "Couldn't you make, I don't know...some gunpowder or something?"

"Not with anything I have on me. It's not as easy as just mixing together a few elements that happen to be handy, you know."

"How about the freezing compound from the sanitarium?"

"Breaking the door handle apart wouldn't get us anywhere. It's barred and locked from the other side." He smiled then. "I see what you're up to, Miss Skye."

"Whatever do you mean, Mr. Barrow?"

"Keeping my mind working in the face of futility," he said, rising to his feet. He nodded towards the pile of rubbish. "Perhaps there's something here we can use to get this door open. Let's see what we can find."

Before they had much of a chance to look, though, Barrow heard a sound he knew well from his own laboratory: a valve, spewing gas. A brass canister the length of his forearm sat among the detritus atop the desk, a valve at one end dispensing a lilac-tinged gas into the room. It carried the sickly-sweet smell of overripe fruit.

"Eldersight!" Barrow coughed, snapping up the canister. "They've gasified the eldersight!" He fumbled with the valve, trying to close it off. "No use. Whatever they used to remotely open the valve—magical or mundane—it fused the metal." He threw the canister into the farthest corner. The gas continued to fill the room.

Pressing a handkerchief to his face, he frantically glanced around. There was a small ventilation grate, high up near the ceiling. Lean though he was, the opening was surely too narrow for him to squeeze his shoulders through. But there were no windows, and the door was solidly locked.

He turned to Emily. "Miss Skye, if I can remove that grating, I think we might escape through the ducts."

She eyed the opening warily, but nodded.

He rummaged through the pile and dragged a wooden chair with a wobbly leg across the room, leaning it against the wall. It wasn't the sturdiest booster, but it didn't have to hold for long. Climbing up on it, he was relieved to find the vent cover was held in place by nothing more substantial than a few small metal clips. He bent these outward, tossed the grate aside with a clatter, and hopped down to the floor.

Heavier than air, the eldersight gas hung low around the floor. It swirled near his knees, even as the canister continued to pump the stuff into the room. Before too much longer, they would both be overcome.

He ushered Emily to the vent, helping her clamber up on the chair to reach the opening. "I'll be right behind you," he told her as she looked back at him. Nodding, she hauled herself up into the opening, swearing loudly as her knee scraped against the duct's metal edge. She disappeared from sight.

His shoulders sagging slightly, Barrow knelt and picked

up the vent grating. He climbed up on the chair, set it back in place, and secured the clips.

Emily's voice was muffled, its echo metallic, but he heard her clearly. "Mr. Barrow, what are you doing?"

"I never would have fit through the duct," he called after her. "You can still escape, though. Get yourself to safety, Miss Skye."

"But what about you? You can't just stay here and wait to die!"

"I'll figure something out," he said, hoping he sounded more confident than the felt. "I always do."

"But—"

"Go," he commanded.

Emily said nothing in response to that. He waited a moment, hearing only the sound of the eldersight gas issuing into the room. Finally, he heard the muffled metallic sound of her worming her way through the ductwork.

Satisfied that she was on her way to safety, he set to seeing what was at hand that he might use to engineer his own escape. He had been right the first time; aside from the crates of memory cylinders, the storage room was full of junk —broken furniture, a roll of heavily-worn carpet, old office supplies.

He gave a moment's thought to using the Webley to blast the door off its hinges, but quickly dismissed the idea. In such close quarters, the overpowered weapon was just as likely to smear his innards across the walls as anything else.

Still holding his handkerchief to his face, he sat on the wobbly chair. All in all, it was utterly useless.

❧

REALITY DETONATED IN A SHOWER OF COLOUR AND sound. He had the sensation of falling at an incredible speed through endless clouds, indigo and crimson light blasting all around him as he tumbled ever downward.

Gravity and the tangible world suddenly returned, and he staggered and lurched under its weight.

Every object in the room turned itself inside out as Barrow saw their innermost workings picked apart and spread before him. Every screw and panel, every wire and filament was laid out as they would be in an exploded diagram of assembly instructions. He saw not just the components, but somehow knew the history of how each piece had come to be.

With rapt fascination, he watched as a small machine—a McGill-style staple punch—pulled itself apart and laid its parts neatly on the table it sat upon. He realized with a start that this was no illusion; the machine had actually disassembled itself under his gaze. *Is this mechanokinesis? Technokinesis?* he wondered, scrabbling to find a word for the impossible phenomenon.

Forcing his eyes shut, he fought against the sensory glut. Exhausted by the effort, he collapsed to the floor. The floorboards gave up the memories of a time before the French and English rowed ashore and fought over this land, when the Mi'kmaq still fished in the inlet they called *Chebucto*. These boards had been trees then, barely more than saplings, but they remembered.

They whispered a song of an unspoiled green world, wistful and sweet. Barrow could smell the foliage in their words. He wanted to weep, knowing he would never be able to recall or recreate the song's simple beauty.

He plunged downward through the floor, or at least felt as if he had. The sickly sweet smell of the eldersight filled his head as the torrent of formless colour surrounded him once more. Anything tangible in his surroundings melted away, and he knew his mind had been wholly divorced from reality.

A woman's face appeared before him, coalescing from the aether, and he needed a moment to recognize her as the woman from the metal capsule.

Annelise, the young wife of Johan Morgentaler.

She was flawless. Sickness had robbed her of her body, but in this non-place, she moved as gracefully as a swan upon still waters.

She reached out, her fingertips lightly touching Barrow's cheek. Warmth flooded into him at her gentle caress. Her expression held concern and, he thought, a gentle sadness.

Thank you, she said with a faint smile, and then she faded away, back into the aether.

23

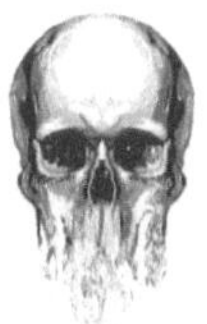

Somewhere in the distance, a clock chimed four.

Barrow forced his eyes open, the effort making his head throb. Lilac haze tinged the edges of his vision like a creeping miasma.

His wits felt like mud as his mind slowly chugged to life, like a locomotive pulling away from the siding. "That's good," he muttered to himself, "if you can draw an analogy like that, you've probably not suffered any permanent brain injury."

As he struggled to get his feet under him, he found with some alarm that his limbs didn't want to cooperate. Several panicked seconds passed before he realized his ankles and wrists were bound with thick cord, his hands lashed to something behind his back. *A post of some kind?* He couldn't tell.

Cold wind against his face helped him shake off some of the cobwebs. He could tell he was somewhere outdoors, and he surmised from the near-absolute darkness surrounding him that he was no longer in the city.

With some difficulty, he separated the pounding in his head from the other sounds around him. Distant peals of thunder played at the edge of his sensorium, but he also heard a lower, constant rumbling. Once he was able to isolate that particular sound in his ear, it became entirely familiar—a massive, idling engine.

He was on the deck of a steamship.

His other senses started to fill in the details. He could smell the acrid exhaust from the ship's engine and feel the rocking of choppy waves beneath him. His mouth felt like it was full of cotton batting and tasted like something scraped off the inside of a malting vat.

Lingering effects of the eldersight gas, he thought, slowly remembering the events that had brought him here.

Another of those details filled itself in. "Ah, Mr. Barrow, good to see you're still with us," said an accented voice. It sounded hollow and faraway. But it was also chillingly familiar.

Barrow looked up, his eyes slowly coming into focus. The foggy aftereffects of the eldersight made that more difficult than it might have been otherwise, but he knew his captor; Johan Morgentaler stood over him, the hem of his black riding cape flapping in the breeze. He held a gun in one hand.

Half-hidden by shadow, a second figure stood nearby. Blinking his eyes several times, it took Barrow a few moments to recognize Lai Jūn. Clad in black silk garments trimmed with red, the mystic said nothing, but seemed relaxed, almost uninterested as he regarded the scene with an uncharacteristic impassivity.

"This is really a rather impressive piece, Mr. Barrow," Morgentaler said, hefting the gun in his hand. The revolver's cylinder glowed a pale blue. Barrow's heart sunk as he realized he was looking at his own enhanced Webley, the persistent effects of the eldersight somehow making the lightning elemental contained within the gun visible.

"Quite impressive, indeed. I can feel the power building within it."

"It's hardly my best work," Barrow deadpanned. "The weapon's payload is well beyond—"

"Yes, yes," Morgentaler interrupted. "Far more lethal than necessary. I saw what happened to that oak tree out on Campbell Road. I would suggest you consider adding an elemental inhibitor circuit to regulate the discharge, were I planning to let you leave here in one piece."

Barrow struggled to shrug his shoulders, which was no easy thing, given his bound state. "Why don't you just kill me, then?"

"Kill you?" Morgentaler chuckled mirthlessly. "I have far grander plans for you, Barrow. Your mind would be an invaluable asset if I could bring it under my thumb. Of course, thanks to your meddling in things that don't concern you, I'll have to rebuild my laboratory before that can happen."

Barrow was distracted by a shadow crossing over the face of the moon. It was a fleeting thing, visible for little more than a second or two, but struck him as impossibly large for any bird, save perhaps an albatross. He shook his head at that; Halifax lay far north of the usual range of the great solitary sea birds. He wondered if what he had seen might be just another aftereffect of the eldersight.

Forcing his drifting attention back to more pressing matters, he leveled his gaze at Dr. Morgentaler. "How do you mean? What plans?"

"You're to be my new laboratory assistant," Morgentaler said. He spoke with confidence, as though the decision had already been made. "Your blundering has set my work back, but I was able to reseal the chamber before too much time had passed. Annelise has lost several months as a result of your interference, but with you working at my side, I'm certain I can perfect the cerebral transfer process in short order."

In spite of his position, Barrow had to laugh at that. "You can't possibly believe I would ever work with you, Morgentaler?" he snarked, his voice acidic. "You may be possessed of a brilliant scientific mind, but you're a sadistic butcher."

Morgentaler waved that aside. "You'll not have much choice in the matter, Mr. Barrow, once I've transferred the contents of your cranium into that of one of my automaton bodies."

That left Barrow speechless.

"Of course, my process is as yet imperfect, so only those select aspects of your mind which are of use to me will make the leap." His lips skinned back in a predatory grin. "The rest —the *refuse*—will remain in this body, not that it'll be of much use to you. In fact, I've already prepared your bed at Hemlock Overlook."

Struggling against his restraints, Barrow cried out in agony. The analgesic effects of the drug must've been wearing off; the pain had returned to ravage his ribs and shoulder. He hadn't realized how blissfully unaware he had been of his injuries while waking from his fugue.

"My Annelise, Barrow," Morgentaler continued. "It was so unfair, the way the sickness took her from me. You can't know what a torture it is to watch someone so full of life slip away an inch at a time." He ran his fingers through his white hair as a tear welled in one corner of his eye, the only hint of emotion Barrow had ever seen from the man. "You'll help me bring her back, though."

"Annelise is already dead, Johan," Barrow said, too exhausted and battered to frame his words carefully. "She was dead before you ever sealed her in that machine of yours. There's no bringing her back, and even if you could, she wouldn't be the woman you loved."

"Ah, but that's where you're wrong!" Morgentaler seethed, crouching down and waving the Webley in Barrow's face. "Simple necromancy couldn't restore her, as you know, and medical science is every bit as impotent. But a marriage of the two, Barrow!" He was raving now, his eyes wild as the wind whipped through his white hair. "Necrotechnology! Now, that would do it! Can't you *imagine* the possibilities?"

The enormity of Morgentaler's loss may have drawn pity, but Barrow had seen enough of the madman's handiwork to feel anything but revulsion. "What you're proposing is an affront to the natural order," he said. "People get sick, Johan. People die, many of them sadly before their time. That's how it's supposed to be."

Morgentaler responded by smacking Barrow across the jaw with the butt end of the revolver. "Simple rules are for simple men, Barrow. Perhaps you'll see the sense of that soon enough."

Barrow spat blood onto the deck of the ship. "And what of Jenny Perkins?"

"She was nobody," Morgentaler answered frostily. "They all were. Insignificant, but I gave their lives meaning. Their gifts to science will be their legacy!"

Now it was Barrow's turn to seethe. "She was a person. She had a little girl named Alice, and a job in a shop, and she attended church on Sundays. She mattered, Morgentaler! Who are you to take that away from her? What gives you the right to take that from anybody?"

"You disappoint me, Isaac Barrow," Morgentaler sneered. "You claim to be a man of science, a man driven by invention! I can see now that you're little more than a mechanic." He spat the word. "A weak fool, whittling away his days replacing worn-out gears and fan belts for what pennies the affluent are willing to toss your way. Why settle for the mundane, when you could be so much more?"

The swiftly-moving shadow crossed in front of the moon once more, spiraling in a ragged arc. Barrow was certain this time that his mind was not playing tricks on him. He could see the bat-like outline of the wings, and he thought he could hear the sound of canvas stretched taut, cutting through the air.

Even with his brain addled by eldersight, the idea of a massive bird had struck Barrow as too far-fetched. He realized, with no lack of amazement, the reality of what he was looking at was even more impossible.

"Miss Skye?" he whispered.

Borne by the wings of his chiropteran glider, Emily darted out of the night sky towards the steamship. Barrow scarcely had time to wonder how she had come to be flying to the scene before she landed in a tumbling heap on the deck of the ship, sending the flabbergasted Morgentaler and Lai Jūn sprawling to the ship's deck as they leapt clear of her wild path.

She fell heavily on her side as she failed to keep her feet beneath her. The glider's wings retracted as she rolled across the deck, folding flat against her back rather than shearing off. The clatter they made against the planks was still dreadful.

"Well, you weren't wrong about the landings, Mr. Barrow," she said as she clambered to her feet and pushed a pair of welding goggles from her eyes up onto her forehead.

Barrow's mouth hung open for a few moments before he was able to frame a response. "How did you—" he started, then shook his head. Bound as he was to the deck of the ship, the details of her arrival didn't really matter just then.

Emily looked over her shoulder as she struggled with the glider's harness straps. She unbuckled the heavy cross strap and let the contraption fall to the deck of the ship with a clatter, drawing a wince from Barrow. "It's tricky to steer as well.

Perhaps you should consider something to emulate tail feathers?"

"I'll take the suggestion under advisement," Barrow replied sardonically, as he had when Morgentaler had suggested improvements for the Webley. *Everyone's a critic.*

Looking at the glider, he fought back a wave of nausea as the lilac tinge ringing his vision churned, as though the elder-sight still in his veins was a retreating army skirmishing against a pursuant force. The glider's mechanical systems began to disassemble themselves in his mind's eye. Soft and glowing, he saw the essence of the wispy zephyr he had bonded to the glider's structure clinging to each piece. The pure silver ring he set in the frame and used to bond the zephyr shone as bright as a lantern.

He shook his head. With no small effort, he forced the fantastic vision aside. "In the meantime, Miss Skye, do you think you might do something about these ropes?"

In answer, she pulled a knife from a sheath on her belt and set to the task, starting with the cord around his ankles. "I seem to be making a regular habit of getting you out of trouble," she observed as the first of the ropes gave way to the blade.

"I assure you, No one is less enamoured of the idea than I," he replied as the blade cut the ropes, twisting his newly-freed feet in small circles to try to get the blood moving. The coarse rope had chafed, leaving the skin inflamed and raw, but he didn't think he was bleeding.

Before Emily could set to the lashing around Barrow's wrists, though, she was hauled to her feet by Lai Jūn. Her knife fell to the deck as the mystic casually tossed her aside. She spun through the air and bounced off a metal railing, landing in a heap and getting tangled in a mess of carelessly-stowed rigging cordage.

Though slower to regain his footing than Lai Jūn had

been, Morgentaler was also standing once more. He made a show of setting his collar and necktie to rights and smoothing back his hair, affecting a more casual and calculating manner than Barrow thought he might have possessed in the moment. In spite of himself, he respected the man's comportment.

Comported or not, Morgentaler had had enough of Emily's interruption. Almost negligently, he leveled a gloved finger in her direction. "Kill the girl!"

With a predacious grin, Lai Jūn stripped off his robes and pressed his fingers to the dragon tattoo tracked along his torso. As it had at the Theatre Royal, the image took on a wraithlike glow as it peeled away from his skin, doubling and redoubling in size as it climbed into the air. Perhaps due to being called forth with more lethal intent this time, the creature looked even deadlier against the night sky than it had under the theatre's lights.

If nothing else, Barrow had to admit the mystic was a masterful showman, arrogant and grandiose even at a time such as this. *Why does he conjure these beasts to do his killing, when he could simply throw Miss Skye overboard and be done with it?* Barrow wondered, thinking back to his own tussle with Lai Jūn in the alleyway. He resigned himself to the fact that the question would have to remain unanswered.

The spectral dragon whirled and twisted through the air, belching steam and gnashing its wicked teeth. It hung in the air, its eyes fixed on Emily. With a mighty roar, it lunged towards her.

And then it stopped.

The beast hung in the air, frozen in place.

Barrow felt something that he could only describe as a vacuum of magic, a sensation that was something between extreme fatigue and having the wind knocked from his lungs.

Sweat running down his face as he stared up incredulously at his halted conjuration, Lai Jūn howled something sharp. Barrow didn't know what the Chinese mystic had actually said, but he would have wagered it was some variety of colourful invective. Some things transcended language.

He twisted to look over to Emily. The girl was back on her feet, her face a mask of fierce concentration. Somehow, she was holding the spectral dragon at bay. She spoke no words, inscribed no markings at her feet, but a small cyclone of raw transmundane force was beginning to form around the place where she stood.

She raised one hand to the sky above. At her gesture, the wind whipped around her, pulling at her clothing and short-cropped hair. The ship rocked from side to side, buffeted by ferocious waves that slopped over the railing.

Horrified, Barrow could do nothing but look on. Minor weather manipulation was a nearly-impossible feat, and here Emily was calling forth a raging squall. He tried to call out to her, to warn her of the danger she was flirting with, but he knew there was no way she would hear him over the gathering tempest.

The ship pitched hard to starboard, its auxiliary sail masts groaning in protest as they swayed. Barrow slid as the ship lurched, the rope around his wrists digging into his skin and keeping him more or less in place. Both shoulders felt ready to pop out of their sockets. Lai Jūn and Morgentaler staggered. But Emily kept her footing, standing in place as though the soles of her scuffed heavy boots were nailed to the deck.

A waterspout far larger than any wave hurdled over the port side railing in a mad arc and crashed down on the deck at the mystic's feet. Caught in the torrent, Lai Jūn scrabbled to keep his feet under him, ultimately failing as the waters sluiced around him.

The spectral dragon lurched in midair as its master lost his balance. It fell to the deck, landing heavily and dissolving into a shapeless mass of stinking protoplasm. The slippery, sticky stuff didn't remain for long. The cascade of Emily's waterspout continued to drench the ship, washing the eldritch substance away. Anything that wasn't bolted down was swept along with it, including Lai Jūn. He clawed madly for purchase—a railing or a rope or a mooring ring, anything to hold onto—managing to catch hold of a length of chain with one hand at the last moment.

Had the rush of water stopped, he may have been able to hold on. Emily set her teeth. Barrow again felt the heaving feeling in his gut as she redoubled her effort, calling another deluge to crash down on the deck of the ship. The full force of the flood struck Lai Jūn, and he lost his tenuous grip on the chain. With a strangled cry, he was swept overboard, clutching one hand to his ribs as he disappeared from sight.

Emily sank to her hands and knees as the waves rocking the ship began to subside, her breathing heavy. Her shoulders slumped forward. She looked over to Barrow with a weak smile, vomited on the deck of the ship, and collapsed.

The knife she had dropped lay a few feet to Barrow's side. He twisted his hips to try to swing a foot over to it, hoping to nudge it closer with his toe so he might cut the ropes still binding both hands behind his back. Trussed up as he was, the awkward motion felt like a heavy boot kicking against his ribs and shoulder. He inhaled sharply through clenched teeth and tried again.

He had almost reached the blade when it was kicked away. Dripping and red-faced, his white hair askew, Morgentaler stalked away a few paces.

"Death would be too swift for you, Barrow," Morgentaler said, kneeling to draw a few items from a leather valise. "You and the girl both! I've something far more interesting in mind."

With that, the necrotechnologist began to sketch out

designs at his feet on the ship's deck. With each ancient symbol Morgentaler laid down, Barrow's dismay grew. This was not a protection circle or a casting ring; Morgentaler was laying down a summoning circle.

The madman was opening a portal to the Abyss.

24

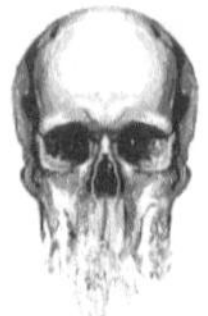

"Don't do this," Barrow pleaded as he redoubled his struggle against his binds. "You won't be able to control whatever you call forth!"

Morgentaler only sneered in response as he began chanting rhythmically in some ancient, guttural tongue. As he spoke, the symbols he had sketched on the ship's deck began to glow, a dull red at first but gaining in brilliance and pulsing in response to Morgentaler's cadence as he droned on toward the awful incantation's diabolical crescendo.

The air crackled with power as a yawning rift opened between realities. Seeming to rise from the deck of the ship itself, the demon Morgentaler called forth from the Abyss blotted the moon from view.

The beast was horrible to behold, standing easily five times the height of a man. It had assumed a roughly human form, though its limbs were exaggerated in length, with its clawed hands falling at the monster's knees. It was nude and grotesquely male. Most chilling of all, the demon's face was a perverse caricature of the man who had summoned it, a mask of Johan Morgentaler's visage twisted in hate and rage.

Barrow knew the body the demon had been forced into did not bear its true likeness. The eldersight still coursing through his veins allowed him to see the fiend for what it truly was, a writhing mass of octopean tentacles and gnashing fangs with a million bloodshot eyes. One moment he saw the demon's hideous true form, the next the body Morgentaler had forced it into, sometimes both at the same time.

Sinuous musculature rippled and writhed beneath its mottled brown skin as its breath steamed in the cold night air. Rationally, Barrow knew what he was watching was the demon's true form struggling to break free of the physical vessel Morgentaler had forced it to inhabit.

"*Caacrinolaas,*" Morgentaler shouted haltingly, enunciating each syllable to ensure he was heard clearly. Hearing its name in a human's mouth, possibly for the first time, the demon's attention fixed on the necrotechnologist. "I have called you forth to act as my servant. You will obey only me until I release you to your own abode!"

The demon snorted and bellowed, a hateful sound, unlike anything the world had heard in centuries. Caacrinolaas, spawned before time itself, was furious to find himself in thrall to this human sorcerer. As long as Morgentaler stood within the summoning circle, though, the demon was powerless to act against him.

The demon kicked out in impotent rage, sending one of the ship's lifeboats spiraling off into the darkness. If it couldn't strike down the one who had enslaved it, the demon would destroy everything else in its path. Barrow was thankful he hadn't yet drawn the beast's notice.

"Come now, Caacrinolaas," Morgentaler chided as though he were admonishing a petulant child. "Such outbursts will gain you nothing. You know what you must do to be freed."

Caacrinolaas hesitated. Though the demon, like all his

kin, was driven by bloodlust, Barrow wondered if his hatred for his captor was strong enough to edge him over from mere recalcitrance to outright defiance. The strength of a demon's will was beyond human measure. Few who found themselves in a position to study such things lived to report their findings.

As things stood now, Barrow would gladly have passed on the opportunity to observe the interplay between summoner and thrall. Some theories, he reminded himself, were better left untested.

The demon turned its gaze toward Barrow and the unconscious Miss Skye. With each step the horror took, the deck of the ship groaned beneath its incalculable weight.

Ice ran through Barrow's veins as he tried to think of some advantage, something he might be able to use to ward off the beast's advance. Try as he might, nothing came to mind.

Perhaps, he thought. *Just perhaps...*

Barrow gave in to the lingering eldersight fugue. Where reality had earlier exploded, now it simply unfolded. With only a fraction of the drug remaining in his system compared to the initial dose, he understood more clearly just how eldersight acted on the mind. The opiate, he realized, increased activity in those parts of the brain—dormant in most people—which made channeling magic energies possible.

No wonder the drug causes permanent psychosis in normal individuals, Barrow mused. *Half a dosage would be the neurochemical equivalent of directing a bolt of lightning through an apple.*

In those with the capacity for magic, though, eldersight would increase their ability. A seer like Mad Ruby would be able to see further into the future and deliver more accurate predictions. A hortimancer might gain the ability to make plants grow with nothing more than a thought.

For a technomancer, it meant an increased understanding and control over mechanical systems. At the moment, that meant the steamship beneath him.

Feeling the idle thrum of the ship's massive engines below, he turned his attention to the deck. Screwing his eyes shut, he focused his mind on seeing through the planking to the workings within.

That wasn't as easy as it had been in the storage room at the customs house; for one, the ship's engines were much more complex system than a mechanical hole punch. As well, several hours had gone by, leaving only traces of the elder-sight in Barrow's blood.

He was distracted as he heard Emily rousing herself. What little colour she still had drained from her face as she stared up at the monstrous beast. Showing impressive fortitude in the face of something she had never, could never have imagined encountering, she hauled herself to her feet and darted over to where Barrow lay.

She had lost her knife, so set to the cordage with her fingers. "These knots are frightfully tight, Mr. Barrow," she observed, trying to prise them loose.

"Leave the ropes," Barrow said shortly, drawing a bewildered look from the girl. "Miss Skye, I need you to get down to the engine room. Open every throttle and give me every ounce of power those engines have."

"But the ship is anchored," she protested, still pulling at the knots. "Even at full steam, we won't go anywhere."

"I'm counting on that," Barrow said. She still looked confused, but he pressed on. "I don't have time to explain. The throttle controls ought to be similar to those in Declan McMurray's steamcarriage, only on a larger scale."

Emily opened her mouth once more, but Barrow cut her off before she could say anything else. "You can do this, Miss Skye, but you must hurry!"

She nodded, still looking unsure, but set off for the engine room.

Hazarding a glance in Morgentaler's direction, Barrow could see the necrotechnologist was struggling to keep the demon under control. Sweat streaked his face, plastering his white hair to his pate. Barrow guessed he hadn't had much experience summoning such powerful entities from the Abyss.

The ongoing struggle between summoner and thrall gave him the few moments he needed. Once more he surrendered his will to the eldersight and used the enhanced sensorium to look through the planks of the ship's deck. He soon found what he was looking for—a steam conduit that ran the length of the ship.

Following the conduit running under the deck, he searched out a joint between sections of the pipe. Four stout bolts through a locking collar held the flanged ends together. He had no reason to believe what he was about to attempt would work, but he focused intently on one of those bolts.

The mental effort was almost more than he could bear, but slowly, impossibly, the head of the bolt began to turn. When he had it past halfway out, he turned his attention to the next one.

The ship's engines roared. Barrow felt a lurch beneath him as the ship strained against the anchor. His tenuous grip on the bolt slipped, and the head sheared off. He swore as it spun away into the bowels of the ship, then fixed his efforts on the third of the four.

It was tougher going this time. Pressure from the engines was building in the conduit, pulling at the opposing sides of the weakened joint. The increased pressure made it harder to twist the bolt free, but if it worked the way he hoped, he wouldn't have to do much more.

The third bolt came free, and fell into the darkness below.

The fourth and final bolt fastening the joint simply gave out.

Wooden planks splintered as the sections of the heavy steel pipe, forced violently apart by the pressure of the steam within, broke through the deck. The eruption wasn't directly beneath Morgentaler's feet as Barrow had hoped, but it was close enough to send the madman reeling.

As he fell to the deck, Morgentaler smeared the charcoal markings he had made around his feet. As long as he remained in the circle, attacks of elemental flame or lightning would not have struck him or broken his tenuous control over Caacrinolaas. With Barrow bound to the deck of the ship, he hadn't been expecting any physical attack.

Lying on the deck of the ship, he twisted, and looked up in horror.

Freed of its master's control, the demon Caacrinolaas howled in triumph as it turned towards Morgentaler. Frantic, Morgentaler hurled first verbal commands at the beast. Caacrinolaas simply laughed. Morgentaler fumbled for the Webley revolver, and fired a blast of otherworldly lighting at the beast. The weapon had felled a tree, but against the demon it did nothing.

Caacrinolaas would not be slowed.

Towering now over Morgentaler, the demon reached down and plucked him from the deck of the ship as a curious child might take a frog from the bank of the river.

"Caacrinolaas, I command you to release me," Morgentaler bellowed in defiance even as his legs kicked impotently at the air. Barrow thought he saw something near a smirk split the demon's face in response, a sinister image he forever after wished had never crossed his vision.

Speaking to Morgentaler as he hauled the panicked and

flailing necrotechnologist level with his own horrible gaze, Caacrinolaas uttered something in one of the arcane and ancient tongues spoken only in the Abyss. The demon's voice was the sound of all things hollow and rotted, his words incomprehensible to Barrow's ears. Morgentaler, though, clearly heard and understood the meaning in the beast's words, and redoubled his efforts to wrest himself from Caacrinolaas' grasp, pounding with both fists against the demon's oversized hand.

Whatever was writhing beneath the mottled skin of the body Morgentaler had forced the demon into was now moving at a frenzied, gleeful pace. Several times, Barrow saw the skin split, shedding only a few drops of ichor before sealing itself shut again; the word *healing* didn't seem appropriate. As the beast's blood fell to the deck of the ship, acrid smoke rose as the stuff burned through whatever it touched. Barrow shuddered, glad to be bound several yards away from the terrible scene that was unfolding.

Emily returned to his side then, either unwilling or unable to watch what was happening. She had picked up another knife somewhere between here and the engine room, though, and set to the ropes around Barrow's wrists. He was free less than half a minute later.

A swirling ring of cold flame erupted from the deck of the ship at Caacrinolaas' feet. Rather than casting light, the dull red flame seemed to drink in the darkness from the night itself as it grew, feeding on nothing but the diabolical energies Caacrinolaas poured into it.

Barrow looked on in horror, thankful his line of view did not offer even a glimpse of the Abyss on the other side of Caacrinolaas' portal. He had been told by his mentors at the Technomancer's Collegeum that one look into the Abyss spelled madness for even the strongest of men. It was another hypothesis he had no desire to test for himself.

"Hold on to something, Miss Skye," Barrow called out as the flaming maelstrom raged, growing in intensity. A vicious wind pulled at his coat. Small bits and pieces not lashed down started to skitter across the deck of the ship towards the portal at the demon's feet. He clutched the mooring ring he had been bound to up until a few moments ago.

Defiant to the end, Morgentaler's screams only ceased when the flaming cyclone snapped shut. The baleful laughter of Caacrinolaas lingered in the empty air, fading away into the night as an eerie calm descended in the wake of his departure.

"What happened just now?" Emily asked as she came to stand beside him.

Rubbing at his chafed wrists to get the blood flowing, he stood up and nodded thanks to Emily. "I lost my hat," he said absently, scanning the deck.

She swatted his arm. "I meant with Dr. Morgentaler," she said impatiently.

"Oh, yes," Barrow said. "Well, simply put, he tangled with something he shouldn't have. The demon broke free of his control, thanks to our intervention, and it dragged him down to the Abyss to deal with later." He shook his head sadly. "I would dare say our Dr. Morgentaler is in for a long, bad time ahead."

"How long?"

"Oh, centuries, at least," Barrow said, "and that's if the beast is in a hurry to be done with him. My understanding is that demons tend to bear grudges against mortals who dare to enslave them, so I expect this one will be looking forward to repaying Morgentaler rather languorously."

Emily shuddered, and not just from the cold. "Why are you going out of your way to not speak the demon's name?"

Barrow smiled broadly, clapping a hand on her shoulder. "You are both clever *and* observant, Miss Skye," he praised her. "Let me tell you why I won't speak the demon's name. The only time a magician should speak a demon's true name aloud is when he's trying to enslave the beast, as Morgentaler did. As our demon has just now departed this mortal plane, some twenty yards from where we stand now, the link he has between this place and the Abyss is still quite strong. I don't know if he's listening to anything on our side of the closed portal, but I'd still rather not give him any reason to notice us just now."

"Hmm, prudent," Emily said, nodding in approval.

"I rather think so."

"Do you know what else might be prudent, Mr. Barrow?" she asked.

"What might that be?" Barrow asked absently, checking his pockets to see what remained.

"Getting off this burning ship," Emily said, pointing to a small but swiftly spreading fire on the starboard side.

THEY NEVER KNEW WHAT STARTED THE BLAZE. PERHAPS some of the demonic, corrosive ichor spilled as Caacrinolaas grappled with his human master had seeped through to the ship's engine room, rupturing one of the boilers. Whatever the igniting cause, Emily was right; it was time to abandon ship.

Caacrinolaas had destroyed one of the ship's lifeboats, but there were still several to choose from. Once he and Emily were safely aboard, Barrow hauled on the ropes to lower the small craft to the water.

As he had in the tunnels a few days earlier, he called a small nimbus of blue light into being. The nimbus swooped and flitted about in the air, cheerily oblivious to the dire straits its master found himself in. "Stop that nonsense at once," Barrow barked. The nimbus dimmed slightly and drooped in the air as if upset at being scolded. "Guide us to dry land," Barrow commanded it. "The nearest point on the mainland we can row ashore." Imbued with purpose, the nimbus flared brilliantly for a moment as it used whatever mysterious senses it possessed, then started off away from the small boat's starboard side.

Pulling at the oars, Barrow managed to get the lifeboat pointed in the direction the nimbus had floated off towards. The small ball of light had gone a good thirty feet before stopping, dancing in the air in one spot as it waited for them to catch up.

He rowed for what felt like hours, the muscles of his shoulders burning with the effort. Now that they were more or less safe, Emily slumped in the bow end of the small boat. Weariness had overtaken her quickly once they had escaped the burning steamship. Barrow didn't grudge her the small rest as he worked at the oars. He was worried that the physical strain of creating the waterspout which had swept Lai Jūn overboard had been too much for her to bear, to say nothing of the horrors she had seen. The girl was powerful, yes, but almost wholly untrained in the use of that power. He had seen stronger mages torn apart by lesser magic than the torrent of force this inexperienced girl had called forth without a second thought.

The sun rose over the eastern horizon, casting the light of dawn over the water. Barrow could see the rise and fall of Emily's chest. She was breathing. There was nothing he could do for her in their current predicament, but at least she was breathing. It was something.

25

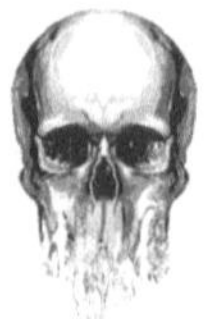

It was raining once more when Barrow returned to the home of Henry Feele. It hadn't stopped raining since the disappearance of Dr. Johan Morgentaler had been reported, but no one noticed the connection between those two things. Barrow wondered if the prolonged inclement weather had anything to do with Emily's haphazard squall that night, but he shook his head. There was no way to know. Halifax was prone to rain at the best of times.

This time the butler, Coleman, made no attempt to direct Barrow to the tradesman's entrance at the rear of the house. Maybe the fellow had been admonished for doing so the last time, or perhaps he simply remembered their previous meeting and had decided the resultant indignity was not worth the effort. Either way, Barrow cared little as he handed his sodden overcoat and umbrella to the unsmiling servant.

As he had before, he carried his black leather valise down the long corridor to Henry Feele's cavernous study. Also as he had found him on the previous visit, Mr. Feele stood lost in thought, studying the large sea chart. Barrow noted with a glance that the colored pins tracking the positions of his shipping fleet had moved about the map, though something about the arrangement pulled at the back of his mind.

"Ah, Mr. Barrow," Feele said as he crossed the room, his hand outstretched. "I take it you've solved my little technical problem?"

"I have," Barrow said, clasping Feele's hand. He placed the valise on the broad oak desk. Reaching into the case, he produced the oversized memory cylinder he had earlier removed from Mr. Feele's erratic autotype machine. It now glowed with a pinkish hue, rather than gray. "I've made some modifications to the cylinder," he said without going into great detail. "Unfortunately, any information you may have had saved in the cell was lost."

Feele shrugged. "Anything I had typed in was of little importance, all things considered," he said. "Were you...were your suspicions correct?"

Barrow nodded. "Yes, unfortunately."

"What a terrible business," Feele said softly. "Just terrible." There was genuine grief on his face. "Did you find out...do you know who it was?"

Barrow regarded his wealthy patron with silent pity. Henry Feele had not murdered anyone himself—indeed, he likely had no idea of just how many poor souls had died at Morgentaler's hand—but he clearly felt responsible for the death to some degree. As far as he was concerned, even using the technology was enough to make him answerable for the killings which made it possible.

"No," Barrow lied after a moment. Knowing the name of Jenny Perkins would in no way assuage the guilt Henry Feele felt, misplaced as it might be. If anything, he worried it might sink his patron into a deeper melancholy over the matter. Barrow decided to keep that knowledge to himself.

He said little else as he set to work fitting the remediated memory cylinder into the cabinet of the idle autotype machine. Installing the part took no more than five or six minutes by the time each of the various wires had been reattached to their corresponding terminals. Like a steamcarriage without a firebox, the beautiful piece of engineering was of no use without the vital component.

"That should take care of it," he said as he snapped the glossy black exterior casing back into place. "You'll let me know, of course, should any further complications arise?"

"Of course," Feele said as he clasped Barrow's hand in thanks. "Coleman will have an envelope for you on your way out."

As he packed up his tools, Barrow had another glance at the map that tracked Henry Feele's shipping routes. Some detail on the map had bothered him at first glance, and now he thought he knew what it was. "Mr. Feele," he said, "unless I'm mistaken, when I was here last, there were twenty-four coloured pins on this map. Is that correct?"

"So there were, Mr. Barrow," Feele confirmed. "What of it?"

"There may not be anything to it, but this morning I count only twenty-three."

"There's not much that gets past you, is there? Yes, we had a ship go missing five nights ago. Piracy is the official story we've been given," Feele said, a dubious expression on his face, "though it's hardly a common thing for a whole ship to be stolen right out from under the watch of the port authority. They may be a useless lot in most regards, but for all their failings, they keep a steady vigil on the harbour." He shook his head. "It ran aground on Sable Island, burnt to cinders and apparently with no one aboard. It's the damnedest thing."

"Yes, I suppose it would be that," Barrow said, deciding to keep quiet on the matter. He had already filled Inspector Eddings in on what had transpired. If Jonathon had seen fit to keep Henry Feele in the dark on the true fate of his ship, he must've had good cause.

⁊

Barrow poured himself a measure of scotch, upended the glass, and downed the drink in one long draught while Inspector Eddings gawped.

"Damnation," the inspector said, pouring a drink for himself. "Everything's all right, then?"

"It's like drinking demon's fire, Jonathon," Barrow gasped. "How do you stand the wretched stuff?"

"That's a twelve-year single malt from the Isle of Islay," Eddings said defensively. "You're supposed to savour every drop, not guzzle it down like some hog at the trough. But that's hardly what I meant, Barrow."

Barrow shrugged his shoulders. "Henry Feele's autotype machine is working properly," he said. "Johan Morgentaler is nowhere to be found, and the Nightshade Cabal hasn't been heard from in days."

"The Cabal," Eddings snorted. "What was its part in all this?"

"As far as I can tell, Morgentaler was simply using the Cabal to traffic the eldersight, and using the profits from that to fund his research. He burned through the family fortune before leaving Europe. I expect with him gone, the supply of eldersight will dry up once more."

"Well, that's all neat and tidy. And where is Miss Skye this morning, then?"

"She's visiting Declan McMurray in the infirmary," Barrow said.

"Is that right?" Eddings grinned and sipped at his scotch. "Good show, Mr. McMurray."

Barrow raised an eyebrow at that. "How do you mean?"

"Do I have to spell it out for you?" The inspector exhaled and shook his head. "Of course I do. I must've forgot who I was talking to," he chided. "There's little better that a young man can do to make a pretty lass notice him than being injured in battle, Barrow."

"The boy took a bullet in the shoulder while driving a steamcarriage, Jonathon," Barrow scoffed. "It's not as though he was off fighting the Boers."

Eddings smiled. "It's all the same, as far as the fairer sex is concerned. You'll note Miss Skye is at his side right now, though, while you're sat here in my office. How is young McMurray, anyway?"

"He's healing well. The doctors say he should regain full mobility of the shoulder when all is said and done."

"And the ruined steamcar he was driving?"

"His employer was outraged about that, of course," Barrow said. "I've offered to help rebuild the machine, and when I told Henry Feele about the incident he insisted on paying for any parts I might need to do the work. Between us, I think we've managed to save Mr. McMurray his position."

"Meanwhile, you get the fun of tinkering with a steamcar engine," Eddings pointed out.

"I'll not deny I'm looking forward to that," Barrow admitted. "Miss Skye is eager to tackle the project as well."

"That's all settled, then? You'll be taking the girl under your wing and teaching her all you know?"

Barrow nodded, steeling himself for what he knew his friend would say next.

Eddings paused and thoughtfully sipped his drink. "I admire your resolve, Barrow," he said with compassion in his voice. "After what happened with Ethan Atherton, you swore off taking on another apprentice."

Two years had passed since the Atherton affair, but Barrow still felt a pang of guilt whenever he thought of the young man who had been his first apprentice. He wondered when he would be able to hear Atherton's name without feeling regret. *Perhaps never*, he told himself.

"Atherton's tragedy was wholly of his own making," Barrow said after a moment. It was true, and he more or less believed the words even as he said them. "Miss Skye is a very different individual."

"And the fact that she's a pretty young girl had no bearing on your decision to reconsider?"

Barrow snorted in derision. "Emily Skye is barely half my age."

"She is that," Eddings agreed. "Meredith Skye, now, she's a good bit nearer your age, isn't she?"

"I doubt Meredith Skye would be remotely interested in some penniless technomancer, Jonathon, and even if she were, I have precious little time for my own work as it is." Rather than endure any further jibes about his personal affairs—or lack thereof—he changed the subject. "Why did the constabulary not tell Henry Feele the truth about his lost ship?"

Eddings frowned. "What would you have me tell him, Barrow? An evil wizard stole his steamship in the middle of the night, planning to raise a demon to kill another wizard, but ended up getting himself killed in the attempt?"

"That's the truth of what happened," Barrow said impassively.

"One of the things you've never yet learned in the years of working alongside the constabulary, Barrow, is that some-times the plain truth isn't always the best approach to the matter at hand. It makes you a good man, but in a lot of ways you would make a lousy copper."

Barrow had no answer to that, as it was more than likely so. He had no interest in being any variety of constable, though, lousy or otherwise. He would prefer to be left to his research and his inventions. *One day*, he thought ruefully, *I may even have the luxury of doing so.*

"There was something I forgot to mention at the customs house, Jonathon. In Morgentaler's basement laboratory, I was attacked by what I thought was a massive automaton."

Eddings puffed his cigar. "Bloody hell."

"Indeed," Barrow agreed, nodding at his friend's frank assessment. "However, while I was struggling against the mechanical brute, I managed to wrench part of the plating from the thing's face."

"You're going to tell me why that particular detail matters eventually, Barrow," Eddings said impatiently. "Why not now?"

"It had a human face underneath," he said, frowning at the memory. "Half of one, at least. A man's jawline and mouth, yellowed teeth, stinking breath and all."

Eddings leaned back in his seat, his face unreadable. "Bloody hell," he repeated.

"Just so," Barrow answered as he picked up the bottle and poured himself another drink.

THE MORNING WAS GIVING WAY TO A BRIGHT AFTERNOON as Barrow left the inspector and headed toward his workshop, and the streets were alive with the day-to-day business of the city.

And then it all stopped.

Carriages halted on a dime. People on the sidewalks paused in mid-step. A small boy chasing a ball down the street was frozen in place, the ball hanging still in the air. Barrow reeled, taking in the tableau as the world around him simply...stopped.

"I should have you clapped in cold iron for all the trouble you've caused, Isaac Barrow," a voice behind him said.

"Malleus," Barrow said, turning to face the Triune Magister. He gestured to the paused scene around them. "Is all this really necessary?" he asked, though he had to admit he admired the feat of chronomancy.

"We've kept an eye on you, Isaac," Malleus said, peering over the edge of his red-lensed spectacles. "Necromancers and demons and deals with the fae...this entire Morgentaler affair has been a debacle from start to finish."

"If you were watching, why didn't you do anything?" Barrow demanded, feeling his cheeks heat as he took a step forward. "People died, Malleus. Where was the Triune Congress? Why didn't you and your Magisters put an end to it before it went so far?"

"We had other concerns," Malleus said, taking a half-step back. As he did, the people on the street slowly resumed their movement, then paused once more as Malleus regained his composure.

It was, Barrow realized, the only instance in which he had ever seen a crack in Malleus's self-assurance. He decided to press the point. "Other concerns? Whatever it was that brought you to MacGowan's Wheelhouse the other night, you mean? Well, whatever it was, I hope it was worth all the lives that were lost."

"You would do well to remember your place, Barrow," Malleus growled. "You have no idea what we are contending with, and as for your own misadventure, the Triune has the authority to question and discipline you for your role in all that happened." He glowered at Barrow for a long moment before he went on, "But we won't."

Barrow gawped at that. "Why not?" he finally asked, feeling foolish as the words left his mouth.

"Dr. Morgentaler was a madman and his research

violated every statute we hold to and enforce. In spite of it all —the demons, the lich, the rampant property damage—the Triune Congress tasked me with thanking you for putting a stop to his machinations." He spoke through gritted teeth.

Barrow couldn't help it—he broke down in a fit of laughter.

"I'll be watching you, though," Malleus said. "You've won their favour this time, but you'll do something brash and thoughtless soon. When you do, I'll be there to take you to task for it."

Before Barrow could reply to that, Malleus disappeared. Perhaps it had been a projection all along? *No matter*, he thought, as the world around him returned to life. A bird in a nearby tree burst into song. *It's rather a lovely day, all in all.*

A STONE THE SIZE OF A FARTHING SKIPPED TO A STOP near Barrow's foot as he fished through his pockets for the key to his streetside office. He glanced up in the direction it had come from, spotting Will Fergus coming up the sidewalk. Rather than his usual well-worn attire, the lad wore a miniature approximation of a grown man's suit, long trousers and all. His face and hair showed evidence of a recent and thorough scrubbing.

Among Barrow's strengths, an ability to note subtle social cues would rank low on the list, but he had little trouble realizing the meaning behind the boy's appearance. "Morning, Will," he said in greeting. "You'd be off to your brother's funeral, then?"

"Just came from, actually," Will said, nodding his head. "Mum and Dad buried him up by Spring Garden, near Saint Mary's. You can almost see out to the ocean from where they put 'im."

Barrow whistled. "That's a nice spot. I hope he can rest well there."

Will kicked a pebble out into the street, watched it bounce and skip about halfway across the cobbles, then looked up at Barrow. "They say you got the man that killed Ian," he said. "They say he was a spellcaster, like you."

"Not like me," Barrow said sternly, taking to one knee to look the lad in the eye. "Spellcasters are just people who can do things in ways others can't. And just like regular folk, most of us are good people who would never do anything to hurt anyone."

The boy sniffled and wiped his nose on his sleeve. Barrow clapped him on the shoulder and smiled. "There are always more people looking to help others than to hurt them, Will. It might not always seem to be so, but it is. Remember that, no matter how dark things look. Now hurry along home. Your parents will be happy to have you underfoot today, I'm sure."

Will nodded and turned on his heel, hurrying off down the block. Barrow watched after him until he disappeared into the mouth of an alley. He reckoned the boy would be heading straight home; if the rest of the Collywobble Boys were to spot him in his formal attire, they would never let him live it down.

The gas lamps were already lit when Barrow descended the iron stairs to his subterranean workshop, a candle lantern in his hand. Feeling foolish, he snuffed the candle when he reached the bottom of the stairs, placing the lantern on a small wooden shelf.

Apparently not one to sit idle while others dallied, Emily was already busying herself by sweeping the dusty floors with a rough straw broom. Barrow felt a twinge of annoyance at the notion the girl had searched through his closets to find the broom, but then he remembered he had left it leaned up against the sideboard countertop when he had hastily swept up the remnants of the failed Experiment 242. *Less than three weeks ago,* he thought with some bemusement as he watched Emily at work. She was humming softly to herself as she cleaned, an old Scottish tune that Barrow recognized but couldn't name. She hadn't heard him as he descended the stairs.

He cleared his throat, loudly, as he crossed the large room. "Good morning, Miss Skye," he said in a bright voice. "I see you've not wasted any time awaiting my arrival." A healthy work ethic was a rare enough thing to find in someone so young, Barrow wanted to encourage the quality wherever he came across it.

"Good morning, Mr. Barrow," she replied, wiping some dusty smudge of something from her cheek with the back of one hand. If anything, the motion just smeared the grime further across her face. "I could hardly sit on my thumb waiting all day, what with this place looking the way it did. I'd swear you were trying to bring the very dust on the floor to life, given the thickness of it," she scolded, though her smile betrayed her mood.

Barrow nodded, conceding the point. With all that had happened in the days following his first visit to Henry Feele's home, keeping up with the general housekeeping of the workshop had fallen by the wayside. He silently admonished himself for letting his laboratory fall into such disorder.

He noticed a parcel on the workbench, wrapped in brown paper and tied with twine.

"A gift," Emily said when she saw he had spotted it. She picked it up and handed it to him. "My way of thanking you for saving my life."

He stared at her. "I should be thanking you. If you hadn't flown in when you did, Morgentaler's demon would've put an end to me."

"That's foolishness, Mr. Barrow," she said, grinning. "If I

hadn't been there to save you from Lai Jūn, you wouldn't have made it that far in the first place."

Mumbling his thanks, he carefully undid the knot and removed the paper, folding it neatly and setting it aside.

"Have you never opened a gift before, Mr. Barrow? Half the fun is in tearing off the wrapping!"

"That seems foolish, Miss Skye," he said, holding up the folded paper. "This way, it can be reused at a later time." He pretended not to notice as she rolled her eyes.

Removing the lid from the box, he pulled out a fine black bowler hat. "Miss Skye, this really is too much," he said, admiring the hat.

"My father always said a new hat means a new adventure, Mr. Barrow," she said, smiling. "One shouldn't skimp on such things."

"Very well then, Miss Skye," Barrow said as he set the bowler atop his head with a grin. "Shall we get to work?"

EPILOGUE

24 June, 1881

Her Royal Majesty, Queen Victoria of England,

Ten days have now passed since the incident at Sable Island in Lunenburg County, some sixty-odd miles south and west from the port of Halifax, Nova Scotia. There has been no sign of the necromancer Johan Morgentaler in the days since. The details of events from that night are scant, but it is believed a powerful demon Morgentaler had conjured broke free of his control and pulled him down to the Abyss wholly in body and, more's the pity for him, alive. May God have mercy on his eternal soul.

The advanced prototype automaton has been recovered from the Hemlock Overlook Sanitarium and will be shipped to London for further examination. It is unknown to us what purpose Morgentaler intended for the machine, but its design and construction is well beyond anything even our top mechanists are capable of. Its study will undoubtedly keep your researchers busy for months to come.

I have debriefed Isaac Barrow at length (using the utmost discretion, I assure you) and have enclosed my full report on the matter. In light of his recent service to the realm, I believe it safe to rule our previous concerns in the case of Mr. Barrow were unwarranted. I do not consider him to be a threat to the Crown, the British Empire, or the Dominion of Canada at this time.

(Indeed, if I may be so bold, I would suggest the Royal Transmundane Division redouble our efforts regarding the young Serbian currently working in Budapest who recently came to our attention. I've only read the reports from our other field agents, of course, but this young man strikes me as a far more unpredictable element than Mr. Barrow.)

I must also mention that in the wake of recent events, Mr. Barrow has taken on a young apprentice in one Miss Emily Skye, previously unknown to us. Though just a girl of seventeen years, Miss Skye seems to find herself in command of an immense arcane power. In point of fact, it seems it may only have been through her intervention that Mr. Barrow survived his encounter with the necromancer Johan Morgentaler at all.

It is our hope that under Mr. Barrow's guidance and tutelage, Miss Skye will learn to master her powers and use them to the benefit of Crown and country. We will continue to keep a watchful eye on the situation.

One final note. In speaking with Mr. Barrow, one part of his story troubles me, and it involves our office specifically; in my opinion, the introduction of an Iron Golem into the current situation seems particularly ill-advised.

· · ·

Ever yours in faithful service,

Agent Jonathon Eddings, RTD.

HISTORICAL NOTES

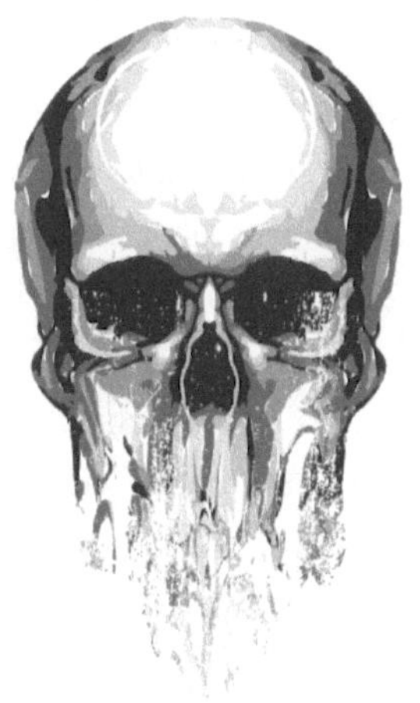

While *The Nightshade Cabal* is a work of fiction, I have made every effort to research the real Halifax of the early 1880s, hoping to give the reader some idea of what the city was like at the time. Of necessity, however, the Halifax of Isaac Barrow, Inspector Eddings, and Miss Emily Skye differs from the Halifax of 1881 in many ways worth noting.

Certain inventions, machines, and devices described are obvious anachronisms. In a world where magic works—technomancy in particular—the timeline of the invention would be rather different. The rasterized display screen on Henry Feele's autotype machine is an example of this; some of the ideas that would lead to the invention of television were known by the early 1880s, but didn't really come together in a workable way until a few decades later. Steam-powered carriages did exist by 1881, but they were not nearly as advanced as the one driven by Declan McMurray. Hydrostone, mentioned in Chapter IV, is an engineered concrete used extensively in rebuilding after the Halifax Explosion of 1917; its use in 1881, though, would've been unlikely.

The automatons and transoceanic airships mentioned in the book are, of course, even more unlikely.

There has never been a sanitarium overlooking Hemlock Ravine. I placed the sanitarium there for no better reason than I needed it to inhabit a location that was outside the city, and I thought the name sounded suitably ominous. Hemlock Ravine was first the home of Lieutenant Governor John Wentworth, and later home to Prince Edward, Duke of Kent, and his mistress, Julie de Saint-Laurent. Today the ravine is a scenic urban park, and a heart-shaped pond Prince Edward had built on the site known as "Julie's Pond" underwent extensive repairs in 2016.

Africville was not known by that name until closer to 1900. Indeed, the area had no formal name in the 1880s, and was simply known as the Campbell Road Settlement at the time this story takes place. For the sake of simplicity and ease of recognition (to say nothing of word count!), I have opted to use the later place name.

There was a lunar eclipse on 12 June, 1881, but it occurred at 6:54 am (well past midnight) and might not have been visible from Halifax.

Underground tunnels—some dating back centuries—do in fact run under the city of Halifax. Local lore says these tunnels were used by smugglers, pirates, and other miscre-ants. This underground network is likely nowhere near as extensive as what is put forth in this book, though. One of the more easily accessible examples today can be enjoyed at the conclusion of the Alexander Keith's brewery tour which, while an admittedly touristy activity, is one I highly recommend if you find yourself in Halifax.

Likewise, the streetcar system in 1881 was a much simpler affair than the one described in this book.

The political scandal referenced in Chapters V and VIII saw Canada's first prime minister, Sir John A. Macdonald, and 150 members of the ruling Conservative party accused of accepting bribes from Sir Hugh Allan's Canada Pacific Railway Company for the contract to build Canada's first transnational railway. Some sources suggest more than $360,000 in bribe money was paid to the Conservative Members of Parliament. Furthermore, Allan had promised no American financial backing would be used to build the railway, which turned out to be a lie.

Macdonald resigned his position as prime minister on 5 November, 1873, and though he offered to step down as leader of the Conservatives, the party refused to accept his resignation. Liberal leader Alexander Mackenzie became prime minister following Macdonald's resignation and, following the election of January 1874, the Conservatives remained in opposition until 1878.

ACKNOWLEDGMENTS

Brent Nichols, Colin Maheu, and Kale Haley read the earliest drafts I was willing to show anybody. Some of that material was still rather rough, but they helped me smooth it out. Additional early feedback on the first few chapters came from Rick Overwater and Michael Gillett. Connie Carolan, Dan M. Hampton, and members of the Shadow Ascension Workshop including Michael Gillett, Celeste Peters, Randy Nikkel Schroeder, Tony King, and Renee Bennett read and offered critique on the revised manuscript. The book in your hands is much better as a result of all of their insightful feedback along the way, and I'm indebted to each and every one of them for their advice and encouragement. Any failings herein, of course, remain my own.

(Actually, there's a real doozy in Chapter XIII that I'm pretty sure is Brent's fault, but I digress...)

I must also thank the membership of the Imaginative Fiction Writers Association. Being in a room with such a diverse assembly of talented writers is truly inspiring. I look forward to many, many more first Thursdays to come!

Iris Morgan at the Spatial and Numeric Data Services office at the University of Calgary assisted with tracking down historical street maps of Halifax and the surrounding region. I'll accept full blame in the few instances where the geography has been fudged to serve the needs of the story.

My thanks to Shayne Leighton, Chantal Gadoury, Amanda Wright, and everyone else at the Parliament House

Press for taking a chance on this book. Thanks as well to my editor, Kelly Beyus, for her assistance in shaping the manuscript into its final form.

Finally, my endless gratitude must go to my amazingly patient and supportive wife, Maggie Knight, without whose encouragement and understanding this might never have happened.

ABOUT THE AUTHOR

Chris Patrick Carolan is an author, editor, and hovercraft enthusiast originally from Glasgow but now based in Calgary, Alberta. He writes steampunk, fantasy (urban and epic), and science fiction, though he has been known to turn to crime to make ends meet. His stories have appeared in various award-nominated anthologies. In 2018, he established ExitZero Books to continue publishing the Enigma Front anthology series on behalf of IFWA, the Imaginative

Fiction Writers Association. He can be found online at cpcwrites.com or on Twitter @cpcwrites but - consider this fair warning - it's mostly wisecracks about McNuggets and Simpsons memes.

BARROW STILL NEEDS YOU

Did you enjoy The Nightshade Cabal?
Remember, reviews keep books alive . . .

Barrow still needs your help by leaving your review on either GoodReads or the digital storefront of your choosing.

He thanks you!